Sanders' first impression was that he was looking at a waxworks or a group of stuffed figures. In a rich shell of a room, with mural paintings on either side of the fireplace, four dummies sat in various broken attitudes at a long refectory table. At the foot of the table was a handsome woman in an evening gown, with her head nearly on her shoulder. At one side of the table sprawled an old man with coarse whitish hair. At the other side was a middle-aged man sitting bolt upright. Finally, at the head of the table sat an immense, fat jovial-looking man with a tonsure of red hair. He looked like a dissipated monk, and dominated them all.

The window-frames shook to the rumble of a lorry in the street below; the silent company vibrated a little.

They resembled department store dummies, but they were people, living people. All but one. He had been murdered.

Carter Dickson

DEATH IN
FIVE BOXES

LIBRARY OF CRIME CLASSICS®

MISTER E'S™

INTERNATIONAL POLYGONICS, LTD.
NEW YORK CITY

Death in Five Boxes

Copyright © 1938 by William Morrow & Company,
Inc. Copyright renewed 1966 by John Dickson Carr.

Library of Congress Card Catalog No. 91-70604
ISBN 1-55882-098-1

Printed and manufactured in the United States of
America.
First IPL printing June 1991.
10 9 8 7 6 5 4 3 2 1

CHAPTER ONE

At ONE o'clock in the morning Dr. John Sanders closed up his laboratory. He was still puzzling over the problem of how arsenic had been introduced into the ice-cream: the Smith case, on which he must make a report by the end of the week. He was tired, and his eyes ached from long strain at the microscope. That was why he decided to walk home and clear his brain.

The Harris Institute of Toxicology is in Bloomsbury Street. Sanders was the last to leave the building, which he locked up with his usual care. A light rain had begun to fall as he turned into Great Russell Street. He welcomed it; it was like clean air. That whisper of the rain was the only noise in the long lane of houses between here and Tottenham Court Road. The quiet glow of street-lamps intensified the darkness of the houses—except at one place.

He never knew why he noticed it at all, except that he was in the idle state of lethargy when the mind fastens on trifles. It was a narrow eighteenth-century house of red brick. It had three floors and an attic with dormer windows, and seemed to be let out chiefly in offices. Two of the little dormer windows in the attic were lighted, shining behind whitish blinds; they stood out alive and lonely over the dead street. He kept glancing up idly at them as he came nearer. Just outside the house was a street-lamp, which partly illuminated the little entry.

Then he saw that there was someone standing by the street-lamp, looking at him.

"I beg your pardon," said a girl's voice.

Sanders was conscious of a sense of shock, for he could have sworn the street was empty. His first thought was that she was an ordinary night-prowler, and he quickened his step. But one glance made him hesitate. She wore a short brown fur coat, with the ends of the collar folded in front like a cravat, and she was without a hat. The gaslight shone down with an air of gravity on brown hair parted at one side; it gave her forehead a waxy look. She had thin lines of eyebrows turning up at the outer corners, very fine brown eyes, and a short straight nose. Raindrops ran along the pavement

7

and pattered under the lamp: the street was now full of their rustling.

"You're Dr. Sanders, aren't you?" she asked.

"Yes, that's right."

"And you're connected with the police," the low, pleasant voice urged, as a statement rather than a question.

"With the police? No, not exactly. I—"

She came closer.

"Oh, please don't put me off!" she said, and clenched her hands. "You are. You know you are. I heard you give evidence in the Holtby case."

"Yes, I do some work for the Home Office Analyst. Is anything wrong? Can I help you?"

He said this against his own natural conservatism. She moved still closer. The rustle of the shower was deepening: a few raindrops winked out on her hair and on the shoulders of her coat. Until she emerged out of the shadows, he had not noticed how attractive she was.

"You see, he made his will before he went out tonight," explained the girl. "That's what scares me."

Sanders stared at her.

"I know I must sound horribly stupid," she went on. "But it's important, really it is, and I'll explain in just a minute. But will you do something for me? Will you? I'm Marcia Blystone. I do sketches. You may know my father, Sir Dennis Blystone. You see those windows up there, the ones with the lighted blinds? Will you go up there with me for just a minute or two? Will you?"

"Yes, of course, if it's necessary. But why?"

"Because I'm afraid to go up alone," said the girl simply.

John Sanders, who was so entirely concerned with forensic medicine that he seldom had time to look at life, glanced up and down the street. A more suspicious man would have hesitated. There was not a suspicious bone in Sanders's body, in anything that concerned himself. He considered the matter as gravely and carefully as he would have considered the difference between the seeds of the poisonous white datura and the seeds of the harmless capsicum.

"In the first place, you had better get in out of the rain," he said, and made a polite gesture towards the entry.

"You see, I didn't want a policeman," she was urging. "But I had to have somebody who knows something about it. And, anyway, I had to stop somebody, and you looked nice, so I did."

The entry consisted of a vestibule with glass doors opening into a long and dingy hall. At the left of the vestibule there was a board painted with the names of those occupying

8

the different floors. He struck a match and inspected it. Ground floor, Mason & Wilkins, Chartered Accountants. First floor, Charles Dellings' Sons, Estate and Housing Agents. Second floor, the Anglo-Egyptian Importing Co. Third and top floor, Mr. Felix Haye—the name newly painted in large letters.

"That's it," she whispered. " 'Mr. Felix Haye.' It's not an office; it's a flat. *Will* you go up?"

He tried the glass doors and found that they were unlocked. Then he struck another match.

"To judge by the light," he said, "Mr. Haye is still up. I don't want to be inquisitive; but what am I supposed to say to him when we get there?"

"If anybody answers the door, just pretend that you're a friend of mine and that we're coming home from a party. I'll do the talking. If nobody answers the door—"

"Yes?"

"I don't know," admitted the girl, and he thought she was going to cry.

Sanders's ideas were in some confusion. A practical instinct said: What the devil am I getting into? A conservative instinct said: I have never done anything like this before. An unexpected instinct said: I want to keep on as long as possible in the company of Marcia Blystone.

He groped for, but failed to find, an electric switch, and went ahead striking matches. There was a strong office-smell about the place, as well as the atmosphere of the eighteenth century. Past the offices of Mason & Wilkins, Chartered Accountants, they groped up a staircase whose treads were covered with tough linoleum, and creaked at each end like a see-saw. They were halfway up to the landing of the second flight when Sanders's hand hit something in the dark.

He was just striking another match, his left hand moving ahead with the matchbox. In the flash of the light he saw that it was nothing more startling than an umbrella. Somebody had left an umbrella standing on the stairs, propped against the inner wall. But it clattered down the stairs with a din that drew from his companion the beginning of a scream; it bumped against the banisters, rolled down a few more treads, and seemed to fall half apart.

Holding up his match, he stared down at it. The crook of the handle was now separated from the rolled umbrella by several inches of shiny metal. He ran down to look at it. It was an umbrella-swordstick. Into the shaft was fitted a very narrow steel blade about two feet long.

"It's the first one of its kind," he said in a startlingly normal voice, "I ever—"

9

But he did not draw the blade more than part way out of its sheath, for he saw that there were bloodstains on it.

Dr. John Sanders, medical consultant of the Home Office, snapped the blade back very quickly just as the match-flame burnt his fingers. He did not know whether or not Marcia Blystone had seen it.

"What's wrong?" she whispered.

There was no longer any necessity for striking matches. A light had been switched on by someone on the floor overhead. Sanders saw the girl standing on the stairs above, holding to the banisters.

"It's all right," he said, with probably the biggest lie he had ever told in his life. "It's all right. Go on up. Somebody's given us a light, and—"

The person who had given them the light was peering out of a half-opened door on the floor above. The front part of the offices here had been enclosed in a series of frosted-glass panels bearing the inscription in gilt lettering, *Anglo-Egyptian Importing Co. Ltd.: B. G. Schumann, Managing Director.* The same inscription appeared on the doors towards the rear of the hall. Out of one of these stepped a mild elderly man of clerkly appearance, craning his neck. Evidently he had just been washing his hands and face; his bald brow looked polished, his crown of grayish hair was ruffled up like the ghost of hair, and he still held the towel. After peering at them over half-glasses pulled down to an almost horizontal position on his nose, he spoke in a natural tone.

"I thought I heard something. Did anybody fall?"

"An umbrella," said Sanders, holding it up. "Yours? We found it on the stairs."

It was a new one, with a shining redwood handle, and it looked as though it had never been used for its ordinary purpose. The other contemplated it with an expression at once sour and vaguely disappointed. His eye wandered to another flight of stairs, the last one, leading up to a closed door which must be that of Mr. Felix Haye's flat.

"Oh, an umbrella," he grunted, as though he had expected something different. "No, it's not mine. Probably belongs to somebody upstairs." He gave a last brisk rub of his hands on the towel, and spoke with sharp dignity. "And when you come down, please, will you kindly remember that the hall light-switch is *there,* and remember to turn it out when you leave? Thank you."

He was about to go inside and close the door when Marcia Blystone spoke.

"Is Mr. Haye at home?"

A pause. "Oh, yes. He's at home."

10

"Has he some guests, do you know?"

"I believe he has," replied the other, as though trying to be noncommittal. An evident desire to talk conquered after a struggle. "And very quiet they've been, too, tonight. Not a sound out of them for hours. I hardly thought it was going to be a quiet evening, either. At first they all started to laugh like a lot of wild Indians, and stamp their feet on the floor. Laugh? Never heard such laughing in your life. I thought it was going to lift the roof off. Why can't people—!"

Checking himself, he flung down the towel on a desk inside the door as though to emphasize his meaning. Then he went in quietly and closed the door.

Sanders glanced up at the door to Felix Haye's flat. Without looking at the girl he went up the last flight of steps and began to press the electric bell. That bell had a bounding sort of ring which pealed out strongly and seemed to penetrate into every corner of the flat before it came back. There was no reply. After he had pressed it for some seconds, he tried the knob of the door. Then he turned back to the girl, who was staring up from the hall below.

"Look here. I don't know what's happened in this place, but I'm afraid something has. The door is open. I'm going in. But I don't want you to come in until I give you the word. Just tell me this: what were you afraid you'd find in here?"

"My father," she said.

Inside, another short flight of stairs led up to the hall of the flat. These stairs, like the hall itself, were carpeted in soft dark brown. Every light was blazing. He was now facing towards the front of the building, so that the simple plan of the flat became clear. Ahead of him, at the end of the spacious hall, was a small kitchen overlooking the street. On his right were three communicating rooms: a big living-room overlooking the street, a bedroom, and a bathroom.

The rooms were spacious, though low of ceiling. When the lower floors had been let out as offices, the owner had not touched this little masterpiece of eighteenth-century paneling. Sanders stood amid unexpected luxury, listening to the loud drumming of the rain on the roof.

He tried the effect of his own voice, and wondered what he would say if anyone answered. No one did. When he went to the living-room he discovered why.

Sanders's first impression was that he was looking at a waxworks or a group of stuffed figures. In a rich shell of a room, with mural paintings on either side of the fireplace, four dummies sat in various broken attitudes at a long refectory table. At the foot of the table was a handsome woman in an evening-gown, with her head nearly on her shoulder.

At one side of the table sprawled an old man with coarse whitish hair. At the other side was a middle-aged man sitting bolt upright. Finally, at the head of the table sat an immense, fat, jovial-looking man with a tonsure of red hair. He looked like a dissipated monk, and dominated them all.

The window-frames shook to the rumble of a lorry in the street below; the silent company vibrated a little.

Dead?

Not quite, anyhow. Even in the doorway Sanders could hear strange breathing. He went softly across to the woman, whose ringed hand was cut on a broken cocktail-glass. Her pulse was very rapid, well over a hundred and twenty. Her skin had a patchy reddish look. He lifted one of her eyelids, and understood. The pupil of the eye was so dilated that it left only a narrow ring round the iris.

Moving quickly round the table, he examined each person. No one was dead or even in danger, but each had the symptoms of having swallowed a narcotic poison. He could hear the painful whimper of their breathing under the noise of the rain.

Most affected was the old man with the coarse whitish hair; his scholarly face lay on the table, and his breathing disturbed the ashes in the ashtray before him. The middle-aged man was in a condition which just escaped being serious. He sat almost upright as though with dignity: Sanders noticed the fineness and strength of his hands, on which the first two fingers of each hand were nearly the same length. A cocktail glass was before the first man, a tumbler before the second.

These three Sanders examined without finding death. But, when he reached the fourth, he drew back. The fat man with the tonsure of red hair had been dead for over an hour.

When he lifted the man up, Sanders found the cause of death.

Well, that was that. First of all, he had got to find a telephone and get an ambulance here for the drugged ones. There was a phone on the table between the two windows with white blinds. Handling the receiver in his handkerchief, he jiggled the hook several times before he discovered that the phone was as dead as the red-haired man.

"Dr. Sanders!" cried Marcia Blystone's voice.

He heard the old boards in the hall creak even under their thick carpet. To keep her away from this, he hurried out into the hall and closed the door of the living-room. She was waiting, with the fur ends of her coat-collar tied so tightly that it was as though she had been trying to hurt herself.

"I couldn't stand it any longer," she said. "Is my father—?"

"Steady, now. It's all right. What does your father look like? Is he big and partly bald, with red hair?"

"Oh, God, no! That's Mr. Haye. But where is he? My father? And what's happened?"

"If your father is in there, he's quite all right. Nobody has been seriously hurt except Mr. Haye. There are several people; they've been drugged, but nobody is in danger. What does your father look like?"

"He's—well, he's a fine-looking man. You'd notice his hands: the first two fingers of each hand are the same length. I've got to go in there."

He put out his arm.

"Yes, your father's there. Listen to me. Those people have been drugged; or poisoned, if you prefer. I think with belladonna or atropine. But the only one who is dead is this man Haye. All the same, I've got to get them to a hospital immediately, so I'm going down to find a telephone. You can go in there and see for yourself if you promise not to touch anything. Do you?"

"I'm all right," she told him after a pause. "Yes, I promise. So Mr. Haye has been poisoned."

He was already on his way downstairs. In passing he picked up the umbrella with the redwood handle, which he had automatically leaned against the wall as he entered. He neglected to tell her, at the moment, that Felix Haye had not died of poison. Felix Haye had died of a stab through the back, from a long and narrow blade like a swordstick.

CHAPTER TWO

"JUST a moment, please," said Sanders.

The offices of the Anglo-Egyptian Importing Company were now dark. The elderly clerk—wearing a dark topcoat and a shabby soft hat—was just leaving, though Sanders observed he made no move to lock the door. He had begun to walk quietly down the hall, with a stumpy stride which suggested the same dour tolerance as his looks, when Sanders hailed him. He peered round.

"Did you speak?" he demanded, as though there had been some doubt of this.

Sanders produced his card. "Yes. May I use your telephone? I'm afraid this is serious. There's been an accident or a deliberate murder upstairs. Several people have swallowed a poisonous drug, and Mr. Haye is dead."

The other man stood still for a moment, and then used a wicked word. It sounded all the more wicked and unexpected, flung out from such a prim figure in such a full-throated way. But he opened the door quickly.

"Phone's on the desk," he said. "Might have known it'd happen, with his monkey-tricks. I'd better go up there straightaway." He added, almost accusingly: "Schumann's there."

"Schumann?"

His companion nodded towards the name, *B. G. Schumann, Managing Director*, printed on the doors of the Anglo-Egyptian Importing Company. Still he glowered and hesitated, while Sanders dialed the Gifford Hospital in Gower Street. Then he demanded:

"How's the lady?"

Sanders spoke with his eyes on the dial of the telephone. "Quite all right. She's taking it quietly enough, considering that her father was one of the—"

"Her father?" The man looked puzzled, and then he made a gesture of exasperation. "Oh, I don't mean *her*. I don't mean the young woman who was with you. I mean the dark-haired lady who's up there. Mrs. Sinclair."

"She's all right too."

But the man had gone by the time Sanders was ringing the divisional police-station. Registering the name "Mrs. Sinclair," and picking up the umbrella again, Sanders went upstairs. He found Marcia Blystone sitting on a carved oak chest in the hall. Her legs, in fawn-colored stockings a little splashed with mud, were thrust out; and she was staring at the tips of her suéde shoes. When she looked up he noticed again the peculiar luminous quality about the whites of her eyes, as though her own intensity invaded everything she said or did.

"Tell me the truth," she began instantly. "Is he going to die?"

"No."

"Who's that woman?" asked Marcia, nodding towards the closed door.

"The clerk from downstairs says it's a Mrs. Sinclair. But I don't know anything about her. Did you recognize anybody, aside from your father?"

"Well, there's Mr. Haye, the one who's—" She stopped. "So that leaves only one person we don't know, the old man with the white hair. But what on earth happened? *Will* you tell me that? You say they were poisoned with belladonna or something—"

"Atropine, more likely. That's the alkaloid of belladonna."

14

"Oh, atropine, then! You mean someone was trying to kill a whole roomful of people?"

"Possibly," he admitted with caution. "Or it may have been used straightforwardly as a drug, to make them all unconscious. Atropine brings on a kind of delirium. Before the victim knows what is happening to him, he can't move. But I thought you might be able to help us."

"Me?"

"Yes. What were you afraid might happen to your father if he came here tonight?"

She jumped up as though this had surprised her, and for a moment looked merely confused. Yet her earlier fear had been real enough, just as she was certainly frightened now.

"I—I don't know."

"But—" began Sanders with a rush of exasperation. He had been about to say, "But my dear good woman," in his dryest lecture-style, as when an earnest girl student at the Institute made hash of an obvious logical point. He did not, somehow, wish to say this. "But there must have been something?"

"There was. I know my father hates Mr. Haye like poison." She paused over an unfortunate choice of words, and seemed to writhe inwardly. "Yet he insisted on coming here tonight. Also, he had his solicitor at our house today, and he made his will. What's more, he has been acting queerly. He—"

"Yes; go on."

"Just before he went out of the house tonight," said Marcia, looking up at him steadily, "he put four watches in different pockets."

"Four what?"

"Watches. Things you tell the time with. Oh, I know you must think I'm the most awful fool; but I'm not! It's absolutely true. Jefferson saw him do it: that's his valet. Jefferson told me about it, because he was worried too. After my father put on his dinner-jacket, he put one watch in each of two waistcoat pockets, and one in each of his trousers' pockets. He went into my mother's room to get one of the watches, and borrowed another from Jefferson, because he doesn't own four watches."

Sanders stopped himself in the act of asking, with a scientific man's curiosity, whether Sir Dennis Blystone was a lunatic. But there had been nothing about Blystone to suggest it: a fine-looking man, as his daughter had said, even propped up at that grotesque table.

"Yes, but look here: what did he want with four watches?"

15

"How on earth should I know? If I did I shouldn't be so worried."

"Has he still got the watches on him?"

"I don't know," said Marcia abruptly. "You said not to touch anything, and I didn't, except to make sure he wasn't dead." Again she looked at him, growing very quiet. "Also, you know quite well that Felix Haye wasn't poisoned. He was stabbed; and I think it was with that little sword inside the umbrella, the one you're taking such care of."

"Yes," he admitted.

There was a pause.

"That's why I asked you what happened," she insisted. "Somebody tried to kill them all, or maybe only to drug them—"

"One of their own group?"

"Maybe," said the girl sharply. "Maybe somebody put a small dose of poison in each of the drinks except his own, and only pretended to drink poison himself. When it made them all unconscious he killed Haye, and then took some of the stuff himself, so that afterwards nobody would know which person did it. Or (and this is much more sensible, I can tell you!) somebody outside the house poisoned the drinks. When all four of the people were unconscious, this outsider came in and stabbed Haye; and went out again knowing one of the people in the room would be suspected."

Sanders was at home with an academic problem. He was one of those excellent young men who like to sit up all night shoveling words: the more abstract and complicated the problem, the better he liked it.

"There are flaws in the argument," he decided. "In either case, wouldn't it have been simpler to poison Haye outright? Why should the murderer bother with the swordstick at all?"

"Well, there's that, of course."

"Furthermore, if the murderer is an outsider who wanted to throw suspicion on somebody in that room, why did he walk out of the house and leave the swordstick propped up conspicuously on the stairs two flights down?—All of which," he added, "means that we're theorizing without data."

"It sounds bad," observed Marcia, and grinned. "You're very funny and rather nice. What do we do about the data?"

Sanders was puzzled.

"We get it," he said. "Who was this Haye, and why should anybody want to kill him?" (Again he could feel her sliding away from the subject, behind a bland and innocent mask, though her eyes looked as intent as before.) "Do you know anything about him? Is he a friend of your father, for instance?"

She had a shrewd habit of anticipating his thoughts.

"If you're thinking that he's any kind of crook," she said, "like a blackmailer or something, get it out of your head. He's an investment broker. He's got pots of money. Everybody knows him. All of his money may not be made honestly, but at least it's all made on the stock market."

"Did you know him?"

"Slightly."

"Like him?"

"I detested the very sight of him," replied Marcia, as though making a measured decision. "I didn't think he was funny, and I didn't think his jokes were funny, though people were always saying how jovial and generous he was. And he wanted to know too much. He didn't want the information for anything; he just wanted to *know*."

She turned her eyes towards the closed door of the living-room; and, as though in response, the door opened. The clerk from the Anglo-Egyptian Importing Company came out, closing the door behind him with something as energetic if less noisy than a slam.

"This is a fine kettle of fish," he said, shaking himself. Sanders realized, with annoyance, that he had forgotten all about the man. "And fine goings-on, if you ask me. How are we going to explain all this. Eh?"

"We don't have to explain it," said Sanders. "You didn't touch anything in there, did you?"

"I mind my own business," the other retorted darkly. He added with a grudging air: "My name's Ferguson. I work for Bernard Schumann downstairs. Bernard Schumann's in there."

"Which one is he?"

Ferguson pushed the door partly open again. They could see an edge of the refectory table, on which sprawled the old man with the scholarly face and the coarse whitish hair.

"That's him. You say you're a doctor, young man. Is he bad?"

"You mean will he recover?"

"That's what I said, young man."

"He'll recover," said Sanders curtly. Something hard-boned and Scottish in his own nature, something that could break down stronger opposition than was likely to be put forward by the clerk, tightened in irritation at Ferguson's manner. "I was just wondering whether you could tell us anything about what happened tonight."

"No. I'm going home."

"Well, that's your business. Go home if you like. But the police will only have to send for you if you do."

17

Seeming to brush this aside without bothering to comment, Ferguson stumped on his way. But before he had taken many steps he hesitated, and turned round glowering.

"What should I know about it? I mind my own business."

"Yes. That's why you probably know something about what happened tonight. You told us you were downstairs in your office for some time. That laughing you spoke of was probably the hysteria when the drug took effect. You would have known, for instance, whether someone went in or out during that time."

Ferguson hunched his shoulder. "I'll answer the proper authorities, if they ask me. Not you."

"You mean you don't want to help?"

"I mean I don't feel obliged to help *you*."

"What about your employer?"

"Well, what about him?" demanded Ferguson, in a full-throated voice that contrasted with his shrunken appearance. "If Bernard Schumann wants to drink cocktails, at his age, and play the giddy goat like that, he can be thankful he's no worse off."

"I wish you'd take the chip off your shoulder," said Marcia, seeming a little awed by him nevertheless. "It wouldn't do you any harm to help us. My father's in there, and—"

Ferguson went so far as to show a gleam of interest. "Your father? Which one is he?"

"Sir Dennis Blystone. Sitting opposite this Mr. Schumann. Tall man, about fifty—"

"The one with the watches," grunted Ferguson, looking at the carpet. "No, I don't know him. What's *he* celebrated for?"

"He happens to be a great surgeon," said Marcia coldly.

Sanders was brought up short with several new impressions. He knew now why the name had been vaguely familiar to him, and why Marcia Blystone had assumed he would know it. Though the matter did not touch his branch of the profession, he remembered that for certain sorts of head operations Blystone was spoken of in Harley Street as *the* man. But this interested Sanders less than the suggestive overtones in Ferguson's voice, that blatant question, "What's *he* celebrated for?"—which hinted at darker forces moving.

"Are they all noted for something?" Sanders asked.

"Are they?" inquired Ferguson, changing his tone. "I wouldn't know, would I? I'm only Bernard Schumann's cart-horse. And you must be a friend of Felix Haye, or you wouldn't be calling on him tonight. So you would know better than I. But Mrs. Sinclair, that fine lady there, is supposed to be a very distinguished art-critic; and collector too, if you care for such things. Bernard Schumann has been decorated by

18

the Egyptian government, at least. He's the only one who has been able to reproduce the embalming process of the Nineteenth Dynasty, or so they tell me."

His tone as he said this made Marcia draw back. Sanders was not impressed. He kept his eyes on the half-open door, beyond which the silent company sat at their table.

"Yes," he agreed. "They're all well-known people in different professions. Then just what were they doing here?"

"Doing here?" repeated Ferguson, with the effect of a pounce. "You ought to see for yourself, young man. Having a party. Acting the fool."

"Do you believe that? I don't."

Ferguson's voice went high. "I'd like to know what you're talking about, young man. Felix Haye was always giving parties when decent people had to work."

"I'll tell you what I'm talking about," said Sanders simply. "It doesn't look like a party; that's just the trouble. Look at the way they're each sitting in a given place, spaced round the table as exactly as dummies in a window, and each with a glass placed exactly in front of him. It doesn't look like a casual gathering: it looks like a board-meeting."

Marcia's expression changed.

"That's it," she interposed quietly. "Something has been worrying me about that picture all along, and I couldn't for the life of me think what it was. But you've got it. My father never went on a party in his life. He drinks practically nothing at all; he's *afraid* to drink. You know, there's something wrong in there; something horribly wrong."

And, as her expression had changed, it was as though the atmosphere in the hall changed as well, and even the patter of the rain on the roof seemed to grow stealthy. Ferguson reached out with a quick gesture and closed the door. Then he seemed to state a flat proposition.

"How much do you know?" he asked.

"Nothing," said Sanders, who hated bluff with a scientist's hatred. "But there is something to know, isn't there?"

"I didn't say that, young man!"

"Well, I wish you'd say something," said the doctor patiently. "You're a queer old blighter yourself. I don't know what to make of you or any of your exhibits; but I think the police will be interested in you."

The clerk regarded him with a strange and fishy smile. It was a startling change from the dour tolerance with which he had greeted everything else.

"The police won't bother me," returned Ferguson, shaking his head skeptically. "They never have and they never will. Didn't I tell you who I am?—I'm only Bernard Schumann's

19

cart-horse. I'm no more alive than one of his scarabs or mummies. By God, I believe you're an honest man!" he added, as though this realization had slowly entered his mind. "All right: I'm going to give you a word of warning gratis. Don't stir up anything with the police. If you've got any respect for your own health you won't. You stick to your bugs and your drugs, and don't you monkey with things you don't know anything about."

"Why not?"

Ferguson suddenly lost his head.

"All right, I'll tell you that too. Take a look at those four inside there. They're well-off. They're famous. They sleep in soft beds and they don't have dreams. They would charm everybody at a church social, and they'd do it naturally. But do you want to hear the truth of it? All of them are criminals and some of them are murderers. You're right about the board-meeting, in a way. There's more cunning, and baby-faced lying, and plain downright evil locked up in their heads than you'd imagine existed in the world. The trouble is, you don't know the kind of crime each of them is responsible for; you don't know which is which. You don't know which are the murderers and which have comparatively clean hands. And you never will know until it's too late. That's why I'm telling you: take a fool's tip and keep away."

He looked at them with a pale and fiery earnestness. Then, before Sanders could speak, he stumped off towards the stairs. Again the silent company vibrated to the passing of a lorry in the street below; and Sanders, not an imaginative man, felt in his stomach a queasy sensation which might have been fear.

CHAPTER THREE

At a little past two o'clock, Sanders sat in the dimly lighted waiting-room of the Gifford Memorial Hospital, turning over the pages of a magazine without looking at them. His hand shook a little from overtiredness. Everything had now been done. The poison was atropine; but, to judge by the treatment, he had come dangerously close to underestimating the strength of the doses. Dr. Neillsen was now in charge here, as the police were in charge at Haye's flat.

That miscalculation, which might have been serious, came of trying to be too cocksure and soothing in front of the girl. He threw the magazine on the table just as Chief Inspector Humphrey Masters came in.

Sanders knew the chief inspector very well. Masters—ruddy of face, bland as a card-sharper, with the grizzled hair carefully brushed to hide the bald spot—was as affable as the circumstances would permit: the circumstances being that he had been roused out of bed at one-thirty in the morning.

"Ah, sir," Masters greeted him heartily. He hitched out a chair and put his brief-case on the table. "Rotten bad business, this. But it's a bit of luck having you here on the spot. Always grateful for somebody we can trust. Eh?"

"Thanks."

Masters became confidential.

"Now, sir, I've just had a preliminary look at that flat. And, while the boys were doing their work, I thought I'd better nip over here and see how the patients were getting on. Of course, it's bad luck they had to be moved before we got there—"

"Better have one corpse than four. That old man, Mr. Schumann, was in pretty bad shape."

"So the doctor here tells me," said Masters, looking at him sharply. "Oh, I don't say you did wrong, sir; I don't say you did *wrong*. I know it had to be done. The doctor says the three of 'em are safe enough now, but that they'd better not be moved or disturbed until tomorrow. Can I depend on that?"

Masters's simple code was to be suspicious of everybody.

"Well, Neillsen knows his business. Even if you did try to question them, you probably wouldn't get anything of importance tonight."

"Just so. On the other hand," said Masters judicially, "the doctor tells me that the lady, Mrs. Sinclair, pulled through in regular A-1 style. Couldn't have had as big a dose as the others. So it mightn't (eh?) it mightn't do a whole lot of harm if I were to ask her just a few questions? Tactfully, of course, and without excitement?"

"If Neillsen says it's all right—"

"Ah! I knew you'd agree, sir. But, first of all, I'd like a detailed statement from you, if you don't mind. Miss Blystone is upstairs with her father, and she's not very anxious to talk. If you would just let me have your side of it?"

Sanders told him in careful detail, while the other took notes. Long before the end of the recital, Masters was pacing about the room, redder of face and with a very worried brow.

"Lummy, we're in it again!" he said offhandedly. "I'm just wondering what Sir Henry would make of this mess." Then he grew thoughtful. "It's a queerer business than even

21

you think, doctor. Let's be clear about one thing. This man Ferguson told you that all four persons in that room were criminals of some kind. Eh?"

"Yes."

"It wasn't just a manner of speaking? A figure of speech, like?"

"I certainly didn't understand it as that. If you had heard him—"

"All of 'em were criminals, and some were murderers," ruminated Masters. "Just so. Since this Mr. Haye is dead, I'm not much surprised at the last part of it. Did he say anything else?"

"No; he went downstairs and shut himself up in the office."

The chief inspector pulled at his under-lip. "Yes, I know that type," he agreed. "Mum as an oyster and sore as a bear about every small point that doesn't matter. And then all of a sudden they'll blurt out the one thing they oughtn't to mention at all. Very useful for us, though. Did Ferguson give you any idea of what those four people might have been doing there?"

"No."

"But you think he knows?"

"I think he knows or suspects."

"Oh, ah. Now tell me, sir," pursued Masters, sitting down again and hitching his chair closer with a conspiratorial air. "What did Miss Blystone say to all this?"

"To what particular part of it?" asked Sanders, on his guard.

"Now, now, sir!" urged Masters, and fixed him with a shrewd blue eye in a way that somewhat disconcerted him. "That's to say: Ferguson said her father was one of a group of criminals at the very least. Well? Didn't it surprise her, or make her mad, or anything like that? What did she say?"

"She said that Ferguson had probably committed the murder himself. When we first met Ferguson on our way upstairs, he had just finished washing his hands. Her idea was that he was washing the blood off."

He spoke in an ironical tone, and Masters permitted himself an indulgent smile; but the chief inspector's eye was serious.

"He may have been, at that," Masters agreed. "But had *she* any idea what they were all doing upstairs?"

"I doubt it."

"All the same, sir, she followed her father there; and she must have been waiting in the street a good long time at an

22

unholy hour of the night. And all on the strength of the fact that her father had made his will and gone out with four watches in his pocket. They tell me Sir Dennis Blystone is a well-known surgeon?"

"Yes, that's true." Sanders moved restlessly. "Aren't we taking a lot for granted on the word of Schumann's clerk? You're a chief inspector of the Criminal Investigation Department. Do you know any of them as criminals?"

"I take nothing for granted, sir," said Masters. "And I can't say I know any of 'em in the way you mention. Trust me not to make a row just on the word of this chap Ferguson. But now we come to it. There are a whole lot of things on which I'd like your opinion: medically and otherwise. Offhand—" Masters bent forward and opened his eyes wide—. "offhand, what would you say was the queerest feature of this case, apart from wholesale poisoning and stabbing with a new kind of swordstick?"

"Sir Dennis Blystone and his four watches."

"Then you'd be wrong. Because that's only a part of it," replied the chief inspector. "When I was upstairs looking in on the patients, I took the liberty of running through their clothes. Most irregular, of course. Well, sir: each of the others, Mrs. Sinclair and Mr. Schumann, was carrying something every bit as odd as Sir Dennis's four watches. Like to hear what they were? Just so. In the right-hand pocket of his dinner jacket, Mr. Bernard Schumann had the ringing mechanism of an alarm-clock—"

"The what?"

"The ringing mechanism of an alarm-clock," repeated Masters with a kind of relish. "Spring, clapper, everything except the bell. It was old and a little rusty, but it would still work. Also, in the breastpocket of his coat he was carrying a biggish piece of convex glass, like a magnifying glass. What do you make of that?"

Sanders considered.

"Schumann deals in Egyptian antiquities," he pointed out. "So it's not at all surprising to find a magnifying glass. But I don't see any reason why he should need the wheels and springs of an alarm-clock. Mrs. Sinclair had something too?"

"She had," affirmed Masters. "I found it in her handbag. Her handbag was lying in her lap when she sat at that table. And in that handbag were two exhibits: a five-ounce bottle of quicklime, and a five-ounce bottle of phosphorus."

There was a silence.

"Now, sir!" said Masters, impressively tapping his finger on the table. "You're a chemist. What does Mrs. Sinclair, a fashionable lady if I ever saw one, want with quicklime and phosphorus?"

Sanders was frankly beaten. "I don't know. Phosphorus is a poison, of course. In fact, I've often wondered why more murderers haven't used it. It's absolutely impossible to trace the poison back to the murderer, because anybody can procure it. You get it from ordinary match-heads; and sixteen of them would contain enough to do the business. As for quicklime—"

The chief inspector was pulled up short, staring at this grave-faced young man whose head contained so many ingenious devices for murder.

"Hurrum, yes," said Masters, clearing his throat. "But there's no suggestion of phosphorus being used as a poison here? No. Consequently, what does she want with quicklime and phosphorus?"

"Well, if it comes to that, what does an Egyptian importer want with the works of an alarm-clock, and why does a distinguished surgeon borrow a lot of watches before he goes out in the evening?"

Masters nodded as though with pained agreement. At the same time, Sanders had a feeling that the chief inspector was concealing something, and that it pleased him mightily to conceal it. A sort of aura of satisfaction radiated from him. Sir Henry Merrivale would have recognized it instantly; but Sanders, who only suspected it, was beginning to feel uneasy.

"Look here, Inspector, what's up your sleeve?"

"Up my sleeve, sir?" repeated Masters, with radiant innocence. "Up *my* sleeve? Nothing at all. I was only wondering if you had any more suggestions."

"Not at the moment. Unless you think they're all murderers, and these articles are somehow proofs of their murders?"

"Ah! That might be."

"Or it mightn't. I shouldn't think by the look of you that you believed it yourself. Phosphorus is a poison; but you can't kill anybody with a watch or a sheet of glass."

To his surprise, Masters laughed uproariously.

"Sounds like a conjuror's equipment, don't it?" he inquired. "Now, now, sir! Don't get your back up. No offense meant. If this is what I think it is, I admit it's nothing to laugh at; it's as bad a business as I've come across. The man I want to see is that fellow Ferguson. Meantime, would you like to come along while I have a few words with Mrs. Sinclair?"

Mrs. Sinclair had been installed in one of the few private

rooms at the Gifford Hospital. She was propped up in a white enameled bed, a shaded lamp over the bed shining down on her hair, and Dr. Neillsen was talking soothingly to her.

Sanders's first impression was that she did not look like a woman who had just gone through the experience of a stomach-pump, follcwed by ipecac and sulphate of zinc. He felt that it would have made her shrink to think of this, for such was the impression of delicacy she conveyed.

The harsh flush was off her skin now, the rigidity gone from her body. Though she had looked somewhat older in Haye's flat, she could not have been more than in the early thirties. Mrs. Sinclair was soft, sleek, and long of limb. Her long, very dark and glossy hair was let down behind her ears. It seemed to draw back with the air of uncovering a round face of great beauty and sensitiveness, with large eyes of a bluish-black color, a small mouth, and a round but strong chin. The chief characteristic of that face, you would have said, was a sort of humorless earnestness and imagination. Though she wore the ordinary wool smock of the hospital, she wore it in the smooth fashion of a gown. Altogether she was a very attractive woman: as Dr. Neillsen evidently thought.

Masters cleared his throat. He hesitated. Alone among the witnesses, Sanders later noticed, she seemed the only one about whom he was uncertain.

"Only five minutes, mind," Dr. Neillsen warned him. "And I'll stay here to see it's enforced."

"Please do talk to me," the woman urged in a low voice. "Dr. Niellsen has been telling me what happened."

The chief inspector resisted an impulse to swear.

"I'm having none of your police bogey-traps," snapped the doctor. "You do your work and I'll do mine. Mine is to look after my patients."

"Just so," said Masters, controlling himself and becoming his usual ingratiating self. "Now, ma'am—as you know, I'm a police officer, and I'm bound to ask you a few questions. Don't mind my notebook; it's just a matter of form."

She thanked him with an earnest smile, drawing her shoulders back with unconscious grace against the pillows. The pupils of her eyes were still a trifle dilated.

"Your name, ma'am?"

"Bonita Sinclair."

"I think they said 'Mrs'?"

"Yes; I am a widow."

"What is your address, ma'am?"

"I live at 341 Cheyne Walk, Chelsea."

Masters glanced up. "Are you—occupied, ma'am; have you a profession?"

"Oh, yes, I work," she told him, as though this were a point in her favor. "I advise about pictures; and I deal in them, sometimes. Then I write a good deal for the *National Art Review.*"

The chief inspector shut his notebook. "Now, ma'am: you know Mr. Felix Haye was murdered tonight?"

There was a silence, while she seemed to flinch. Then tears gathered in her eyes; Sanders saw them gleam under the light of the shaded lamp. And Sanders was willing to swear they were genuine tears.

"That is what the doctor was telling me. It is horrible. I hate thinking about horrible things."

"Well, ma'am, I'm afraid we've got to think about them for a minute. I want you to start at the beginning, and tell me everything that happened tonight."

She sat up, shakily. "But that's just it. I don't know. I truly and honestly don't know. The last thing I remember is that someone at the table was telling a story—a joke, you know. It seemed to me wonderfully funny, the funniest thing I had ever heard. I laughed and laughed until I was ashamed of myself. But by that time things went all out of perspective, and—"

"Just begin at the beginning, if you will. How did you come to be at Mr. Haye's flat?"

"Why, it was a party. Not a loud party or anything unpleasant, of course. Just a little gathering."

There was a certain tone of prudery in her voice which went with the complete absence of make-up on her face. Whether or not this had been washed off, she now wore only a little powder. She was still undeniably very weak and shaky; and, when she took one hand from under the bedclothes, they saw that it was bandaged.

"What time did you go there, Mrs. Sinclair?"

"About eleven o'clock, I think."

"Just so. But wasn't that a bit late to begin a party?"

"I—I'm afraid it was my fault, really. You see, I had three very important phone-calls to put through tonight, at stated times; and I told Mr. Haye I couldn't possibly be there before eleven. He said he wouldn't think of inconveniencing me, so he wouldn't ask the guests until eleven."

Despite her eager and earnest expression, Masters seemed to feel that he was beginning to grope in a fog.

"But couldn't you have phoned from Mr. Haye's flat?"

She smiled. "I'm afraid not. One call was to New York, one to Paris, and one to Rome. They were business calls,

26

you see. It was a bore, and I'm terribly stupid at such things; but I'm afraid I had to do it."

"What I am trying to get at is this, Mrs. Sinclair. Was it *necessary* to have a party?"

"I'm afraid I don't understand."

"Did Mr. Haye have any purpose in asking you there?"

"But—really, I don't know. He was a very good friend of mine, and he asked me, so I went."

Masters, apparently not quite sure of what he meant himself, switched his attack. The fog was growing. "Did you know all the other guests?"

"I knew Mr. Haye, of course, and Sir Dennis Blystone. Sir Dennis picked me up—" despite her pallor, she reddened—"picked me up at my house and took me on to the flat. But I had never met Mr. Schumann. I thought him charming."

"When did you get to the flat?"

"It was nearly eleven, I think. About five minutes to eleven. Mr. Schumann was already there."

"And then you started drinking?"

Her blue-black eyes smiled, if her mouth did not. "Hardly that, you know. I had one cocktail, and not all of that."

"Only one—" Masters checked himself, clearing his throat hard. "Just so, ma'am. Who mixed the cocktails?"

"I did."

"You admit that?"

"Admit it?" she repeated. Her forehead, almost too smooth under the sweep of dark hair, wrinkled as though in perplexity. "But what is there to admit? Of course I mixed the cocktails. I don't know whether you know it, but when I was there Mr. Haye would never drink anything except White Lady cocktails. I—that is, he had some stupid joke about me. And he always insisted that I should mix the cocktails, so that he could make the joke. He would say, 'Have you tried my White Lady?' or something quite meaningless." She flushed.

"You all drank the cocktails, did you?"

"No; Sir Dennis had an American drink called a highball. But—"

"And you didn't have anything else to drink or eat?"

"Nothing."

"Well, ma'am, you see why I ask this. The drug you all swallowed was in those drinks. So if you could tell me—"

"But that's impossible!" she cried weakly. "Please don't talk like that; you don't know what you're saying. I've thought about it and thought about it, and I tell you that there can't have been any poison in anything we took. No, I am quite

27

sane and I'm not hysterical. If you doubt me, don't take my word for it. Ask the others. You'll see that we couldn't have taken a poison, and you'll understand why."

There was a click as Neillsen shut up his watch.

"Time's up, Masters," he said.

"Now, now!" growled the chief inspector, waving his hand vaguely and paying no attention to this. "You see, ma'am—"

"I said, time's up," repeated Neillsen.

Masters turned round. "Here, stop a bit! You don't mean that?"

"Don't I, though," said Neillsen grimly. "I'm not going to risk what often follows these things. Sorry, Masters; but this is one place where I give the police orders. Will you go quietly, or shall I have a couple of orderlies escort you?"

The chief inspector went quietly. Sanders knew that he was simmering, that he had barely begun, that he was even cut off from mentioning phosphorus and quicklime; but Masters had long known the literal nature of obedience. It did not prevent him, however, from making some strong comments going down in the lift.

"She's having us on," he insisted. "Lummy, doctor, how I distrust women that look like poetry! There's a game there, and I mean to find out what it is. Patient mustn't be disturbed! They don't hesitate to wake me up in the middle of the night, and tell me to come and investigate; and, once I get here, it's a fat lot of investigating I'm allowed to do. I tell you—"

"Correct me if I'm wrong," said Sanders, "but it strikes me that there's something more on your mind than that."

Masters lowered his defenses. "All right, doctor. That's got me. Yes, there is. It's that word 'impossible.' I'd hoped that here at last I was going to get a straightforward case; no locked rooms or bodies alone in the snow or any flummery. And the first word I hear is 'impossible'! But it can't be impossible. Blast it, there's nothing impossible about somebody getting a dose of poison, is there? Could be done in a hundred ways, couldn't it? And if I discover that there is—"

He stepped out into the dimly lighted lower hall of the hospital, in time to hear the swish of the revolving door in the vestibule. Trying to make as little noise as possible on the marble floor, a young man whom Sanders recognized as Detective-Sergeant Pollard hurried up to the chief inspector. Sergeant Pollard seemed to be bracing himself.

"You'd better come over to Great Russell Street, sir," he said. "That fellow Ferguson—he's gone."

Masters put on his bowler hat with an effect of corking himself. Then he seemed to remember where he was.

"So he's gone," whispered Masters, with powerful restraint. "He's just up and gone, is he? I suppose you let him walk right out of the front door?"

"No, sir," said Pollard quietly. "He didn't go out the front door. And I don't think he went out the back door either."

"Now keep your shirt on, Bob," whispered Masters with sudden urgency. "Just take it easy! Where is he?"

"You see, sir, I didn't think we'd have to keep a man watching him. And anyway, Wright was guarding the front door. The last time I saw Ferguson, he was sitting in his office, waiting for you to come back. He said he'd be there when we needed him. But I went down a few minutes ago, and opened the door—and he wasn't there. His linen sleeve bands, those things clerks wear, were on the table, and so were his spectacles. But no Ferguson."

"I'm asking you," said Masters, "how did he get out of there?"

"He must have gone by the back window, sir. But there's no way to climb down from those old-fashioned windows; that's what causes the trouble when there's a fire. He must have jumped."

"Goddelmighty!" whispered Masters, lifting both fists. "An old man like that jumped down forty feet in the dark, and then got up and walked away?"

Sanders tried without success to form a mental picture of this. More than ever this dour clerk, with his spinsterish fussiness and his sudden accusations, became the enigmatic figure round which the whole case centered.

"I admit that's difficult too," he said. "We can't find any marks on the wet ground where he must have landed if he jumped. But the back door is bolted and chained on the inside; and Wright was standing by the front door the whole time. So the only thing he could have done was jump."

"Is it, by George!" said Masters. "We'll talk about this later, my lad. In the meantime—"

"But that's not all," went on the sergeant, bracing himself again. "It seems there's no such person as Ferguson."

Masters took off his hat again. The whole unnatural colloquy, taking place in mutters in the echoing foyer of a hospital, seemed to have prepared the chief inspector for anything.

"While we were looking for him," Pollard continued, "we woke up the caretaker of the building, who was asleep in the basement. He's an Irishman named Timothy Riordan; as suspicious as they make 'em, and more than half full of whisky. I've got an idea that the reason why the commotion didn't wake him up beforehand was that he was drunk. But—"

"Look here, Bob: what the hell are you trying to tell me?"

"Just this, sir. He tells us that there's nobody called Ferguson in Mr. Schumann's employ. Mr. Schumann's only employees in the English office (he's got one in Cairo too) are two assistants, one of 'em an Egyptian who's been with him for ten years. Ferguson doesn't exist, that's all."

CHAPTER FOUR

IT WAS nearly eleven o'clock next morning when Sanders returned to Great Russell Street, where he had arranged to meet the chief inspector. He had not gone home that night after all. There was a bed at the Harris Institute, which he sometimes used when he had been working late; and Masters had asked him to do a great deal of work in a short time.

In his transport box he was carrying a remarkable collection of glasses and bottles from Felix Haye's flat. He had spent most of the night and all of the morning analyzing their contents, with results which made him stare when he tabulated them.

But he did not feel tired. It was a pleasant enough April morning, with a smell of spring in the cool air, and an edge of sun broadening behind the old houses. The house in Great Russell Street went on with business as usual; Mason & Wilkins, Chartered Accountants, and Charles Dellings' Sons, Estate Agents, moved incuriously on the first two floors. But the Anglo-Egyptian Importing Company was locked up, with a policeman before the door.

Masters, brisk, freshly shaven, and bland, met him in Felix Haye's flat. Only Masters and Sergeant Pollard were there. Sunlight streaming through the little windows from the street made the flat a cheerful place, though it still had an air of secrecy.

"Morning, sir," said Masters. "Good morning, good morning, good morning! We'd just about given you up, Bob and I. Took a long time, didn't it?"

"Curse your hide," said Sanders amiably. "It's the one time we can accuse the police of getting their ideas from detective stories. The inspector always says to the chemist, 'Analyze this!' The chemist in the story walks into his laboratory, immediately walks out again, and reels off the smallest measurements of the most obscure poison. Have you any idea how long this sort of work takes?"

"Never mind," said Masters soothingly. He led the way into the living-room, where there were now no stiff figures sitting round the refectory table. "Point is—is the news good or bad?"

"Bad, I should say."

Masters's face clouded. "Oh, ah. I might have expected that. Well?"

From the transport box Sanders took out the nickeled cocktail-shaker from which last night's drinks had been poured. They had found it standing on an occasional table near Felix Haye's chair, and it was still half full.

"Three of them," Sanders went on, "had been drinking these White Lady cocktails. Composition: gin, Cointreau, and lemon-juice. But in the dregs left in the cocktail-shaker here —no atropine. Nothing."

The chief inspector whistled.

"But that means—?"

Sanders nodded and set out the three cocktail glasses. "In the dregs of the glasses," he continued, "amounts of atropine ranging from one-fiftieth to one-tenth of a grain. Judging by the dregs, Schumann had the biggest dose, Haye the second biggest, and Mrs. Sinclair the smallest. The original drinks must have been loaded with it."

He then set out a tumbler.

"Sir Dennis Blystone, as you know, had an American highball composed of rye whisky and ginger-ale. He only half finished it; and there was about a third of a grain of atropine in the remainder. Finally, there was no atropine in any of the original bottles from the kitchen: gin, whisky, Cointreau, even the dregs from the lemon-squeezer.

"Consequently, you see, if the poison wasn't in the cocktail-shaker or any of the original bottles, it means that atropine was dropped individually into each of the four glasses."

"You mean that somebody sneaked round and poisoned all the drinks after they had been prepared?"

"Yes."

"Just offhand," remarked Masters, after a pause, "I can't think of anything more risky. Somebody drops atropine in four glasses—and never gets caught. You might do it once without being seen, or maybe twice. But four goes!" He brooded. "By the way, doctor, what's a fatal dose of the stuff?"

"Half a grain, usually."

31

"And in those glasses, just the dregs after they'd drunk," persisted the chief inspector, "there were still amounts up to a third of a grain? Lummy! Wasn't the chap who did it in danger of polishing off the whole lot of them with atropine alone?"

"In very great danger, it seems to me."

Masters stared at the refectory table, as though he were still trying to visualize the four victims sitting there. Sunlight through the narrow windows brought out the colors of the paneling, and of the murals painted on either side of the fireplace. The murals were admirable eighteenth-century work of a somewhat suggestive kind; they dealt with nymphs beside pools, and retained their original hues in a shade like water-color.

Idly Sanders wondered what had been the original purpose of this room, high up in someone's house. The fireplace had a carved over-mantel, on top of which a few bright-jacketed novels were now shoved together between bookends. There was a box of cigars open on one of the many occasional tables, and two ashtrays on the refectory table itself. The umbrella with the rosewood handle now lay on that table like a sword.

"A big dose of poison," Masters was going doggedly, "in each drink. And do you remember what Mrs. Sinclair said last night? She said she could swear, she said they would all swear, that no drug could have been put into any drink. Now why did she come out with that? Why was she so quick to let us know that? You don't suppose they all *knew* they were drinking atropine, do you?"

"I shouldn't think it was likely," observed Sanders. "It would be rather a dangerous social amusement. Have you discovered anything else?"

The chief inspector was sardonic.

"Fine crop of fingerprints here; probably lead to nothing. The handle of that umbrella's no good. I'm afraid you mucked it about yourself, doctor, when you came up. It's the weapon that stabbed Haye, right enough. But nobody seems to know whose it is or where it came from. I'll find that out when I get on to the witnesses. They were sent home from the hospital this morning, and I've got a fair field."

"What about Ferguson?"

"All right. Rub it in. All I know about Ferguson," snapped Masters, "is that he really did vanish and no mistake. I've half a mind to try it out on Sir Henry. Bob was right: he didn't go out the front door, and he didn't go out the back. I've gone all over the rear wall this morning. There's a rain-pipe on that back wall; but it's nowhere near the window, and

Ferguson would have to be first cousin to a gorilla to reach it. No, that won't do. He must have jumped—without marks on the ground. We've got only one clue."

"Which is?"

"He left his spectacles behind," grunted Masters, "and he left his fingerprints on the spectacles. Not that that'll probably help us a little bit. Unless he's in the files at the Yard, which isn't likely, we're no better off than we were before. Meantime, I've got the address of Haye's solicitor, and I'm sending the sergeant round to see him. As for me, I'm going to tackle Mrs. Sinclair again. Like to come along, doctor?"

Sanders did like to come along; he felt he deserved it. They drove to Chelsea in a police car, and along that Walk by the river which seems to have an autumnal tinge even in spring. You could almost have predicted what sort of house Bonita Sinclair would have: it was more like a cottage or a doll's house. The dark bricks had careful lines of white mortar between them; there were many window-boxes, which would be full of roses in the summer; and the green door had a brass knocker shaped like a cat.

But this was not what made Masters yank on his handbrake with some violence as he stopped the car. Despite spring and budding trees, the long windows to the right of the door showed the reflections of fire-light. And a man's figure passed across one window, as though pacing in thought.

"That," said Sanders, "looks like Sir Dennis Blystone."

"It is Sir Dennis Blystone," snorted the chief inspector. "Oh, the fatheads! The eternal, blistering—I told Sugden to keep an eye on him! I had 'em all watched, every single one of them, to keep 'em from getting in touch with each other before I got here. And now look what's happened! He's got out, somehow. Come on."

A neat maid took Masters's card. They were led into a drawing-room, a sort of bower, where Bonita Sinclair and Sir Dennis sat on either side of the fire.

It had a domestic look about it. The woman wore a loose blue morning-robe, and was sipping a morning sherry; her beauty was heightened by the firelight, or by its rather theatrical surroundings. Blystone got up abruptly from his chair.

"Good morning, Mrs. Sinclair," said Masters. "Morning, sir. You made a good recovery."

"Fortunately, yes."

Blystone had (it is a contradiction in terms, yet nothing else conveys the meaning) a personality which seemed at once forceful and hesitant. He was tall, with a somewhat hatchet-faced impressiveness, and a pair of fine eyes which won confidence. Next to this you noticed the careful tailoring of his clothes, which was somehow like the careful tailoring of his gestures: both subdued, both directed towards inspiring confidence and ease. Dr. Sanders liked him at once.

"All the same, sir," Masters went on, "I thought I requested that none of you would leave your homes this morning."

Blystone nodded gravely.

"So you did, Inspector. The trouble was—I had to know."

He smiled in a reminiscent way. If he was still shaky from the after-effects of the drug, he concealed it well. His tone now had a homely air which carried conviction.

"I don't often lose my memory. The last time I did was a good many years ago, on a Boat-Race Night. But I still remember that. When I woke up next morning—well, Inspector, I suffered untold agonies about what I might have been doing the night before. I couldn't rest until I had gone round to see every one of my friends, and pestered them for an hour with questions about my smallest action. I had to know. So I had to know what I did last night."

Masters became affable. "Just so. Well, sir, you didn't kill Mr. Haye, did you?"

"Not to my knowledge," answered Blystone, returning the smile.

They all sat down.

"Now here's the position," Masters pursued. "The difficulty I'm finding is to get anyone to admit *anything,* even the smallest facts. But there're certain things we can't deny. We can't deny Mr. Haye is dead. Eh?"

"Hardly."

"Then somebody killed him. And it's no use denying," said Masters, deliberately and casually baiting his trap, "that we're pretty sure he was killed by one of the three other persons in that room."

He did not need to go on, for he had got his effect. Bonita Sinclair put down the glass of sherry on a table beside her, and looked at him with wide-eyed horror. Blystone, though he remained nodding slightly as though he were following Masters with close attention, stopped him.

"In other words, by Mrs. Sinclair, by Schumann, or by me?"

"If you must have it, sir: yes."

"Inspector, that is ridiculous."

"Why?"

"Because it's plain damned nonsense," retorted Blystone, with a commonsense sharpness. "None of us had any reason

34

to kill him. I tell you he was our friend, and I think I speak for all of us."

"Why is it necessary to speak *for* all of you?" asked Masters quietly.

Blystone regarded him with grave irony. But there was a very slight pause before he spoke.

"And it won't be necessary, Inspector, to pick me up on every shade of meaning. Say that I speak for myself, then, though I think it would have been more courteous to speak for Mrs. Sinclair first. That's all." He hesitated, and then burst out as though anxious to end subterfuge: "Oh, look here. We may as well have this straight. Haye was sometimes annoying, and some might have called him a common-or-garden variety of bounder. But he was a good friend; he did me a lot of favors; he was always interesting, and—if the man who killed him isn't hanged higher than Haman, it won't be for lack of help *I* can give you."

After this outburst, of which he seemed a little ashamed, Blystone resumed his consulting-room manner and sat back.

"Good!" said Masters cheerfully. "That's the sort of talk we like to hear. Now, sir: didn't it surprise any of you to be invited to Mr. Haye's flat as late as eleven o'clock last night?"

"No, not particularly."

"But your daughter tells us that you never go to parties."

"My daughter has nothing to do with this," said Blystone, suddenly annoyed. "I am told she gave you some trouble last night, for which I apologize. And I hardly know what she means. I am not one of this 'Bright Young Set' we hear so much about; but I don't consider myself old enough to qualify for a bath-chair just yet."

"For instance," argued Masters, "Mr. Haye didn't ask you to come there and say he had some information to give you. Eh?"

After making the last remark, Blystone had glanced across at Bonita Sinclair, who smiled back at him in a cryptic way. But at Masters's question he turned round again sharply.

"Information? No. I don't understand."

"You say he did some favors for you. What sort of favors?"

"He had invested some money for me, always successfully, and he gave me a number of—outside tips."

"Oh, ah? And did he invest money for you too, ma'am?" asked Masters, turning to the woman.

She assumed the same earnest air she had shown last night. Her dark hair was now bound round her head and into wheel-like plaits over her ears. Bending forward in the fire-light, she had one arm and hand braced stiffly on her knee as in the pictures of old actresses. But the posture seemed neither stiff nor theatrical; it was as natural to her as the sincerity of her gaze.

"Quite often, Mr. Masters. I'm a dreadful idiot at business, and Mr. Haye was always willing to help."

"Now, ma'am," pursued Masters with his cat-like deceptiveness, "I'd like to have you go on telling me what you began last night, when the doctor interrupted us. I mean about the atropine. You were all given a dose of atropine in *something,* you know. But last night you told me it was impossible that anybody could have dosed the drinks. What did you mean by that?"

She looked puzzled. "I—I don't think you can have understood me properly. Or else I was still under the influence of the drug, and perhaps I didn't make myself quite clear. I'm so sorry. What I meant, of course, was that none of us could have poisoned the drinks."

"Us?"

"Any of the four of us at Mr. Haye's flat."

Masters stared at her. "Excuse me, ma'am, but that wasn't what you said last night! You said N-o-b-o-d-y at all."

"Surely you misunderstood?" she suggested, with such earnest candor that Masters was a little staggered. "Let me tell you what happened.

"As soon as we all arrived at Mr. Haye's flat, he asked me to make the cocktails—as I think I told you? Yes. Of course, I know you don't think *I* put the poison in them. But I couldn't have done that, even if I had wanted to. And neither could anyone else. They were all there in the kitchen, watching me."

"All three men?"

"All three, standing round me."

"Go on, ma'am."

"To begin with, Denny—I am so sorry—Sir Dennis rinsed out the cocktail-shaker with hot water. And he rinsed out the glasses too, with us watching. I made the drinks, and Mr. Haye shook them. Sir Dennis made his own highball, of whisky and ginger-ale." (In reply to Masters's inquiring look, Blystone nodded firmly.) "Then Mr. Schumann put the shaker, and the highball-glass, and three empty cocktail-glasses on a tray, and carried them into the living-room. We saw him put them down on the little table, and then he came back; and poor Mr. Schumann certainly didn't tamper with them. We can testify to that. Also, I *know* there was nothing wrong with the drinks at that time."

"How do you know that, ma'am?"

"Because I tasted them," she answered, with a triumphant smile. "People always do, you know. I mean, when you've

36

made a batch of cocktails, you sample it to see whether it's all right. When I had made the White Ladies I took a drink of them, and I'm afraid I drank straight out of the shaker." She made a face as though delicacy had been outraged. "Also, I tasted Sir Dennis's highball. I had never had a 'highball' before, you see, and I wanted to know what it was like."

Masters was growing more uneasy. He cleared his throat.

"Just a moment, ma'am. You say Mr. Schumann carried all the things from the kitchen to the living-room, and 'came back.' Didn't you all go into the living-room?"

"No, that's what I wanted to tell you. We stayed in the kitchen, because Mr. Haye was showing us a trick with an orange. You cut the peel in a certain way, and wriggle it or something, and it's got a face like a laughing or crying baby." A shade of gentle tolerance, of sad indulgence, went over her face. "There never was such a man as Mr. Haye for tricks and jokes and appliances of all kinds. Whenever he could get some new ingenious thing, like a mirror for the bathroom that wouldn't cloud with steam, or a new way of making a ten-shilling note vanish out of an envelope, he was as pleased as a schoolboy. I don't think I shall ever forget him standing up in front of the electric refrigerator in the kitchen, making that orange baby say, 'Ma-ma', and bursting with laughter all over his face." She paused, shuddered, and added in a casual way: "That horrible umbrella-sword-stick belonged to him, you know."

There was a silence.

"I did not know it, ma'am," Masters observed grimly. "Did he have it at the flat last night?"

"Oh, yes; he's had it for a long time. It used to stand in the ordinary umbrella-rack in the hall."

"But about the poison. Mrs. Sinclair, are you willing to swear nobody tampered with those drinks?"

She clasped her hands together. "I do. I am. That is, I know none of us could have done it. We were watching each other all the time. You can understand, Mr. Masters, it simply wouldn't have been possible. But of course it must have been done afterwards. Mr. Schumann put all the things down on the little table, and returned to the kitchen with us while Mr. Haye was showing us the orange baby." She paused impressively. "We all stayed in the kitchen for—how long, I wonder?"

As though anxious to have the thing right down to a fraction of a second, she appealed to Blystone.

"Three or four minutes, at the least," Blystone decided, his hard eye on Masters.

"And during all that time," Mrs. Sinclair continued, "the

37

drinks were in the other room, exposed on the table. You know—of course you would know—that the kitchen doesn't communicate directly with the living-room. The door from the kitchen to the hall was nearly shut, because Mr. Haye was standing in front of it. So we couldn't see out into the hall. Isn't it horribly clear? During that time, someone must have crept into that living-room—some outsider—and put the drug in."

Masters made another note. He was becoming dangerously bland and affable; he seemed to swell.

"Just so, ma'am," the chief inspector said with interest. "One thing, though. Are you quite certain Mr. Schumann didn't drug the things when he took them to the living-room?"

Both Mrs. Sinclair and Sir Dennis Blystone spoke at once; there was no doubt of this.

"We watched him from the hall," she explained. "The tray was a bit wet, and I didn't want him putting it down on any of Mr. Haye's fine furniture."

"I see. Had any of the cocktails been poured out when they were taken to the living-room?"

"No; they were poured out later. The only drink actually in glass was Denny's highball. Oh, Inspector, isn't it simple?" she urged. "A person would only have to slip into the living-room, drop the atropine into the cocktail-shaker and into the tumbler, and—it's a dreadful thing, but there you are."

" 'M, yes. Quite. The atropine must have gone into the cocktail-shaker. Eh?"

"Of course."

"Go on, ma'am."

She hesitated. "There isn't much else, really. Afterwards we went into the living-room. Mr. Haye poured out the cocktails and handed them round. We sat down round the table. Mr. Haye put us each at one side of the big table because he said he had a little speech to make." Once again she seemed on the edge of tears. "He got up like a chairman at a meeting and said, 'Friends, Romans, countrymen.' I mean—chairmen at meetings don't usually say that; but it was the way Mr. Haye talked, and he would shake all over with laughter when he said something like that. He said first we would drink a toast to me. 'Our White Lady,' he said. So we drank the toast. Then he said he had something to tell us: that this was a sort of celebration—"

"And what did he have to tell you, ma'am?" demanded Masters, while she looked at the fire.

"But that's just it. He never finished. He said, first of all, that it reminded him of a story about two Scotchmen. He told that story, and looked excited, and said it reminded him of another, which he had got to tell us before he forgot it. It was one of those long stories, which seem to go on forever, and are all full of dialect—Mr. Haye loved to imitate dialects, especially Lancashire.

"Well, at the beginning I didn't think the story was so funny. But all of a sudden I burst out laughing. We were all laughing, and we laughed harder and harder. I was feeling queer and overheated. Mr. Haye certainly looked overheated, because the perspiration was running down his face, and his red hair stood up, and he was laughing so much he could hardly talk. The oddest thing was to see Mr. Schumann—who looks like a saint, really, and frail as he is—almost doubled up with his hands pressed to his sides, and stamping on the floor.

"The last thing I remember is Mr. Haye's face seeming to swell up until it filled the room, and red as fire with the hair round it. He was saying, 'Eee, bah gooom!' or something in dialect, and pointing at us. Everything sort of scrambled up and grew horrible; and that's the last I recall."

She told the story with a far-away air, staring alternately at the fire and at Masters. But the narrative had an extra-ordinary vividness—her artist's eye for a picture?—which she emphasized with one or two slight gestures.

"I don't even like to think about it," she added.

The chief inspector turned non-committally to Blystone. "You, sir. Have you anything to add to that?"

"I'm afraid not," said Blystone, passing one of those curious hands across his forehead. "I realized that something was wrong, of course. But there was no time to do an thing about it. I wanted to sing, as a matter of fact. I was going to strike up, 'Pull for the shore, sailor; pull for the shore.' But I can't remember whether I actually did."

"You agree that none of your party could have poisoned the drinks?"

"Isn't that obvious?"

"And it's certain the atropine must have been put into the cocktail-shaker by some outsider while you were all in the kitchen?"

"Yes."

"But, with the exception of your highball, the drinks were not actually poured out from the shaker until you had all gone to the living-room? You saw the cocktails poured out?"

"Certainly."

Masters leaned back with ferocious geniality.

"Now, then!" he said. "I don't mind admitting I've enjoyed this little ride on the roundabout. But I'm bound to warn you both that it's time we got down to business and you told the truth. The point is, there was no atropine in that cocktail-shaker. You follow me, sir? Consequently, the atropine must have been put into each individual drink, *after* the cocktails were poured out. And you say you were all there, sitting round the table in the living-room. I want to know which one of you poisoned those drinks. I also want to know why you had four watches in your pocket; and why you, ma'am, were carrying a bottle of quicklime and a bottle of phosphorus. Well?"

CHAPTER FIVE

DR. SANDERS had been waiting for it, watching it draw closer, wondering how the woman's spiritual candor and Blystone's dogged positiveness would stand up under it. But the result was not exactly a triumph for Masters. Both of them stared at him. For one brief instant you seemed to see through their opened eyes into their brains, as at the drawing of a curtain; and what you saw there, Sanders would have sworn, was honest bewilderment.

Sir Dennis Blystone got up from his chair. His astonishment seemed to chill slowly into suspicion.

"It will not be necessary," he said sharply, "to try any police tricks on us. We are trying to help you."

"It's not a trick, sir," the chief inspector told him. "It's the gospel truth. Ask Dr. Sanders here, if you don't believe me. There was no atropine in that cocktail-shaker."

Blystone contemplated him for a time, while the implication of Masters's grim straightforwardness seemed to filter into his own mind like poison. Then he turned to the woman.

"God, Bonny," he said in a different voice, "what *did* happen?"

"I suggest you'd better try to remember, sir. Now, come! No hard feelings: let's just have the truth. You see the meaning of that. If the cocktails had been poured out before you all came back to the living-room, if they had been standing there exposed while you were all in the kitchen—well, your story would have held water. But they weren't. You say (or rather the lady does) that the drinks were all right when they were made, because Mrs. Sinclair tasted them. Very well. They were all right up to the time they were poured out into the glasses, because there's no atropine in the shaker. But after they were poured out for a toast, somebody slipped

40

the drug into each glass. You were all sitting at the table; you must have seen who did it. Now, then: have you anything to tell me? Do you want to change your story?"

Blystone lifted his hands and let them fall.

"I do not want to change my story," he said. "It is the plain, literal truth."

"Oh, what's the good of all this, sir?" demanded Masters, beginning to show a frayed temper. "You don't deny the cocktails were poisoned, I hope?"

"No."

"Just so. But, if you keep on like this, you'll be saying it was impossible the drinks could have been poisoned at all."

Blystone gave him a glance from under craggy eyebrows. "That is precisely what I am saying. I will take my dying oath that nobody tampered with those drinks round the table. Man, do you think I—we—haven't got eyes? Do you think it would be possible to sit at a table and not observe a drug being put in?"

The chief inspector, fuming, looked from one to the other of them. Bonita Sinclair was tapping her slipper slowly against the carpet; at the moment, with her thoughtful expression, she resembled a Madonnaesque schoolmistress.

"Please let me say something," she interposed. "What is this 'atropine' like? I mean, is it solid or liquid? Has it got a color?"

"Well, doctor?" prompted the chief inspector, turning to Sanders.

"It is a colorless liquid," Sanders told her. "You have probably seen it many times without recognizing it. Atropine comes from belladonna, and there is belladonna in most ordinary eye-lotions."

She looked startled.

"Eye-lotions? But I have—" She paused. "And how much of it would be needed to make a person unconscious?"

"Of pure atropine, only a few drops. This was pure atropine, by the way; not the weaker medical preparations."

"Then I think I can solve your problem," said Bonita, with a certain air which (Sanders thought) was ghoulishly like humor and which struck him as all wrong. "It's quite simple, too. Someone came in from outside, just as we thought. But he didn't put the atropine into the cocktail-shaker, for he wouldn't be able to gauge how much to put in, and he might put in too much and kill everybody. So he put a little of it into the bottom of each glass, where he could measure the quantity. You say it is colorless. So nobody would notice it. Most cocktail glasses are damp or wet anyway; and, if it were noticed, the person would simply assume it was

41

water from the washing, and pay no attention.—Don't you think I'm clever, Denny?"

She had turned the full power of her personality on Blystone, who colored a little. But he remained staring ahead.

"I must say, ma'am, you've got an eye for these things," Masters said grimly. "I hope you don't take to poisoning, or you'll have most of 'em backed off the boards."

It was her turn to redden. She lowered her eyes, and she was breathing more rapidly.

"I'm sorry, Mr. Masters; but I don't think that was very funny."

"Nor I," he assured her. "What about it, doctor? Could that have happened?"

"No," said Sanders.

It caused a minor sensation. Both Bonita and Sir Dennis became very quiet.

"I mean," Sanders went on, "that it doesn't seem very likely. Where were the cocktail glasses standing?"

"In the middle of the refectory table," she answered, after a slight hesitation. "Mr. Haye leaned over and poured out the drinks."

Sanders considered. "You see, the largest amount in those glasses was almost big enough to kill, if the whole cocktail had been drunk. It amounted, in bulk, to something between a teaspoonful and a tablespoonful. If there were three glasses, little ones, and all with so much white liquid at the bottom of them—well, wouldn't someone at least have noticed it? Did anyone notice it?"

"I—I believe I did," the woman told him earnestly. "But, of course, I shouldn't like to swear to it."

Though Masters must have been furious, he tried not to show it. After glowering at the placid face, and at the hint of rather sinister amusement in Sir Dennis's expression, he opened his notebook again.

"We'll leave that for a moment," he said, "until you think you can remember. In the meantime, sir: would you mind telling me just what you were doing with those four watches?"

Blystone threw back his head and laughed. He had just been lighting a cigarette, and the quiet violence of his amusement blew the match out. Laughter changed and lightened his face; it seemed to be good for his whole system.

"I beg your pardon,' he corrected himself gravely, and put down the cigarette on the mantelpiece. "But may all your riddles be solved as easily as that! I understand that a simple thing like my four watches has been giving the police a thundering headache. You'd better hear the explanation. By the way, Mrs. Sinclair gave you the clue last night—though you don't seem to have spotted it. Didn't you tell them, Bonny, that I was to pick you up here at your house before we went on to Haye's?"

"Yes, sir, she told us that," said Masters. "What of it?"

"And she further told you, I think, that she had three very important telephone-calls to put through at various times? One to New York, one to Paris, and one to Rome?"

Masters's eyes opened, and then narrowed.

"You've already guessed it, Inspector," said Blystone heartily. "Those cities do not operate on Greenwich time. In the case of New York, for instance, there is five hours' difference. Midnight here would be seven P.M. there. Paris and Rome have different times as well. But, if from various cities like that you are told to ring up at an hour indicated by them, you are going to find it extremely complicated; and you are likely to muddle yourself badly. Bonita cerfainly would have.

"I found the solution," he explained with amusement. "One of the four watches, my own, is set with ordinary English time. The other three were set to the corresponding times in New York, Paris, and Rome. One glance at my watches, and you could tell the time in any of four cities. It was a great help. And it's all very easy when you know the answer."

Masters, it must be recorded, looked at him with something very like admiration.

"You don't tell me, sir?" said the chief inspector. "As you say, all very easy when you know the answer. Is there any answer to the quicklime and the phosphorus?"

It was the woman who laughed now.

"But surely that didn't bother you? I suppose it would, though, in a way," she remarked thoughtfully. "You see, I took the wrong handbag out last night. Naturally I don't carry such things in the ordinary way. Quicklime and phosphorus are used for removing paint from canvas when you suspect there is another painting, a valuable one, underneath. You've heard of that? They're both calciums, you see—calcium oxide and calcium phosphate. I can really recommend the preparation, Mr. Masters."

"You seem to have quite a knowledge of chemistry, ma'am. And I don't mind saying this: *I* can recommend your ingenuity if all this don't happen to be true."

"You don't doubt our word?" asked Blystone sharply.

"Well, sir, after all—that's my business, isn't it?" said Masters, who now seemed to be enjoying himself. "Where would the police be if I never doubted anything? Eh? Oh, yes, I'm willing to believe you." He looked doubtful. "But I don't suppose you could tell me, could you, what Mr. Schumann was doing with the works of an alarm-clock?"

Blystone hesitated. He was stroking his chin with that curious hand, whose first and second fingers were almost the same length; in certain lights it had almost the aspect of a deformity.

"Alarm-clock?" he repeated. "I don't understand. What about it?"

Masters described the find.

"So we all had a treasure-trove," the other observed, looking into space. "No, I can't tell you anything about it. You'll have to ask Schumann."

"If you will allow me," interposed Bonita gently, "I think I can read the hideous enigma. You men are so very nice, and at times you are so very stupid. Mr. Masters, did you ever hear of Andrew J. Borden?"

"Not to my knowledge."

"Surely you have? I dislike to mention such things, because I think it's really morbid to talk of them: but Andrew Borden was the victim in a great American murder-case nearly fifty years ago. He and his wife were killed with a hatchet in broad noon of a summer day in their own house. Their daughter Lizzie—Lizzie Borden of Fall River—was tried for it and acquitted. As I say; I think it is most unpleasant to talk of such things—"

"Just so. But what of it?"

"In Mr. Borden's pocket," she continued dreamily, "they found an old, rusty, discarded lock-mechanism. He had picked it up off the street that morning. Nobody could understand why it was there until they learned he had a habit of picking up things like that; things that interested him or that might come in useful. Mr. Schumann, I think, is very much like that. Don't you read character, Mr. Masters?"

"Why, you might say I'm reading character now," declared Masters gravely. "And very interesting it is too. But, for the moment, I won't trouble you any more. There's just one other thing I think you ought to know. Are you aware," said the chief inspector, in his best witness-box manner, "that all three of you have been accused of being criminals?"

Bonita Sinclair sat up, as though startled beyond speech. Sir Dennis Blystone suddenly put his hands behind his back.

"I don't think that is very funny either," the woman said reproachfully. "Who told you that?"

"Information received, ma'am. Very useful. Is it true?"

"It's utterly ridiculous. Why not murderers as well?"

Masters nodded. "Yes. That was a part of the idea too."

"By George!" exploded Blystone, in an awed tone. "This

44

is going beyond slander. This takes your breath away to such an extent that you don't even think of denying it." At length he chuckled. "Our professions will give you some very sinister suggestions. The story books will be useful. Bonita, of course, sells faked paintings—"

"I do not! It really isn't a joking matter."

"—whereas I undoubtedly sell drugs or perform illegal operations. You might investigate us in that respect. What about poor old Schumann? The novelist in you will immediately come to the conclusion that he murders people, wraps them up in mummy-cases, and sells them as mummies. That's more spectacular than our offenses, but just about as true. No: look here: seriously, who has been stuffing you with all this rot?"

Masters kept an imperturbable face.

"Information received. Now—"

"Who has been stuffing you with all this rot?"

"You seem concerned, sir."

"Of course I'm concerned," said Blystone impatiently. "If somebody walks into your office at Scotland Yard, and says that it's well known you have been taking bribes, wouldn't you be concerned? If a man is accused of something, he's got a right to know what he's accused of and who accuses him."

"What are you accused of, sir?"

"Well, good God, man, that is what I'm trying to find out! Isn't this carrying police reticence a bit too far?" Blystone's extreme dignity had broken down again. "If it gives you any pleasure to take us for—er—what my daughter would probably call a sleighride—"

Masters shook his head. "It seems to me, sir, I've heard some sleigh-bells jingle while I've been talking to you. Hurrum! However, that's as may be. Maybe I can answer your question by asking another. When you and Mrs. Sinclair went to Mr. Haye's flat last night, was Mr. Schumann already there?"

"Where? At Haye's flat? Yes. But I don't see—"

"Was Mr. Schumann's office closed up?"

"Yes. No. Now that I come to think of it, there was someone in the rear office. A clerk or someone. I did not notice particularly. Why?"

"The clerk's name seemed to be Ferguson," observed Masters. "A very interesting chap. Good morning, and thank you both."

His retreat was full of sinister dignity. But, as they went out into the hall, Masters grinned wryly and spoke to Sanders in a low voice.

"Now I wonder," he said, "which of us came off best there?

I've got me doubts. But I'll lay you a tanner I've scared both of 'em, which is what I tried to do. They'll have a tail put on them straightaway. If they knew Ferguson, they'll try to get in touch with him; and it may lead us straight to the old chap."

He scowled, with an expression of wry admiration.

"But just keep in mind what you've heard today, doctor. No wonder Ferguson said they were smooth customers. For pure perverted cleverness, their ways of wriggling out of things with explanations are as good as anything I ever heard. Oh, they're mustard, all right! You heard the explanation about the watches."

"Didn't you believe it?"

"Believe it? Not likely! The trouble is, how am I going to prove what I think?"

"You mean there's still another reason for the four watches? And, for that matter, another explanation of the quicklime and phosphorus?"

"Of course there is," grunted Masters with broad skepticism. "The point is, I can't make the woman out. Hurrum!" He struggled with an innate caution about talking too much. "All I'll say is that I don't see how the quicklime and phosphorus applies to her, unless we've come across a new wrinkle in crime. All I'm certain of is that she's got an A-1 head on her shoulders, and an A-1 imagination for thinking up jiggery-pokery and general ghost stories. She's got—um—possibilities. Sir Dennis Blystone isn't a patch on her for cleverness or maybe other things. But . . . hullo!"

He spoke very softly. They had come to the front door, and Masters was opening it, when he paused. Against the wall in the little front hall there was a low carved chest, not unlike that in the hall of Felix Haye's flat. The lid, Sanders noticed, was raised a crack; and sticking in that crack at one side was what looked like a gray-gloved finger.

The hall was dusky, with frilled curtains over the glass panels at each side of the door. On the wall hung a curious unfinished sketch, the beginning of a sketch, which was signed with the name of Dante Gabriel Rossetti. To Sanders's surprise, the chief inspector looked at this picture carefully before he leaned over and lifted the lid of the chest.

Mrs. Sinclair was evidently a slovenly housekeeper under the spick-and-span exterior. The chest was full of old lumber pushed out of sight: several umbrellas, a tennis-racket going to pieces, a grimy jumper, and two raincoats.

And on top of the pile lay a man's arm.

It gave Sanders an unpleasant shock until he realized that it was a dummy arm. It was composed of a black coat-sleeve stuffed with wool, the edge of a white cuff, and a stuffed hand in a gray glove; and it had an unpleasantly natural look which conjured up all manner of images in the gloom of the hall.

"Ah," said Masters, lowering the lid again.

Sanders spoke quietly as they both hurried towards the door.

"For God's sake, chief inspector, what's going on here? What are they up to? And why does she keep a stuffed arm put away in—?"

"Easy!" muttered the chief inspector, making sure the maid was not in sight. "You'll know soon enough, doctor. Besides, I don't think the arm is her property. You may be able to guess where it came from and why it's here. Eh? In the meantime, we'll just run out to Hampstead and see Mr. Schumann."

CHAPTER SIX

PAST the steep streets of Hampstead, the road still seemed to curve up interminably to the heights overlooking Hampstead Heath. The police-car circled a broad pool of ornamental water and drew up at one entrance to the roads down across the heath.

In contrast to the rolling vastness of the heath, the houses towards their left looked flat and gray. The trees were as yet only touched with green; in the distance they still looked spiky and bluish, with dips and hollows where the hard brown paths wound down under them. A sharp wind was blowing, chasing a discarded newspaper up one of the paths. They seemed here to be at the top of the world, under a sky faintly brittle with sunlight and an air alien to London.

Masters drove the car down the road to the left, in the direction of Schumann's house. His companion was still pursuing the subject.

"I don't want to make a nuisance of myself," Sanders insisted, "but I should appreciate a hint, anyway. Four watches, quicklime and phosphorus, the works of an alarm-clock, and now a dummy arm. Honestly, and man to man: *have* you got an idea what the whole mess means?"

The chief inspector chuckled.

"Just between ourselves, sir—I have," he admitted. "What's more, I've got a good notion to drop in and see Sir Henry Merrivale today. Do you know him?"

"I've seen him. I was in court when he defended Answell on that murder charge. But why do you want to see him?"

"Ah! Not a bad bit of work, that Answell case," Masters conceded, "even if he did do us down. But it would please me a whole lot to see him, because this is one case that will make the old man wild. It's out of his line, you see. He won't be able to make head or tail of it, and—I can. Would I like that? Yes, sir, I would!"

"One other point. Why were you so interested in that drawing hung up in Mrs. Sinclair's hall?"

Masters grew serious.

"Well, I'm not what you would call a connoisseur. Objay dart, as I said in that Peacock Feather case, are a little out of my line. But I do know what touches police work, and my missus has taken me to the National Gallery once or twice to improve my mind. I don't know whether you noticed, in Mrs. Sinclair's parlor, another picture hung up on the wall opposite the fireplace? Painting of a girl in a Dutch cap?"

"I can't say I did. It was darkish in there."

"H'm. Maybe she meant it to be," said the chief inspector. "Anyhow, I'll take my oath I saw the dead image of that same picture in the National Gallery. It's by this chap Rembrandt. I always remember his name, because," confided Masters, "he's the one artist that I think is thundering good and that everybody else admits is good too. Every time *I* like a picture, you can bet your shirt everybody will say it's rotten and that it's an example of my bourgeois taste. That's how I remember."

Sanders studied him.

"There must be a good many Rembrandt copies in existence," he pointed out. "Hold on! Is it true after all—" he was conscious of a sense of disappointment as he said it— "that Mrs. Sinclair deals in fake paintings?"

"Oh, no. Lordlovus, no!" said the chief inspector heartily. "If Mrs. Bonita Ruddy Sinclair is half as clever as I think she is, she'd never be as crude as that. It's a new dodge, doctor. You'll enjoy it.—This is our house, I think."

He stopped the car outside a low wall fronting the path. Bernard Schumann lived in a semi-detached house of solid Victorian respectability. It was built of gray brick, with white stone corners and window-facings; and there was someone watching them from the bow-window as they went up the path to the steps.

A grim-faced old woman in a housekeeper's dress admitted them into the stuffy hall, and waved away Masters's card.

"I know who you are," she told him. "And, if I had my

say, you wouldn't get in at all. We've got doctor's authority for that. But he insists on seeing you. In there."

Before a bright coal fire in the drawing-room, a horsehair sofa of ancient pattern had been drawn up as close as comfort would allow. Schumann, wearing a dressing-gown, lay propped up on the sofa with a quilt tucked closely round him.

He was an appropriate figure for that high bow-windowed room, where the knick-knacks of sixty years ago made a kind of jungle. Schumann's wool nightshirt was buttoned up closely round his neck. His scholarly face, with its pinched darkish eyebrows and gentle wrinkles from nostril to mouth, had something of the air of a clergyman's or a minor statesman's; nor was this effect greatly lessened by the coarse texture of his whitish hair. It was a flaw in the china, that was all. His eyes were candid and pale blue, though they looked troubled. His hands, very delicate ones, were crossed on a book in his lap.

But in this room Sanders found an atmosphere, even a culture, older than Victorian. Among the ordinary gew-gaws there stood a long glass case containing ornaments that were not ordinary: blue canopic jars, statuettes smoothed to grayness, a clay seal, glazed scarabs for signet-rings or pendants. And, in the corner by the windows, stood a mummy-case some seven feet high.

"Please sit down, gentlemen," said Schumann, with a gesture that was almost courtly. His voice corresponded to his appearance; but he had at first some difficulty in getting it clear. "I have been expecting you. I understand you wish to ask me some questions about an alarm-clock."

He spoke without any surprise or apparent sense of incongruity, though he kept on clearing his throat.

"Just so, Mr. Schumann," agreed Masters, also without surprise. "How did you know that?"

The other smiled. "Sir Dennis Blystone telephoned to me."

Then he half straightened up on the sofa. "Let me be frank, and make our position clear. I know you wanted to prevent us from communicating with each other; and I suppose you were quite right, according to your lights. But consider our point of view. We wanted to know what happened even more than you did. That was only natural. Again to be frank: I gather that you suspect us of concocting some story among ourselves, some story we should all agree on and which should be the reverse of true. I gather you suspect us of saying, 'That's our story, and we stick to it.'"

Masters shook his head.

"If you don't mind, sir, I'll ask the questions."

"As you wish," said Schumann courteously. "But I can

tell you in advance that I have nothing to add to what my friends have said. They told you the truth, and the whole truth."

"Suppose we take it in order," suggested Masters. "First of all, since you mentioned it, what about that alarm-clock? You can explain what you were doing with that?"

"I was doing nothing with it."

"Doing nothing with it?"

"I never saw it before in my life."

Again Schumann seemed to conquer a dry and tickling throat; he regarded Masters with a smile of sober charm.

"Now that's too bad, sir," Masters told him. "I was hoping you'd have some good reason for carrying it. Mrs. Sinclair and Sir Dennis both had good reasons."

"No doubt. I can speak only for myself."

"Then you don't speak for 'us' any longer?"

"Now what in the world, I wonder," asked Schumann, with every appearance of straightforwardness, "am I supposed to say to that? I give you my word there has been no prearranged story. If there had been, I should probably have had a lie ready for you."

"How do you think the alarm-clock works got into your pocket?"

"I don't know. I imagine someone must have put it there."

"While you were unconscious? Then you're suggesting that the other things found in Sir Dennis's pockets and Mrs. Sinclair's handbag were also put there while they were unconscious?"

"Not in the least. I have no doubt they are telling the truth."

For a long time Masters carefully led him over every incident that had happened the night before. His story varied in no particular from the account already given by the other two witnesses. And, while Schumann's smooth voice flowed on, Sanders found his own attention wandering.

It wandered most frequently to the big sarcophagus in the corner by the windows. Blurred by time to the mere ghosts of colors, the painting on that mummy-case blended with shadows in the room as the sky grew overcast. The background of the sarcophagus was black, with transverse hieroglyphed bands in red; the mask or face was gilded, and a vulture was depicted on the breast, where the arms were shown as folded. In front of it, a little to the right, stood a Victorian tripod bearing a brass pot without a plant inside.

Whether or not from mere association of ideas, it seemed to Sanders that there was an aromatic odor in the room. This, he thought, was impossible.

"—and I can only repeat," Schumann continued, with no hint of impatience, "that there was *no* ulterior motive in our gathering at Haye's flat: at least, that we were aware of."

"That we were aware of?"

"If you prefer, that I was aware of. I did not even know who the other guests were going to be."

"What time did you arrive at the flat?"

"At about a quarter to eleven."

"Was Mr. Haye already there?"

"Yes; he told me he had just arrived there."

"How did he—um—behave, sir? What was his manner like?"

"Well, he seemed annoyed that the caretaker of our building, Timothy Riordan, had not made a good job of tidying up his flat. He had told Riordan to attend to this earlier in the evening, it appeared." Schumann smiled, and his expression changed. "Otherwise he was in excellent spirits. He made one or two jokes about dragons."

Masters blinked. "Eh? Dragons, sir?"

It was a like a change of atmosphere, a skidding of the wheel; yet for a second Dr. Sanders could have sworn their host was trying, almost with a gulp in his throat, to tell them something. But Schumann drew back again.

"I suppose," he said unconvincingly, "that Timothy may be considered something of a dragon. But what did you wish to ask me? I am waiting."

"When you went up past your office last night, Mr. Schumann, was the office open? Was anybody working there?"

"No, certainly not."

Masters leaned forward. "Just the same, you know, there was a man in your office last night. He said his name was Ferguson, and that he worked for you. He knew his way about: knew you by your first name: identified you: he made himself at home, to the extent of washing his hands there?"

Throughout this, Schumann's changes of expression seemed to reflect darkening sky outside. He pushed himself upright on the sofa, showing the outline of frail arms under the Victorian dressing-gown. But he spoke ve·y quietly:

"Sir, are you raving mad?"

"Of course," said Masters, "we know there's no such person—"

"I don't think I quite follow you," interposed Schumann. "Certainly there is such a person."

For the first time Masters was honestly taken aback. If he did not exactly jump up out of his chair, his posture conveyed that he had been on the verge of it. It was the one development for which he had not been prepared.

"Here! You don't mean to say you've got a clerk named Ferguson?"

"Not now; that is what makes it so extraordinary. But he, or a man such as you describe, did work for me eight or ten years ago. He—he left: there was some trouble. I understood he was dead. Surely you can't be serious?"

Staring straight ahead, Masters was evidently rearranging thoughts.

"Lummy, what a lot that would explain!" the chief inspector muttered. "How he was at home there, how he knew about you, even how he might have got into the office when it was locked up. . . . But it still wouldn't explain how he got out."

"Got out?" repeated Schumann.

"You might as well know it, sir. After we got there, Ferguson disappeared out of a building locked up back and front. How did he do that?"

If possible, a look of even more mild blankness passed across Schumann's eyes like a shadow; the eyelids winked slightly. Sanders had seen just that expression on the face of a man in parliament, preparing to deal with a problem without committing himself.

"I'm afraid I cannot tell you that." He became lightly humorous. "The Ferguson I knew was not a magician."

Masters scented evasion, and was after it like a terrier.

"Ah! Possibly not, sir, as you say. But you tell me that there was some trouble at the office, and Ferguson 'left.' What was that?"

"I don't think it would interest you."

"Anything about Ferguson would interest me, sir," observed Masters grimly. "If I could find out who Ferguson is, and what he wanted, and just how in lum's name he figures in this case anyway, I should feel a whole lot closer to a solution. Just let's hear about it, if you will."

"He absconded with some money," answered Schumann, showing a certain fastidious distaste.

"Didn't you prosecute?"

"No. He went abroad. What he was doing there last night, what he meant or what he wanted, I have not the remotest idea." Schumann's eyes narrowed. "I know there has been no robbery or even any disturbance, because I talked to my chief clerk this morning. The whole affair is irrational. It is mad. Think back over it. A group of us meet for a—an ordinary social evening."

The words here seemed to stick in his gullet, but this may have been the dryness of his throat.

"We are drugged. Poor Haye is stabbed. Certain outlandish articles are placed in our—in my pocket. A former clerk of mine is pottering about in my office below: doing nothing, stealing nothing, acting nothing except a senseless masquerade. Then this clerk, according to you, vanishes through locked doors. I must believe it, since I must believe the evidence of my eyes and ears. But I shall be interested to hear what you make of it. Did Ferguson—for instance, did he say anything about me?"

Learning forward, Masters regarded him with a hypnotic eye.

"Yes, sir, he said two things. He said you had been decorated by the Egyptian government for being able to reproduce the embalming process of the Nineteenth Dynasty, whatever that may be. He also said you were a criminal."

"The first statement is correct. The second is not."

There was a pause.

"But haven't you got anything else to say, sir?" demanded Masters. "Anything to show—?"

"I have my whole life to show," said Schumann quietly. "I think it compares very favorably with that of an absconding thief whom I failed to prosecute, and who dares not remain behind to say this to my face."

Seldom in his life, Dr. Sanders thought, had he heard a speech more convincing, or one more convincingly spoken. But there was something else as well. As Schumann lowered his head, there was again that unspoken struggle to tell them something.

And Masters showed an intuition for which Sir Henry Merrivale would never have given him credit.

"Mr. Schumann," he said, "who killed Haye?"

"I do not know.

"Atropine is a curious drug," Schumann went on, as though irrelevantly. "I have been looking up its properties this morning. I had some experience last night with the hallucinations it brings. At that table last night, I was facing across the room towards some murals on the wall and some bright-jacketed books with lurid titles on a shelf over the fireplace. It seemed to be hilariously comic, the way in which the murals came to life and the titles of the books grew like electric-signs. Persons, non-existent persons, seemed to walk in and out of doors—"

"Mr. Schumann," said Masters, "who killed Haye?"

"I do not know," their host almost snarled.

Masters's tone became colorless. "Very well. Now, about the drugging of the various drinks. I'm bound to tell you your story agrees with the others. But it's been suggested that a little atropine could have been brought to the flat by an out-

53

sider, and put into the glasses themselves while they were unattended in the living-room. Do you agree?"

"No, sir. The glasses were quite clean. I noticed it later
when Haye was pouring out the cocktails."

"Ah!" said Masters with satisfaction. "Then how was the
atropine put into the drinks?"

For the first time a twitch of annoyance crossed Schumann's face. He lifted one hand and shaded his eyes with it.

"My friend, I am not a subtle person. I cannot produce
ingenious explanations for you to disbelieve. But to my
homely mind that seems so simple that I cannot understand
your attitude. Now, you deny that during that three or four
minute interlude the work could .have been done. Why?
Solely and simply, if I understand you, because you later
found no atropine in the cocktail-shaker. But think again:

"Suppose an outsider had come in, and has poisoned both
the contents of the shaker and Sir Dennis Blystone's highball? We drink, and become unconscious. The outsider has
then a free hand to do as he likes in the flat—which we can
hardly deny, since he took that swordstick out of the umbrella-stand and stabbed Haye. What on earth is to prevent
him from washing out the shaker, filling it half-way up
again with harmless cocktails, and leaving it where you
found it?

"It will then be assumed, as you did assume, that atropine was put into each individual glass. Thereby suspicion is
thrown on one of us. And, but for the fortunate chance that
we had stood by to watch while the drinks were prepared, we
might have believed it ourselves."

Schumann coughed from the distinct enunciation and
weight he had tried to give every word. At the end he looked
worried.

"Surely you had thought of, that?" he asked.

"Oh, yes, sir; I'd thought of it," said Masters gruffly;
"whether or not I believe it. Then you accuse Ferguson of
being the murderer?"

"Not at all. I am more charitable than Ferguson."

The sky had grown heavier and darker over the heath outside the windows. Now the colors of the mummy-case were
barely discernible in the corner; color had faded from furniture, from curtains, even from the brass bowl on the tripod
near the sarcophagus. Masters made a last entry in his notebook.

"Just one more thing," he said, "and I'll leave it at that—
for the present. I'd like to get a full description of Ferguson
as you last knew him: his address, his habits, where he went,
everything about him. I daresay you can supply that?"

"Not offhand. It has been at least eight and nearer ten years ago, and I am a little hazy. But I think I could get you the details. Ferguson! Yes, I will get you the details; I am as interested as you are. You see, I thought he was dead."

"Dead?"

"I will send you the details this afternoon, sir," repeated Schumann, sliding off the sofa with an effort and standing upright. "In the meantime, I must ask you to excuse me."

The reason for this abrupt dismissal Sanders did not understand: unless Schumann was at the end of his strength. He looked a little paler than when they had entered. Standing with the padded quilt draped round him, he was smaller and yet even more courtly than they had imagined; it was impossible to disregard his proffered hand. Schumann's eyes, and the blank painted eyes of the mummy-case, followed them as they went out. Yet it is a sober fact that the stolid Chief Inspector Masters, when he glanced behind and noticed it, seemed uneasy.

"Anything wrong?" inquired Sanders.

"Urr!" said the other, flinging out his arms as though he wanted room. And, once outside the house, he breathed deep as though he wanted air.

"Explanations! And more explanations! If I hear any more ruddy explanations—"

He had his hand on the front gate when another person, who had been lurking just outside and smoking a cigarette, stepped in front of him with an air of concern.

"Please don't say that," requested Marcia Blystone. "I've been following you all morning, and now you've got to listen to me. I know who killed Mr. Haye, and how the poison was put in the drinks."

Masters stopped and stared. It was the first time Dr. Sanders had seen Marcia in honest light. She looked more robust, more smiling, than the rather-too-intense girl he had seen last night. Her brown eyes were shining as though with triumphant excitement, there was color in her cheeks, and she wore a bright scarf round her head.

"You too, miss?" demanded the chief inspector. "What are you doing here?"

"I took a taxi out," she explained. "And I dismissed it. Honestly, I'm afraid you'll have to give me a lift home in your Black Maria or police car or whatever you call it. Hello, doctor."

"Now, now, miss, I'm afraid—"

"You wouldn't leave me stranded, would you?"

"Of course you wouldn't," said Sanders sharply. "Good

God, where is your chivalry, Chief Inspector? The girl can't walk home. And if she has some valuable information—"

Masters tried a tone of fatherly reasonableness. "Now miss, you're entirely welcome to ride back in the car, of course. But as for any more theories—"

"It's not theories," she said calmly. "It's facts. Or, at least, some of it," she amended carefully. "Do you mind if I sit in the front seat with you? So I can explain."

Throwing away her cigarette and taking a large sketching pad from under her arm, she got into the car beside the chief inspector. Sanders, hoping the latter would not see his grin, climbed in at the back. Masters drove off rather vigorously down the curve along the steep edge of the heath.

"Very well, miss," he said. "Let's hear it. Were you going to say that the atropine was put into the cocktail-shaker and that the murderer washed it out afterwards?"

"No, of course not," said Marcia, evidently surprised. "It's much more ingenious than that. The murderer—"

"Just so," said Masters. "To tell you the truth, I was afraid of that. But let's get it in order. Who's the murderer?"

Very carefully she opened the sketching pad and placed it across the steering-wheel—to the discomfort of Masters, who is a steady-going two-handed driver. But he risked a look. On the pad she had drawn in pencil a really brilliant sketch of Bonita Sinclair. Glancing over their shoulders, Sanders saw that it emphasized the physical points he had noticed: the long, soft lines of the body and the smooth spiritual lines of the face. It wore now a yearning look which the artist had strongly parodied.

Marcia added in an offhand tone:

"There's the hussy."

"Miss," roared the chief inspector, "will you kindly take that thing off my—Anyway, what makes you think she did it?"

"She murdered her husband," said Marcia, "and I've got evidence to prove it."

Regarding what happened next, Masters maintains to this day that the girl, in her triumphant excitement, held the sketch in place on the steering-wheel and at the same time trod on his foot. It is certain that the police-car shot like a projectile down the long curve of the road descending the hill. But Marcia, in turn, maintains that no damage would have been done if the other vehicle—vehicle by courtesy—had been on its proper side.

Majestically in the middle of the road, an enormous fruit-barrow was creaking its way up the hill. The man who was pushing it could be seen only with difficulty behind gentle pyramids of oranges, apples, lemons, Brazil nuts, greengages, and bananas. But his despairing howl rose up an instant before the collision.

Yanking the wheel over hard, Masters avoided a head-on smash. Otherwise he could not have made a more skillful cannon-shot at billiards. In one majestic crash, the barrow whirled, rose, and pirouetted like a dancer; at the same time it exploded with oranges, apples, lemons, Brazil nuts, greengages, and bananas. They did not merely issue from the barrow: they sprayed. The man who had been pushing the barrow escaped its weight, but he went into the ditch under an avalanche of oranges, apples, lemons, Brazil nuts, greengages, and bananas.

Bumping on a broken wheel, the barrow coquettishly turned turtle and stayed there. It was not so with the man who had been pushing it. He struggled up, an avatar of wrath, and even then they were startled to see that he was stout, that he wore a loud-colored bath-robe, running-shorts, and spectacles.

"What the goddamholyblazes do you think you're doin'?" howled a familiar voice, blasting the birds out of the trees above. "You tried to murder me, that's what you did! Oh, gimme me breath! Just gimme the goddam strength to get my hands round your neck—"

His spectacles down on his nose, distorted with a rage beyond apoplexy, there peered from the ditch the malevolent face of Sir Henry Merrivale.

CHAPTER SEVEN

IT WAS, Sanders thought, an impressive sight. Standing fat and straddle-legged on the edge of the ditch like an all-in wrestler, with his bald head gleaming malevolently and his gaudy bathrobe flying, H.M. gibbered. He looked, in fact, like an all-in wrestler after a losing decision, as had been the case with the oranges, apples, lemons, Brazil nuts, greengages, and bananas.

"Well, what were you doing on the wrong side of the road?" shouted Masters. "Just tell me that. What were you—"

"What was I—" After one tremendous blast H.M. stared, and his voice grew awed. "That's not Masters," he declared. "Don't tell me that's Masters?"

"I tell you I couldn't help it, sir! The young lady was leaning across me with that drawing, and her foot was on top of mine—"

H.M.'s eyes opened.

"So you're at it again," he said in a strangled voice. "Burn me, Masters, you're not decent. Ever since you met Mrs. Derwent in that peacock feather case, no gal is safe with you. You assault 'em in broad daylight, in a police-car—"

With a powerful effort Masters conquered himself. "Let-him-rave-miss," he said out of the corner of his mouth. "That's the old man. That's Sir Henry Merrivale. And you, sir. Will you kindly tell me what in blazes you're doing in the middle of Hampstead Heath, with nothing on but a bathrobe and pants, pushing a blazing fruit-barrow up this hill?"

"I'm takin' exercise," said H.M. with dignity.

"You're what?"

"I'm reducin', curse you," said H.M., drawing his bathrobe round him like a Roman toga. "Everybody in Whitehall, from Squiffy down to my very typists, never gets tired of tellin' me what a corporation I'm developing. They've got no call to. Look at that! Hard as iron!" He thumped on it. "But I'm gettin' tired of it. I'll show 'em."

Sniffing, he peered up and down the road as though looking for enemies.

"But that fruit-barrow—"

"I got a friend named Giovanni," said H.M., "who owns a gymnasium down the road. I also got a friend named Antoinelli, who did own a fruit-barrow. He bet me I wouldn't push it up the hill, and he was right. How far did I get with it, hey? Just twenty-nine paces, and along comes a joy-ridin' policeman and swipes it to glory. Oh, my eye. Look at it now. I never saw anything like it since the Bolivian earthquake. It's persecution, that's what it is. Burn me, I'll—"

"You're not hurt, are you?"

"This is a fine time to be asking that, ain't it? Sure I'm hurt. Good and hurt. Probably—"

"In that case, sir," Masters urged soothingly, "you'd better get in the car with us. Never mind the barrow. As soon as we get to the nearest A.A. box, I'll see that the damage is attended to. You don't want to do any more exercising today, do you?"

"Well . . . now. I expect I've taken off enough inches for today," said H.M., inspecting his waist-line hopefully—as we all do. "You're smackin' well right I don't want to do any more exercising today. I don't mind dumb-bells or road-work; but I draw the line at turnin' flip-flops into a ditch every time a police-car tries to run me down. And if you think *my* damages can be attended to at an A.A. box, then you got no idea as to the position or extent of the injuries. *Gor!* I could—"

Hitching the bathrobe higher round his shoulders, he waddled over to the car across a plain strewn with oranges, apples, lemons, etc. Though he still simmered occasionally, he seemed in a better temper. After inspecting the wreckage, he sat down on the running-board of the car, picked up a banana, peeled it, and malevolently began to eat it.

"Aren't you afraid you'll put it all back on again?" said Marcia.

"Ur—sorry," interposed Masters, and performed introductions. At mention of Sanders's name H.M. looked up with interest.

"So? I know your boss at the Home Office Analyst's. I say, son, are you the fellow who wrote that book, *Post-Mortem Analysis of the Larger Intestine?*"

"How terribly romantic," said Marcia, gurgling. "Did you really, doctor?"

Sanders, who was young enough to glow with pleasure at mention of this work, felt his enthusiasm dimmed. The book, his literary ewe-lamb, was eighty pages long, had sold eleven copies, and was probably not known even to the Recording Angel. But frequently he had read it through again and thought that it was good. Also, he hoped that it would impress Marcia Blystone.

"It's a good book," asserted H.M., and made himself Sanders's friend for life. "A thunderin' good book. Somebody's got to write these things, my wench. It can't be all moonlight and roses."

"Not in the larger intestine, anyway," said Marcia.

"Don't be indelicate," howled H.M. "How the devil did we get into all this, anyway? What was I going to say? Ah, I got it. Look here, Masters: I seem to see omens and portents, and a glimpse of dirty work at the crossroads. Were you three conferrin' about the Haye case?"

Masters drew himself up in his most official manner.

"May I ask, sir, what makes you think that?"

"Ho ho," said H.M. "Were you?"

"Possibly, sir. As a matter of fact, I'd thought of dropping in on you this afternoon—"

"Masters, confess! You were goin' to walk in and crow over me like billy-o, and strut and grin with all the trumps in your hand. Weren't you? Burn me, *why* does it give you such pleasure to do me in the eye? Why does it give *everybody* such pleasure to do me in the eye? Well, you can save yourself the trouble, because—"

"Because?"

"I've already been consulted about it," said H.M. with sour dignity. "And I'll bet I know a thing or two you don't."

"Consulted? By whom?"

"Do you know the firm of Drake, Rogers & Drake?"

"Mr. Felix Haye's solicitors," stated Masters. "I sent Sergeant Pollard round there this morning."

"Then he'll have an awful lot to tell you, son. It was old man Drake who came to me. He must be gettin' on for ninety; but last night something occurred at the offices of Drake, Rogers & Drake that hasn't occurred there for a hundred and fifty years. It so scandalized Drake that he had to get extra-police aid or bust."

"Well, sir?"

"They had a burglary," said H.M. "Haye deposited some things there for safe keepin', and they got pinched."

"Money? Valuables?"

"No, nothin' valuable. That is, nothin' financially valuable. Just five little boxes. Five little sealed boxes, to be opened by the solicitors in case Haye died. The solicitors never got a chance to open 'em. And I'm afraid, Masters, they might contain five little motives for murder, all in a row."

H.M. dropped the banana-skin, licked his fingers, and fished up another banana. The Chief of the Military Intelligence Department sat on the running-board and gobbled bananas with concentration. As for Masters, he had assumed a stuffed look which meant business—and which he also meant as a warning.

He spoke warningly: "Just so, sir. Miss Blystone here is the daughter of Sir Dennis Blystone."

"Sure; I know," H.M. agreed, looking up. "When I saw the mention of Haye's death in 'stop press' this morning, I thought I'd better ring up Boko and ask what was what. Boko put me through to your superintendent, and I got the details. I don't like it, Masters. It's not pretty."

"Do you think we'd better discuss the case: at the moment?"

"Masters," said H.M. querulously, "I wouldn't have your nasty suspicious mind for anything in the world. Burn me, I never could understand this tendency to hush-hush and look mysterious in front of witnesses! If they're goin' to lie, they'll lie. If they're goin' to tell the truth, they won't. Why not say it in front of the gal? She looks like a nice gal. And she may be able to help us."

The chief inspector grinned.

"You might say, sir, it was helping us that wrecked your friend's fruit-barrow. Miss Blystone was just about to tell us

60

who committed the murder, and how the poisoning was done—"

"Oh, never mind that now," cried Marcia, getting out of the car. "But what did you mean about five little boxes?"

"Just that. Haye deposited five cardboard boxes, wrapped in brown paper, tied, and sealed with red wax. They were to be opened in case of his death. Each box had a certain person's name written on it."

"What names?" she asked quickly.

"Well . . . now. I wrote down the list, but it's back in my trousers at Giovanni's gymnasium, and I don't recall offhand. But your father was one of 'em."

"I don't believe it."

"Why not?" inquired H.M., with wooden interest.

She had grown very quiet. "Because I know what you're thinking. I'm sensitive to atmospheres. I can feel things, and I know. You think my father is a criminal. You think there was a kind of—of board-meeting of crooks in Mr. Haye's flat last night. But you're wrong about my father, because I can tell you this:

"The only reason why he was there at all was that he went with Mrs. Sinclair. My mother doesn't know anything about it —I hope. *I* didn't know anything about it until this morning. But I saw Stella Erskine, who knows everything there is to know in London. And the plain truth is that the way my father has been carrying on with that Sinclair woman is a public scandal."

She drew a deep breath, and her face was flaming.

"H'm," said Masters. "To tell you the truth, miss, I'm not surprised. Well?"

"She's *notorious*," said Marcia. "She's known all over Europe. It seems she really is a quite genuine authority on paintings, but that's not her only profession. In spite of all her demure shrinking ways, she's nothing but a common—"

"Now, now!" growled H.M. "Here, have an apple. Or something. I mean, there's no point in gettin' upset—"

"I'm not upset about that. I shouldn't have minded if he had taken up with some nice sensible steady-going bit of fluff who wanted a good time. But I don't want to see him make a fool of himself. And I don't want to see him divorce my mother, get married to this—this machine, and then get himself poisoned for his money."

Masters whistled. "Look here, miss. You said she was a murderess, and you could prove it. You didn't honestly mean that, did you?"

Marcia lifted her shoulders.

"Oh, nothing was actually proved against her. But here's

what I heard from Stella Erskine, and you can trust Stella to know the dirt if there is any.

"About three years ago Mrs. Sinclair was going about with a man in Monte Carlo, a rich Italian. He was taken with a seizure after having dinner with her one night, and he died. The trouble was that they were having dinner on the terrace at the Splendide, in full sight of a dozen people and two lynx-eyed waiters (there's nerve for you!). It was proved beyond any doubt that he had eaten nothing she had not eaten; he had drunk nothing she hadn't drunk—because, in her coy way, she drank out of his glass. The matter was hushed up somehow; and nobody knows the details, except those details.

"Then there was the death of her husband. Nobody knows or knew much about him. One day he simply up and died, that's all. It was at Nice or Biarritz. He was buried quickly; the old doctor, who was a friend of Mrs. Sinclair, granted a death-certificate; and she collected the insurance.

"That," admitted Marcia, who seemed relieved to get this off her mind, "is all the real dirt. The rest is just a whisper. Even Stella, who'll embroider if she gets half a chance, couldn't tell me much. But it seems she has had some rows, also hushed up, with a museum in New York, an art-dealer in Paris, and some private collectors. She does get about."

There was a silence. H.M. wrapped the bathrobe closer round his big bulk, and scowled at the half-eaten banana.

"Phooey!" said H.M., uninformatively.

"You're sure this isn't just gossip, Miss Blystone?" demanded Masters. "Because, if it isn't—"

"It's what they all say, that's all I can tell you. Couldn't you ring up the police in Monaco and France, and find out?"

"Oh, yes. I could and I will. But this Italian in Monte Carlo: was it shown he was poisoned? That ought to've been easy."

"Nothing was shown. As I say, it was hushed up."

"Still—under the circumstances, evidence that he couldn't have been poisoned—?"

"She poisoned the Italian," answered Marcia, "in the same way she drugged the drinks last night. I told you I was following you all morning. You went to her house, didn't you? And my father was there. I went right in when I saw you come out. I was never so scared in my life, but I was mad enough so that I didn't care. I'm afraid I caused rather a dust-up; but I got the facts. Remember, I told you that when she had dinner with the Italian she drank out of his glass?"

"Yes."

"And she drank out of my father's highball-glass last night, didn't she?"

"Well, now, miss, that's what she told us," grunted Masters.

"And, what is more, she also tasted the batch of cocktails just after she mixed them. But she drank straight out of the shaker. Didn't she?"

"Yes."

"It's unnatural," said Marcia, with another deep breath. "Did you ever in your life see anyone pick up an open cocktail-shaker, and tilt it up, and drink over the edge? Especially a re-fained long-legged prude like Bonita Sinclair?"

"I don't drink cocktails, miss. Beer for me every time. But—"

"She had a reason, of course. I've tried the trick with mouthwash, and I know it works. You put a little of the liquid in your mouth, in the hollow under the tongue. You don't have to keep it there long. She could have put it in her mouth under pretext of looking in a cupboard after a bottle, or something.

"All right! Then you pick up a tumbler or a cocktail-shaker, and pretend to drink from it. But you don't drink from it, really. You add something to its contents: in this case, you add the atropine you've got concealed in your mouth. And in full sight of several witnesses you've drugged the drinks in such a way that everybody will swear they couldn't possibly have been drugged in any way whatever."

As though a little fearful now that she had completed her speech, Marcia took a firm hold on the door of the car. There was a silence amid the holocaust of fruit.

H.M. was amused, as far as a flicker of amusement could go over that wooden face.

"That's torn it," he said. "Masters is shocked. You mustn't mind him. He thinks it's unsanitary. He also thinks it's unladylike of the wench, which seems to indicate that he was a bit impressed. 'When in silks my Julia goes—' "

"I don't care whether it's unladylike," snapped Masters. "The point is, is it practical? What do you say, doctor?"

"Considering all the factors involved—" Sanders was beginning after some reflection, when Marcia interrupted him in a temper.

"Oh, for heaven's sake!" she cried. "When I saw you last night, and asked you to walk upstairs blindfold into you-didn't-know-what, you went right ahead as cool as you please. You didn't ask a question; you just took charge of everything; and I thought you were quite the nicest person I'd ever met. Then you began to talk. You and your 'data' and your 'considering all the factors involved'! Why can't you be human?

Why can't you have an opinion on something, yes or no, like a human being? There you are! When somebody asks you a straight question, you pull in your chin, and lift up your finger, and sort of squint your eyes shut like the Delphic Oracle—"

Sanders went red to the roots of his hair.

"I am beginning," he said through his teeth, "to have a decided opinion as to the course that ought to be pursued with *you*."

Marcia froze.

"Well, really," she said.

"Will you two shut up?" ordered H.M. austerely. After he had glared everybody down, he went on: "There's a question before the house. I got my own opinion, but just the same I'd like to hear yours, son. D'ye think this atropine-gargling trick could have been worked?"

"It's remotely possible," Sanders replied, "provided she could hold enough pure atropine to do the business, which I doubt. And there are two 'human' objections to it. First: if Mrs. Sinclair did anything like that, why did she afterwards clean out the cocktail-shaker so that there was no atropine in it? She herself told us the stuff must have been put into the shaker, so why make herself out a liar? Second: the great objection to the method is that it's comic. If you ever tried to prove a case like that in court, you'd have the jury grinning at you, and counsel for the defense would laugh you to pieces."

That, he thought, was better.

With some effort H.M. hoisted himself up from the running-board, and began to climb into the car.

"I want some trousers," he growled. "Fine thing it'd be, hey, if I caught pneumonia and died now! Then you never would get out of the mess. And, Masters, my son, you're in one awful mess. I wonder if you know how bad it is."

"Oh, I wouldn't say that, sir." Masters was complacent, almost smugly complacent. "In fact, I might say I've put together the whole affair, with the exception—hurrum!—of a few little trimmings. Of course, I don't expect you to see it. It's a bit out of your line. I don't know whether I told you the newest developments?"

Rapidly he sketched out the events of the morning. H.M.'s expression of evil satisfaction deepened.

"And there you are, Sir Henry. I don't blame you for thinking it's a mess, or being puzzled—."

"Puzzled?" said H.M. "Who's puzzled? Not me. If you think I'm bluffin', I'll prove it to you. I'll tell you just exactly what you can explain and what you can't explain. You can explain the four watches, the alarm-clock guts, the magnifying-glass, and the dummy arm. You know why there's an unfinished Rossetti sketch in Mrs. Sinclair's hall and a Rembrandt in her parlor. You can explain the quicklime and the phosphorus too; but you don't see how they apply to her. That's got you beaten to blazes. Also, even grantin' that there's a real Ferguson after all, you can't for the life of you think of what he's doin' in the picture: to say nothin' of how he vanished out of it."

He looked vaguely at the windscreen of the car.

"H'mf. Ferguson and Mrs. Sinclair. Ferguson and Mrs. Sinclair. Yes, son, they're your two crooked puzzle-pieces.

"Masters, there's an old stratagem in puttin' together a puzzle. Say you've got a lot of bits that fit together. And you've also got a couple of extra bits, but neither of 'em will slide into the pattern with relation to anything else. So what do you do? You try the two extra bits together, to see if they'll fit each other. Try Ferguson and Mrs. Sinclair together, just for the sake of argument."

"Together? How?"

H.M.'s little eye opened in the direction of Sanders.

"You, son. According to the information I got from Boko, you were the first to speak to Ferguson after the discovery of the murder?"

"Yes, so far as I know."

"Uh-huh. Did he say anything, son? Make any comment?"

Sanders considered. "Yes. He said he might have expected it, and told me that Bernard Schumann was upstairs."

"Anything else? I don't know. But I'm almighty curious."

"Yes, he did," answered the other, startled. "He said, very sharply, 'How's the lady?' I thought he meant Miss Blystone; but he seemed to get mad all of a sudden, and said in no uncertain terms that he meant the dark-haired lady, Mrs. Sinclair. Then he hurried upstairs."

H.M. shut his eyes.

"So. And consequently, Masters, we got a connection between the two already. I was hopin' for that. Not much of a connection, maybe; but enough to lead straight through hypothesis to Q.E.D. Think of what you know about the quicklime and the phosphorus. Think of what you know about Ferguson. Think of what you know about Mrs. Sinclair. Then tie 'em all together like a string of sausages; and see if you can't tell me straightaway just what Ferguson is, and how he evaporated out of that building."

There was a pause.

"Lummy!" breathed Masters. "You've got it. Not a doubt in the world. It's as clear as daylight."

Dr. John Sanders looked from one to the other of them, at such a point of maniacal curiosity as he had never known before. Intellectually, he was in danger of blowing up.

But the rift which had threatened between him and Marcia Blystone was closing up again by the alliance in cryptic utterance between H.M. and Masters. Marcia had literally come over to his side; for she was now standing close to him with her hand on his arm. Or was she quite as puzzled as she seemed? He could not help wondering, because—as in a few moments last night—he could not read her expression. Since her outburst, her eyes had been as expressionless as the painted ones on the mummy-case at Schumann's. But her words confirmed their alliance.

"Don't mind me," she said. "Is it really as clear as daylight? I know I'm here only by courtesy, but if you've gone as far as that you might be a little more explicit."

"All right," said H.M., abruptly. "Get into the car."

But he still sat silent, glaring at the windscreen, while they drove. He was silent when Masters arranged at an A.A. box for the disposal of the fruit holocaust. He was silent when he went to get dressed at the Garibaldi Gymnasium and Physical Fitness School; and even when he stemmed with banknotes the torrent of woe from the owner of the fruit-barrow. In fact, it was not until the car drew up before Felix Haye's building in Great Russell Street, at two o'clock in the afternoon, that he spoke.

"If I was talkin' like that," H.M. said to Marcia, as though there had been no interruption, "it was because I want you to tell the truth. Here we are; and you can tell me the truth now, can't you?"

"Me? Why?"

H.M. indicated. "You were standin' by that street lamp, weren't you?"

"Yes." She looked at him curiously.

"And how long had you been waitin' here last night before the doctor came along?"

"A little over an hour, maybe."

"Uh-huh," said H.M., with the same air of sour but apologetic patience. "Then you saw the murderer, didn't you? You must have."

CHAPTER EIGHT

AT`ABOUT the same time on the same afternoon, Detective-Sergeant Robert Pollard—acting on instructions received from Chief Inspector Masters—was entering the offices of Drake, Rogers & Drake in Gray's Inn.

Pollard's own morning had been devoted to collecting what information he could about the various persons in the case. The result left him depressed and rather dazed. According to underground sources in Fleet Street, Sir Dennis Blystone was unimpeachable. An affair with Mrs. Sinclair, of course, had been hinted at. But he did much work for charity; he was of sober reputation; there was no swank about him; he never took a taxi when a bus would do; and so on in the same fashion.

Since both Mrs. Sinclair and Bernard Schumann were well-known dealers, the Yard as well as Pollard's journalistic friends could supply information. The most suspicious art-dealers spoke of Mrs. Sinclair in terms so glowing that their sincerity could not be doubted. Schumann not only appeared to be an honest man: he was a much-persecuted man who once had ten thousand pounds' worth of completely uninsured stock wiped out in a disastrous fire at his warehouse in Cairo. Even Felix Hayè himself dwelt in an odor of sanctity throughout the City.

Tears on the Stock Exchange are unusual. They made the sergeant swear. Pollard, who had crept into the Force by way of Harrow and Cambridge, usually found his theories ignominiously crushed by the chief inspector. But by this time he had certain definite ideas, which evidently did not square with those of Masters.

To two leads, he felt, Masters was not paying half enough attention: (1) the swordstick; (2) the girl, Marcia Blystone.

That morning Pollard had questioned the caretaker at Haye's flat, the gnarled little Irishman whom he had seen the night before. Timothy Riordan still breathed an air of whisky and suspicion, but at least he was coherent. He knew nothing, he swore, about the events of last night. He had not seen or heard anything all night. The last time he had seen Haye alive was at a little past six o'clock in the evening, when Haye had gone out to dinner; he had met Haye on the stairs, and Haye had asked him to tidy up the flat, because there were guests coming that night.

Had he tidied up the flat? Yes, he had. About this part of it old Timothy seemed still more snappish and suspicious. He had tidied it up immediately and then gone down to his basement again. He had not seen any of the guests arrive that night, because he had gone to bed at half-past ten.

That umbrella-swordstick? Indeed he did know that umbrella-swordstick. It belonged to Mr. Haye himself, and he (Timothy Riordan) had noticed it in the flat last night when he was tidying up.

This interested Pollard. Masters, the sergeant thought, was so obsessed with the question of atropine that he thought little of the weapon with which the actual crime had been committed. Why a swordstick at all, if the murderer were able to poison any given glass with atropine? Why that particular swordstick? And why, after the murder, had it been left standing so conspicuously on the stairs?

Marcia Blystone had also been neglected.

"Not my type," Pollard had decided, after inspecting her. From what he had seen of the two, he much preferred Mrs. Sinclair. Mrs. Sinclair, said the Fleet Street gossip, had buried two husbands. The latest had been an aging business man, whom nobody remembered at all except for his startling agility on a tennis-court. She had also had a string of admirers along the Riviera: one of them a rich Italian who—during an intimate dinner at Monte Carlo—had got so excited about her charms that it brought on an attack of appendicitis, and he died of it.

Privately, Pollard could understand this. In Marcia Blystone there was too much of the boy; and the sergeant detested boyish women. He could not in honesty deny that Marcia was very good-looking, but he suspected her of certain pawky humors, moods, and artistic tempers. He was quite sure she was a fluent liar.

Was Ferguson a witness, a witness for whom they were frantically searching? Yes, but so was Marcia Blystone. She had been hanging about outside the building where Haye was killed. For how long? An hour at least, she said. The police-surgeon could not report with certainty just when Haye had been stabbed, beyond the fact that it was not before eleven o'clock and not later than twelve. Well, had the girl seen anything? Had she gone into the building? And how did she figure in the affair anyhow?

Pollard had got to this point when he groped up the breakneck stairs of the old red-brick house in Gray's Inn where Drake, Rogers & Drake had been an established firm before the birth of Queen Victoria. The almost gruesome integrity of Drake, Rogers & Drake, who always acted and spoke together like Siamese triplets, was well known to Pollard. He felt the atmosphere as soon as he entered. An ancient secretary took him into the presence of Mr. Charles Drake, the junior partner.

The junior partner looked worried. He was a brisk, aggressive, no-nonsense man of fifty-odd, with a rolling walk like a sailor and a pince-nez which pushed up the bridge of his nose into a hump. His manner may have been intended to intimidate clients; but behind it Pollard now sensed an uncertainty about the first catastrophe that had overtaken his firm since the French Revolution.

"This is awkward," he said, greeting Pollard in a little office barely large enough to turn round in. "I suppose my father knows best; but I understood he wasn't going to the police. Er—just yet, in any case. Stop!"

Charles Drake's eyes through the pince-nez were large and gray, having about as much human sympathy as two oysters. But at least they were human enough to show consternation. He held up his hand as though he were really stopping Pollard like a traffic-policeman.

"You mean you've come about Haye's death?"

"Yes, sir, of course. Why else should I have come?"

"Burglars," said Drake briefly. "But I guessed as much. Stop!"

Nothing could be done here without a quorum of the firm being present. Through a series of ambassadors Charles Drake requested the presence of Mr. Wilbert Rogers, the next in command. Mr. Rogers was a lean and dignified man who spoke only once or twice, but with powerful weightiness.

"Yes, I guessed as much," Charles Drake went on. "I saw a mention of it in the paper this morning. But I haven't told my father yet. It isn't wise to upset him before lunch. May I ask if Mr. Haye was murdered?"

"He was murdered, sir."

"I guessed that too. Very well: you're here. It will have to be discussed. Get out your notebook, and I'll give you the facts."

He had the air of one about to begin dictation, and his knuckly hands opened and closed. After exchanging a nod with Mr. Rogers, he settled back in his chair and talked like a machine-gun.

"Mr. Felix Haye," he said. "Mr. Haye was an investment broker, and had offices at 614 Leadenhall Street. He has been a client of ours for eleven years. (You will correct me if I am wrong, Mr. Rogers? Thank you.) He was a bachelor, and his only surviving relative is an aunt in Cumberland.

Exactly a week ago, April 7, Mr. Haye came to us and stated that someone had tried to kill him."

Pollard sat up with a jerk. Drake's tones were merely businesslike.

"Yes, sir. Did he say who had tried to kill him?"

"No," said the other, drawing a pad of notes towards him. "For our mutual inspection he produced a half-flagon bottle of Ewkeshaw's Pale Ale. With this he had a cardboard container, wrapping-paper, and a covering letter. The letter was a sheet of Ewkeshaw's stamped stationery, on which were the typewritten words, 'With the compliments of Horace Ewkeshaw & Co. Ltd.' Mr. Haye stated that he had reason to believe the letter was a forgery, and that the contents of the bottle were poisoned."

"I see, sir. An old dodge," commented Pollard, like a detective of ripe experience.

"As you say, an old dodge," agreed Drake with a cynical air, like a poisoner of even riper experience. "He asked our advice. My father suggested the police, although I did not concur in this view, and neither did Mr. Haye. He asked us to send the bottle to an analytical chemist's; and, if it should prove to be poisoned, to put the matter into the hands of a reliable firm of private inquiry agents. Have you got that?"

"Yes, sir."

"Good. I followed his instructions. Two days later, April 9, we received the analyst's report. The bottle contained ten grains of a narcotic poison called atropine."

"Atropine!"

"A-t-r-o-p-i-n-e," spelled Drake conscientiously.

"Thank you, sir. What happened to the bottle?"

"One moment," said the solicitor with asperity. "You must have the facts in order, or they will be of no use to you. Mr. Haye called on us that same afternoon, and we informed him of the analyst's report. He was upset. He then went away again, saying that he would return after he had thought things out.

"He returned on the following morning, the tenth. My father doesn't usually come to the office on Saturday mornings. But Mr. Haye was so insistent that we were obliged to bring my father from our house in Bloomsbury Square, so that we should all be represented.

"Mr. Haye then showed us five small parcels or packages, which he spread out on the desk—er—like a conjuror. Each was a cardboard box about six inches long by four inches broad. Each was wrapped in heavy brown paper, tied with strong string, and sealed in two places with red wax bearing the imprint of his own signet-ring. On each box he had printed a name in ink. Here is a list of the names."

Taking a blue-bound folder out of the drawer of his desk, he copied some words on a sheet of the writing-pad and pushed it across to the sergeant. Pollard read:

1. Bonita Sinclair.
2. Dennis Blystone.
3. Bernard Schumann.
4. Peter Ferguson.
5. Judith Adams.

Uncertainly Pollard put the sheet away in his notebook. Peter Ferguson? Peter Ferguson? A real Ferguson, then? But this did not trouble him so much as the fifth name on the list.

"This last name, sir.. Who is Judith Adams?"

"I can't say. Probably some friend—I mean, some person he knew. If you search long enough you will undoubtedly find her; *I* don't know."

"Never mind for the moment, sir. What did Mr. Haye tell you?"

"He said that he wished to deposit the boxes with us, to be opened by us in case anything happened to him. We accepted the charge. And last night someone broke into the office and stole every one of them. There. That's the whole story. Unfortunately."

Drake's large eyes, magnified behind the pince-nez, showed a suffusion of blood which concealed a powerful impatience and curiosity. But he asked no questions. Instead he picked up a pencil and began to tap the desk.

"Yes, sir; but what did Mr. Haye say about the boxes?"

"He said," answered the other carefully, "that they contained evidence about certain persons who wished him dead."

"Evidence against, you mean?"

"He said, 'evidence about.' He may have meant evidence against. I do not know."

"Do you know what was in the boxes?"

"Certainly not. Stop: except in one case. Eh, Mr. Rogers?"

"Yes," agreed Mr. Rogers grimly. "It ticked."

"It what, sir?"

"Sergeant," said Charles Drake, putting down the pencil, "did you know Mr. Haye? I don't say that to lead you away from the subject; I say it to emphasize a point. Mr. Haye was said to have 'a sense of humor.' *I* don't have a sense of humor: I can't afford one: and I may say that I get along very well without it. But Mr. Haye had. *In pace requiescat!*

71

Say, as one lady said to me, that he was 'just an overgrown boy'—" a twitch of cold nausea passed over Drake's face—"and let it go at that."

"Young Charles!" said Mr. Rogers sharply. "No!"

Charles Drake caught himself up at this correction.

"In any case! Miss Rawlings, my secretary, picked up the boxes to put them away in Mr. Haye's deed-box here. One of the small boxes began to tick. T-i-c-k, tick. Miss Rawlings almost dropped it. I believe the poor lady thought she had got hold of a bomb. Mr. Haye was amused. He said something to the following effect: 'You must have started up one of the watches. There are four of them in there. They should have run down long ago.' "

"Do you remember which box that was?"

"I do. It was the box bearing the name Dennis Blystone."

"Yes, sir. Go on."

"That (I repeat) was on Saturday, the ninth. On the following Monday I received the bottle of Ewkeshaw's ale back from the analytical chemist's. I dropped Mr. Haye a line, asking him what he wished me to do with it. On Tuesday—in short, yesterday, the day of the murder—Mr. Haye rang me up. He asked me if I would bring the bottle round to his flat yesterday afternoon. I did so, and I arrived there about six o'clock."

"Yes sir?"

"He spoke of a 'great design' he had in mind; but he would not tell me what it was. Haye was in his worst mood: or his best, if you prefer. When I arrived at the flat, he was dressing for dinner and taking a drink or two. I found him standing in the hall in his evening-trousers and under-vest, waving a cocktail-shaker in one hand and a cavalry saber in the other. Yes: I said a cavalry saber. He was making passes at the air, squaring off and fighting imaginary duels.

"I told him I had brought the bottle. He instructed me to put it in the kitchen somewhere. I told him for heaven's sake to be careful with the bottle, and asked him if he wanted anyone poisoned. He said he rather thought he did. To make sure nobody got the bottle by mistake, I took a piece of paper and wrote, 'Poison; do not drink,' on it. I put it in a conspicuous place on one of the lower shelves of the pantry, with the paper stuck round its neck."

Pollard made a note, staring at the past. He must find that bottle. For it was Felix Haye himself who had had ten grains of atropine in his possession the night before. Of course, it was not 'loose' atropine; it was contained in Ewkeshaw's ale; but all the same—

"You say, sir, that this was at about six o'clock?"

72

"It was."

"And then?"

"I asked him why he was in such a hurry to get the bottle of ale. He said—I don't vouch for the exact words here, but this is the gist of it—he said, 'I want to exhibit it at a little party I am giving tonight.' At this time he was dressing, and shouting out to me from the bedroom."

"Did he say anything more about the party?"

"No, he did not. He would not. He finished dressing, and we left the flat together. He said that he was going on to dinner somewhere, and then to a music-hall; but that he meant to return before eleven o'clock. I am sorry, sergeant. That is all I can tell you."

"But wasn't there anything else, sir? *Anything* at all? You realize how important this is: a reference to any guests—?"

Drake frowned rather angrily.

"Stop. You shall have it, anyhow. As we passed the Anglo-Egyptian Importing company on our way downstairs (you are acquainted with Mr. Bernard Schumann, the owner?), we met one of Mr. Schumann's assistants, who was just going home. He is an Egyptian; I cannot remember his name. But I can't say I like the look of the fellow. All eyes and teeth and polished hair. Haye asked him whether Mr. Schumann was in the office. The Egyptian said that Mr. Schumann had not been there all day; and that he was (if I remember correctly) entertaining some out-of-town friends."

"Did Mr. Haye say anything to this?"

"Only that he rather expected to see Mr. Schumann that night," replied Charles Drake, looking at him sharply. "He accented the word 'rather.' That was all."

"Nothing else, sir? Nothing at all?"

"I believe not. Why?"

"For instance, when you were on your way out of the building did you meet the caretaker, and did Mr. Haye speak to him? The caretaker is a little oldish man named Timothy Riordan."

Drake's manner showed a cold impatience and an even colder wish to help.

"Am I omitting vital facts, young man? Come to think of it, we did meet the caretaker. At least," he corrected himself cautiously, "I have reason to believe it was the caretaker. He carried a mop, anyhow. Haye asked him if he would go upstairs and tidy up the flat."

"And did he?"

"I cannot say. He went upstairs, anyhow."

"Was he drunk, sir?"

Drake was puzzled to such a bursting point that even his

mouse-colored hair seemed to stand on end with it; but he would not ask a question.

"Not that I observed. Er—he made some reference," said Drake with an effort, "to a book which he seemed to have loaned to Haye, and asked whether Haye had finished with it. I only tell you this because he has probably told you already; and I don't wish to be accused of keeping back 'vital information.' Haye said nothing."

"Book, sir? What book? He said nothing about a book."

"I have not the remotest idea. Something scurrilous, I daresay."

Pollard grunted. "Finally, sir, if you'll just tell me about this burglary at your office last night—?"

"Ah, that is better. Well, the burglary took place at twelve-thirty. At twelve-thirty the night-watchman here, Beasley, rang up my house—or my father's house, I should say. I got up and answered the phone, and then I waked up my father. Beasley had just seen someone climb out of the window of our rear office here, and go down the fire-escape."

"At twelve-thirty," said Pollard musingly.

"Beasley chased this person, whoever it was, without result. Then he came up to the office. Nothing had been touched in the rear office except the large 'deed-box' painted with Mr. Haye's name. It was one of a number of such boxes on our shelves. This box was broken open, lying on the floor. I got dressed and came here as soon as I could. The five smaller boxes were all missing.

"I never thought before," said Drake, staring in a somewhat cross-eyed way through his pince-nez, "how easy it would be to rob an office like this. These windows are two hundred years old. A knife would open the catches like—like cheese. But who robs solicitors' offices? All valuable documents—I mean of the sort a burglar would steal—are in our safe, which has not been touched." He looked round quickly at Mr. Rogers. "I *hope* it has not been touched? No matter. Not that I can't imagine what happened. But that's your job. Perhaps you'd like to go and see the scene of the burglary?"

He got up.

Pollard got up too. But he was not looking at the bunched and somewhat frog-like countenance of the solicitor. He was looking beyond at a solution to all the inconsistencies, at an outline of the case which had now taken on hard clarity. It was not theory: Pollard knew that he grasped facts.

Felix Haye had called a "board-meeting" with sardonic purpose. He meant to exhibit the poisoned bottle of ale to his guests. He meant to announce that evidence against each

74

of them, which might mean anything from a prison sentence to the gallows, had been packed away in five boxes; and that these boxes would be opened if another attempt were made on his life.

But somebody had been prepared for all this. Somebody's stock of atropine was not yet exhausted. Somebody drugged the drinks of those in Haye's flat. It might have been one of the three guests themselves; it might have been the elusive Ferguson or the altogether mysterious "Judith Adams" whose name they now heard for the first time.

Then "somebody" stabbed Haye with the swordstick. Leaving a group of unconscious persons at the table, some-body let himself—or herself—quietly out of the house in Great Russell Street. This person hurried to Gray's Inn, no great distance away; this person broke into the solicitors' office and took away the damning boxes. But, obviously, all five boxes had to be taken. If the murderer removed only one box, the box on which his own name was written, it would betray the person who had taken it. So all five had to be removed in order to protect the thief.

And then?

Pollard could hardly stifle a whistle of enlightenment. He saw it now. The essential clue lay in those four watches.

In the box bearing the name *Dennis Blystone*, Haye had deposited four watches. Consequently, unless you wished to believe a coincidence too wild for credence, they were the same four watches that were found in Blystone's pockets on the night of the murder. Therefore Marcia had lied when she said Sir Dennis had taken them to Haye's flat himself. On the contrary, they were placed there by the murderer while Blystone was unconscious.

The murderer's actions, became apparent. After breaking into the solicitors' office, he had returned to Great Russell Street with the contents of the boxes. The four watches (con-tained in Blystone's box) he put into Blystone's pockets. The alarm-clock works (contained in Schumann's box) he put in Schumann's pocket. The quicklime and the phosphorus (evidence of some sort against Mrs. Sinclair) he put into her handbag. In all probability Haye had written a letter which would explain the meaning of these curious articles. But the murderer, while wishing to throw suspicion on everyone, was not willing to go so far as to expose everything.

And that murderer's movements could now be traced.

According to the doctor's report, Haye had met his death between eleven and twelve. During this time the murderer had been in the building, since he drugged the drinks and stabbed Haye with the swordstick. He then left the building

75

and went to Gray's Inn for his burglary: and the time of the burglary was established at twelve-thirty o'clock. Consequently, since the murderer afterwards returned to Great Russell Street in order to plant curious clues in the pockets of drugged guests, he must have done this between twelve-thirty and one o'clock.

Therefore the key to the whole case was Marcia Blystone.

Sergeant Pollard, rapidly setting these thoughts into line, was a little dazed at the ease with which a net could be woven. By her own confession, Marcia Blystone had been waiting outside the building for over an hour: that is, between twelve and one o'clock. During that time the murderer had both left the building in order to go to Gray's Inn, and returned to it after the burglary. There was only one way in or out of that building—the front door. As had already been established, the windows were inaccessible and the back door bolted and chained on the inside. Therefore the murderer must have used the front door. And therefore Marcia Blystone must have seen him.

The girl had been lying, just as she had been lying about the four watches.

Afire with excitement, Pollard wanted to hurry away with a certain query for Marcia Blystone. He did not know that this was not necessary. He did not know that Sir Henry Merrivale, sitting in a police-car before the house in Great Russell Street, was already glowering upon Marcia and asking her exactly the same question.

CHAPTER NINE

"—IF I saw the murderer?" repeated Marcia Blystone, staring at H.M. "Is that what you want to know? Honestly, I don't know what on earth you're talking about."

Neither, it appeared, did the chief inspector; though with native caution he checked himself on the edge of speech.

"Oh, Masters, my son," said H.M. despondently, answering his look. "You haven't heard the story of the burglary, from old man Drake. I have."

H.M. was now wearing his ancient top-hat, tilted forward on his brows. He peered malevolently up and down Great Russell Street. He studied the building in which Felix Haye had died. And, with some feeling comment, he sketched out the account of the burglary.

"You see what's happened?" he asked with ghoulish hopefulness. "The murderer hocussed the drinks and stabbed Haye. He got out, raided Drake's office, came back here with the loot, and festooned people's pockets with the contents of those boxes. The crib was cracked at Drake's at twelve-thirty. I've verified that. So," insisted H.M., "who went in and out of here during that time? Because I'm smackin' well certain the murderer did."

The idea was novel: so novel that Masters momentarily forgot the girl in order to go in pursuit of it.

"I can understand," the chief inspector admitted, "how the real murderer might have destroyed all those boxes. But why should he bring any of the—um—trinkets back, and put them in people's pockets? Why?"

H.M. seemed bothered by an invisible fly.

"I dunno, son. But that's what happened. It has to be. All those trinkets were relics of antiquity. The clockwork was rusty, the phosphorus dull, the watches had run down long ago. Burn me, you don't think Mrs. Sinclair or Blystone or Schumann run around normally carryin' keepsakes like that, do you?"

"No, I admit that—"

"And it's why they were so worried when they woke up and found the stuff in their pockets. Blystone and Mrs. S. tried to acount for it by tellin' stories that wouldn't deceive a baby, if what you've been repeatin' to me is correct. That tale of phosphorus and quicklime being used to clean paintings is not only a lie; it's smooth and staggerin' cheek. Did that woman really think she could make people believe it? Schumann did better. He at least acknowledged he wasn't in the habit of carryin' the works of an alarm-clock, and that someone must have put it in his pocket when he was unconscious."

Masters pondered this.

"Very well, sir. If you say so," he growled. "But I still ask, *why?* Why did the murderer take a big risk in coming back to the house here? Of course, if he wanted to incriminate the others—sow suspicion broadcast, as it were—"

"It seems to me," said H.M., "rather a good move. In fact, I can't think offhand of a better. He'd both throw suspicion and keep the others quiet with somethin' on their consciences to worry 'em. But there's more in it than that, son. You follow it?"

"I follow this much. If this is true, we've—well, almost—eliminated the three guests at the party. If Mrs. Sinclair or Sir Dennis or Schumann were the murderer, whoever it was would hardly have put damaging evidence in his own pocket along with the rest."

"Is it so very damagin'?"

Masters frowned inquiringly.

"I repeat, is it so very damagin'?" inquired H.M. "Just think that over for a while. You've got a very neat case on your hands, son, with a very neat and slippery murderer in the middle of it. For the love of Esau don't take anything for granted, or you'll find yourself on a butter-slide. In the meantime—" he turned round from the front seat to look at Marcia—"why not tell us the truth?"

She raised her eyes and looked at him quietly.

"I am telling the truth," she said in a low voice. "It's quite true I waited out here for over an hour last night. But during that time nobody went in or out of that door. *Nobody*. I'll swear it with any oath you like. Or you can arrest me."

There was a silence. H.M., who seemed about to flare up, grew disconsolate and concluded by scratching his nose. Masters glanced suspiciously between them.

"Now, miss!" he warned. "It had to be by this door. There's a back door to the building; but, as we happen to know, it was bolted and chained on the inside—"

"What about Ferguson?" Dr. Sanders put in mildly. There's a fellow who gets out of buildings without using either the front door or the back door. Every confounded theory seems to come straight back to Ferguson. Ferguson is a kind of testing-acid for everything. But you can't test anything until you do find him; and, if you'll allow an opinion, it wouldn't do any harm to look for him first."

Masters got out of the car in order to draw himself up sternly, but H.M. intervened.

"Now, now, son! Keep your shirt on. He's quite right, y'know. I see I've got to make it my business to get Ferguson by that scruff of the neck. Because, if the wench has been tellin' the truth, some very intriguing possibilities have just opened up to me. Still, there's part of it we can verify." He blinked at Marcia. "You weren't tellin' the truth when you said your father left your home last night carryin' those four watches, and that he took them to Haye's. Now were you?"

She folded her arms.

"If I don't answer you," she said, "I suppose you'll send me to prison. All right. Go ahead."

"Oh, my eye," said H.M. "I never did see such a crowd of people for wantin' to go to jail! Who's goin' to send you to prison? Honest, now, there's no reason for heroics. All I asked you—"

"No."

"Y'see," continued H.M., tilting his hat still further over his eyes, "it will save an awful lot of fuss and bother if you do tell us. Now, Masters and I know what the four watches mean. We know what's inside that dummy arm your father hid away at Mrs. Sinclair's. But we can't *prove* anything, can we? Your father's got the watches. And the only thing Masters is interested in is the murder."

"You're not joking? You really do know?"

H.M. quite seriously crossed his heart. But, if he had any hope that this would allay either her fears or her worries, he was wrong. Marcia got out of the car and slammed the door. Her eyes had that strained, glazed look which speaks of danger from nerves in spite of a calm face.

"Then I'll tell you something else," she said. "If this ever comes out, I'll—I'll kill myself or go to Buenos Aires or something. If there's one thing I can't stand, it's being laughed at. So you can go along and investigate and accuse just as you please; but that woman killed Haye. You'll see."

Without another word she turned round and walked quickly away. H.M. stared after her for a moment; then he turned to Sanders.

"After her, son," he said out of the corner of his mouth. "I wouldn't say this once in umpteen times, but this time—after her! She's the wrong type to worry. Stop a bit. Burn me, I'll go with you!" Glaring at a dumfounded chief inspector, he crawled out of the car, and held tight to his hat. "You stay here, Masters. Why do you think I'm mixin' myself up in this business, anyway? Denny Blystone is one of my oldest friends. You sit tight and I'll see you later. Come on, son."

They overtook Marcia as she was crossing Bloomsbury Street. H.M. waddled at one side of her, Sanders strode at the other; and she was so elaborately unconscious of their presence that she nearly walked into a passing taxi.

"I don't suppose you'd care for a spot of lunch?" suggested H.M. hopefully.

"No, thank you."

They walked on still more rapidly. On their left rose now the vast, spiked, prison-like fence of the British Museum; and, beyond the courtyard, the vast, gray, prison-like bulk of the Museum itself. Round the gates hung a cluster of newspaper-sellers and a pavement photographer with his tripod.

"How about havin' your picture taken?" suggested H.M. He likes being photographed himself, and considers this a temptation of honeyed guile.

"No, thank you," said Marcia. Then, struggling against it, she leaned against the fence and shrieked with laughter.

"All right," she said, beaming on them both at last. "We'll have our pictures taken. And then we'll go to a pub or somewhere, and you'll jolly well tell me what you really think about this business."

After the ceremony of having their pictures taken—H.M. at his most dignified, his top-hat cradled in one arm, his other fist on his hip like Victor Hugo, and glaring at the camera in such a way that even the pavement photographer was moved to remonstrance—they settled down in the saloon-bar of a smoky and comfortable tavern in Museum Street. Two pints of bitter and gin-and-tonic were on the table when Marcia spoke over the last drink.

"I didn't let on before that policeman," she informed him, "but I know all about you. You see, I know Evelyn Blake, Ken Blake's wife. She says you've got the most anti-legal, un-moral, altogether cussed nature of anyone she knows. She says every time her husband goes out with you he always lands in jail. That's why I think you're on my side, really. So—"

"So you ran away from Masters a-purpose, curse you," said H.M. without surprise. "I know. All right; I followed you. What are you goin' to tell me?"

"I don't mind talking in front of you," Marcia said coolly. "But I'm not sure I ought to talk in front of Dr. Sanders. After all, Dr. Sanders is connected with the police, in a way. And Dr. Sanders thinks I'm comic."

"The devil I do," said Sanders, putting down his tankard with a thump. "Here, what are you talking about? I don't think anything of the sort."

"That's what you said."

"I said nothing of the kind."

"You certainly did. You said my idea of how Mrs. Sinclair had poisoned the drinks was comic."

Sanders's exasperation was now full-blown. "And so it is. But that has absolutely nothing to do with my opinion of you. Can't you see—"

"Do you think it's comic, Sir Henry?"

Moving his tankard round on the table, H.M. regarded her with sour amusement. "Well . . . now. You can test it out right here, you know. You got liquid in front of you. And I'm afraid you'll find, my wench, that it's whackin' awful nonsense. Sure you can hold liquid in your mouth. Sure you can introduce it into drinks in just the way you said. But there is just one thing you can't do while you're holdin' the liquid there: and that's talk. It's absolutely impossible, my gal. Try it. Now Mrs. Sinclair, before tastin' your father's rye highball, asked him for a sip of it. But how was she goin' to ask him for a sip of it unless she did talk? No. I'm afraid the whole thing won't wash. You've got to find another way for the drinks to have been poisoned."

"Oh—!" Marcia checked herself. "Then how do *you* say they were poisoned?"

H.M.'s forehead was wrinkled, and he muttered to himself before he spoke.

"Suppose," he said absently, "we sort of run over the alternatives we've got. Hey? Now, let's assume for the sake of argument that the whole crowd of guests were tellin' the truth when they swore no atropine could have been sneaked into the cocktail-shaker or the glasses up to the time Schumann carried the drinks to the living-room. Let's assume it's not all a preconcerted story between Mrs. Sinclair and your father and Schumann."

"And in that case?"

"In that case," declared H.M. laboriously, "we seem to have only one alternative. Only one. I mean the original thesis that an outsider sneaked in and poisoned the shaker while the guests were in the kitchen; and that the outsider washed out that shaker afterwards." He turned to Marcia. "Now you tell me the truth or I'll skin you. *Did* anybody go in or out of that building while you were watchin'?"

"No. That really is true."

H.M. studied her for a long time.

"Uh-huh. We'll accept it, then. In that case we're bound to admit that the murderer is (1) Ferguson himself; or (2) a confederate workin' with Ferguson. Now don't yell at me and ask how Ferguson got out of the building! That's simple; I'll explain it before you finish that gin. But that's not the point. If Ferguson or a confederate did all the dirty work, why should Ferguson hang about the building for so long after the dirty work was done? And potter round the Anglo-Egyptian office? And accost you two on the stairs and talk to you? And go to inspect the corpse after you discovered the murder? And talk some more? And make himself so ruddy conspicuous before he decided to vanish? It's all wrong. If he's guilty, why should he want to appear in the mess at all?"

"I don't know," acknowledged Sanders. "I'll admit I got the idea that he was genuinely startled when he heard about the murder."

"Yes, that's what I mean. Oh, my eye! Suppose neither Ferguson nor any outsider did the dirty work, then?"

Sanders stared at him.

"You mean that Ferguson had nothing to do with the real business? And the murder was committed by one of the three guests in Haye's flat?"

"That's a possibility, son."

81

"I don't see it," returned Sanders. "On the contrary, that would make the whole crime absolutely impossible. One of them would have had to drug the cocktails—which is impossible. One of them would have had to get in and out of the building without being seen—which is impossible."

"Uh-huh. I know. But," said H.M. gently, "I've had to deal with these impossible things before."

During this debate Marcia had been looking across the almost empty room with absent, half-shining eyes and eyebrows that were gradually raising with inspiration. If Sanders had known her better at this time, he would have known that such signs betokened trouble ahead—for someone. Now she turned to them, making a gesture as though begging them not to interrupt her.

"I've got it all now," she said almost wearily. "And you're quite right; it is simple. I know how Ferguson got out of the building."

H.M. put his head in his hands and groaned.

"All right," he said. "Let's have it. What's your shot?"

Marcia nodded in a somnambulistic way. "Right, then! The murder was committed by Ferguson and Mrs. Sinclair acting in collusion. She supplied him with the poison; he did the drugging, stabbed Haye, and stole the boxes. You said those two were connected, didn't you? Didn't you? Yes!—As for the way he got out of the building, he never did get out of the building."

"I hope you're havin' a good time," said H.M. malevolently. "But go on."

"Listen, please! I'm sure of this part of it, because that rather nice sergeant who took me home last night told me all about it. You'll immediately say that Ferguson wasn't hiding in the building. Of course he wasn't: just the reverse. But who definitely *was* in the building? Just tell me, who was the only other person—the only one at all—known to have been in the building all the time? It was the caretaker, a short stocky Irishman named Riordan. Don't you see it? Ferguson *is* the caretaker."

A somewhat awed expression passed over H.M.'s large face. He did not say anything. He seemed incapable, at the moment, of saying anything.

"Ferguson, the real Ferguson, is in disguise," said Marcia earnestly. "He got a job as caretaker in that building, where he had worked before as an employee of Mr. Schumann. You were telling Mr. Masters that Schumann thought Ferguson was dead. Last night Ferguson took off his 'caretaker' disguise and appeared upstairs as himself. That was why he let himself be seen and talked to! He *wanted* to impress the picture on us—then he would disappear. The story would be that a 'dead' man had first appeared and then vanished. It would drive the police wild looking for a phantom who didn't exist. And all the while Ferguson, in his rôle of Riordan the caretaker, would be sitting downstairs unsuspected among the hotwater pipes."

"Hand the lady a cokernut," said H.M. "That's idyllic, that is. Do you honestly believe all that?"

"There happens to be proof. Were Ferguson and the caretaker ever seen together? No. Just where was the caretaker during all that horrible fuss before and after the police arrived? Dr. Sanders and I didn't see him. The hospital-people who took away the drugged guests didn't see him. Nobody saw him—until the police started looking for Ferguson. *Ooo! Am I right!*" It was not a question; it was an exultant statement.

"No," said H.M. "For God's sake will you shut up before Ferguson turns into a howlin' nightmare? He's already got sixteen faces and all the colors of the rainbow. He's the original India-Rubber Man. He's beginnin' to gibber at windows and jump up out of inkwells. I'm being haunted by Ferguson, and burn me if I'll stand it. I tell you there's nothin' very strange or extraordinary about Ferguson at all. He—"

Marcia dropped her triumphant air and became earnest again.

"Please tell me, then: do you deny that Ferguson and Mrs. Sinclair are mixed up in this together, somehow?"

This stopped H.M., who was simmering.

"No. No, I don't necessarily deny that. I've already said so, ain't I? Consequently—"

"And you'll admit that it's quite likely Mrs. Sinclair supplied the atropine?"

H.M. looked worried. "Stop cross-examinin' me!" he roared. "I'll admit it's a probability; but as for provin' it—"

Marcia subsided before that blast. But this was the point at which Dr. Sanders felt he had got to assert himself. All the pin-pricks of the day against his sense of humor and his judicial air, all the pompous traits which she had accused him of having, and which he swore in his soul he had not, all boiled up together to point out to him the proper course.

"If that's the case," he observed, lighting a cigarette with some deliberation, "there's only one thing to do. Crack Mrs. Sinclair's house and find out."

"Crack Mrs. Sinclair's what?" asked Marcia, startled.

"Her house. Burgle it," he explained. "I'll do the job, if you like."

There was a silence. "Darling, you mustn't!" cried Marcia. "I won't let you. You'd get caught!"

A pleasantly warm feeling flooded from Dr. Sanders's chest and shoulders up round his collar. To him it seemed exactly like the first long drink on a cold day. For her face was radiant.

"Not at all," he said.

"But do you know anything about—burgling, and things like that?"

The temptation was great; but Sanders was honest. "From a practical standpoint, no," he admitted. "But scientifically, yes. You leave it to me. I'll bust her wide open."

"But would you—I mean, could I come along with you?"

"Certainly, if you like."

H.M. was looking from one to the other of them with sour but wide-eyed amusement.

"Ho ho," said H.M. "Do you really mean it, son? Honest-Injun, I believe you do. Not that I'd want to be a damper or spoilsport regardin' such an idea—"

"I should think you wouldn't," Marcia told him. "Evelyn Blake says you've got a positive pathological obsession on the subject of burglary. She says you'd rather see somebody burgle a house than walk in at the front door. She says—"

"Well . . . now," muttered H.M., rubbing a hand across his big bald head and peering at them from over his spectacles. "I may have engineered rather a lot of funny business in my time, it's true. I'm not objectin', you understand. All I'd like to know is the point of this idea. Supposin' you do break into Mrs. Sinclair's? What in the flamin' acres of Tophet do you expect to prove by it? What do you expect to find there?"

Sanders was calm. "Evidence. I'm not certain what evidence; but surely it's the sensible thing to do. Consider it. You believe that there is a connection between Ferguson and Mrs. Sinclair. You believe that there is still more atropine where the last batch came from. Her house is the obvious center. We couldn't get a search-warrant on the evidence we've piled up so far. So the thing to do is get inside that house and—"

He gestured. H.M. contemplated him.

"You speak awful persuasively, son," he observed, breaking off to look at the girl. "Simple as that, hey? But, I say! Maybe there's something in the idea. Maybe I could help you."

"Like to come along, sir?"

"No, I would not like to come along," returned H.M. with dignity. "I got a position to maintain, I have. I'm an important man, curse you. Fine thing it'd be if I went roarin' round the country jemmyin' windows and pickin' locks!" He reflected. "What I mean is that I might be able to arrange a few things, like seein' that Mrs. Sinclair was out of the way, and a couple of details about the neighbors that probably wouldn't occur to you. How do you propose to go about it?"

"The—er—the usual way."

"Oh. The usual way. I see. Well, I admit I'm awful curious about certain things you might find. If a ghost of me sort of turned up in the neighborhood later, to sort of inspect your findin's, don't be too surprised. But understand this: don't expect any help from me if you get into trouble. I can't be mixed up in any cloth-headed monkey-business like that. I'm not in it. I'm not near it. I don't know you. Before I begin givin' you your instructions," insisted H.M., with a face of extraordinary malignity, "is all that clearly understood?"

Marcia and Sanders nodded; but powers beyond their control did not. Poetic justice does not always sleep. H.M., with the best intentions, had in the past put many men into equivocal positions and under the fingers of the law. Before many hours were up he was himself to figure as chief actor in one of the ripest burglaries on record.

CHAPTER TEN

LATE on a fine April night, Sanders—wearing a dark suit and a dark hat—called for Marcia at Sir Dennis Blystone's house in Harley Street. The usually calm Sanders was not only eager; he was ablaze with excitement. For, while he had been poring over the best scientific works on crime to pick up a few pointers on house-breaking, he had discovered the answer to one of the chief problems in the case.

At first he could not believe his eyes. With certainty came doubt, and then certainty again. He had devoted himself to his studies with the earnestness of one swotting for an examination, making neat notes and occasionally sending out for purchases which were now stowed away in his clothes. But now, with regard to certain mysterious articles, he *knew*.

But he found a strained atmosphere when he arrived at the house in Harley Street.

It was a placid, dignified place like Sir Dennis Blystone himself, with yellow-shaded wall-lamps in the hall, and a suggestion of the office as well as the home. Yet there was something wrong with it. Sanders had a feeling similar to one he had known some years ago when he was eighteen or nineteen, and had gone to take a girl out to a dance. The girl's father had just recovered from a spree; he was wandering round the house with steady but nervous-looking dignity; the mother was on the edge of tears; and neither wanted the girl to go out, but a good face had to be put on the whole affair.

Sir Dennis Blystone he saw almost as soon as the maid admitted him. Blystone wandered out of a door at the rear of the hall, wearing a rumpled-looking lounge suit, his fine face heavy with an expression of domestic trouble. At the same time Marcia hurried down the stairs, buttoning on a pair of dark gloves.

"Marcia," her father began uncertainly. "You're not—"

"Sorry," she informed him. "They're taking me to Scotland Yard to be questioned."

Blystone, who had seen Sanders with the chief inspector that morning, did not question this. But a tall, stately woman with waved grayish hair hurried out from the door behind. Ordinarily, Sanders thought, her stateliness would have been overpowering; but now she almost flew towards him, and she also was on the edge of tears.

"Surely that is absurd?" the woman demanded. "What *would* she know about it, a poor little child like that?" (Marcia gritted her teeth.) "She knows nothing. She wasn't even there. And do you know what time it is? It's past eleven o'clock. You can't—"

It's that damned dance all over again, thought Sanders, feeling acutely uncomfortable. But he assumed his heaviest manner.

"Can't be helped, madam," he said. "Orders."

"Of course. Don't be absurd, mother," said Marcia crisply. "Don't bother to wait up for me. All right, Inspector; I'm ready."

Lady Blystone turned. "And Marcia. What on earth do you mean, going out in those awful rubber-soled shoes? Go upstairs and change immediately. Dennis, are you going to allow this? Can't you do something? Can't you at least go along with her?"

"Now, Judy—" the other began pacifically.

"Oh, my God," cried Lady Blystone, "haven't you brought enough disgrace on us already, without seeing your own daughter taken to Scotland Yard like a common jail-bird? I should think you would be ashamed to look any of us in the face after this. I dare say you think that since your friend Mrs. Sinclair has been taken there tonight, it's all very well for your own daughter to go too. There will be reporters, you know that. They'll wait outside the place with cameras. You know what will happen. I tell you I won't—"

"Sorry, madam," thundered Sanders, feeling that if this went on he would bolt himself. "Orders. This way, Miss Blystone. I've got a taxi waiting."

In the taxi, slipping through cool darkness and peace, he spoke again.

"We shall have to cruise round a bit first. We're to meet H.M. at Mrs. Sinclair's house at midnight, and we're not to budge an inch until we see him. So Mrs. Sinclair has been taken to the Yard! That must be his doing; it keeps the way clear for us. But what made you tell that fat-headed lie about being taken for questioning yourself? I hope she doesn't ring up about it. She's in the mood to."

"Well, it sounded more romantic," said Marcia, looking at him curiously. "Oh, don't preach. Not tonight, of all nights. She's always in the mood to. Do you understand now why my father might be inclined to take up with a little bit of fluff?"

"Yes."

"Are you all ready for the—?"

"Quite ready. And I think I've got some things that will surprise you."

He saw in her face an absolute confidence in him, a questionless faith which made him throw out his chest. Dr. Sanders was a trifle light-headed. Before leaving his flat he had taken two jolts of Dutch courage, but no stimulant out of a bottle could produce quite this effect. The glow had only increased—dangerously—when the taxi set them down a few streets away from Cheyne Walk.

Mrs. Sinclair's house was dark. So, Sanders observed, were the houses on either side. More than ever, in the distant glow of a street lamp, the place looked like a doll's house; the green door stood out against toy bricks, the brass knocker shone. There was a smell of green and growing things from the garden. Over Chelsea and the river a dim moon made the scene as unreal as the adventure on which they were embarking. The two conspirators walked very slowly towards the low brick wall and green-painted iron gate leading into Mrs. Sinclair's front garden.

Through Sanders's mind was running a sentence out of one of the treatises he had been reading. *There must be,* whispered this author, *an immense sum total of energy wasted in this country every night by the locking, bolting, barring, chaining, and generally barricading of front doors. No good burglar would ever think of tackling a front door. It is too public, too heavily fortified, and too obvious a means of ingress. He prefers the comparative privacy and weakness of a scullery window . . .*

"Here we go," Sanders whispered to himself. "Ready?"

He heard her draw a breath, but she jumped back.

"Ugh! I say, what on earth is that? What have you got on your hands?"

"Rubber gloves."

"Well, take them off! They feel horrible."

"I'm not going to put them on you. Shh!"

"I should jolly well think you weren't! Oh, you lunatic, what are you doing now? Take it away! It's on my hands; it's mucking me up; I can't let go of it. Oh, my God, what have you got there?"

(This is a fine beginning for a burglary, Sanders thought.)

"Let go of it. Ss-t!" he hissed. "It's only fly-paper."

"Fly-paper? John Sanders, have you gone completely and utterly ma—"

The infernal stuff was sticking to his own gloves now. He pulled it loose and reached out to open the front gate. And, at the same time, there appeared just inside the gate the large figure of a policeman.

It would be untrue to say that Sanders's heart did not give a violent bump, like someone jumping off a shed. It was the unnerving suddenness with which a symbol of the law had appeared in Mrs. Sinclair's front garden. He was a large policeman with a cropped mustache, and he loomed even larger in the dim light of the street-lamp.

But Sanders's wits did not jump from the shed as well.

"Good evening, constable," he heard himself saying calmly. He folded up the fly-paper and put it in his pocket.

"Evening, sir," answered the policeman sharply, but without sinister inflection. "Who lives in this house?"

It was the turn of the evening, the determining throw of dice. If Sanders lost it, the adventure was over before it had begun. He knew that. And in his desperation not to lose his first shot at knight-errantry Sanders risked it.

"You're new to this beat, aren't you, constable?"

"Yes, sir. Just transferred this week."

"I thought so," said the amateur liar. He took a key out of his pocket. "*I* live here. Or my wife and I, rather. Why?"

He ushered Marcia inside the gate, holding the key conspicuously. Either from the gate or from the girl at his side, he heard a small awed squeak. If the constable waited for him to use that key, he was done; it was the key to the Harris Institute of Toxicology.

"Oh," grunted the policeman, saluting. "Glad to hear it,

sir. Well, we'd better have a look around. There's a suspicious-looking character here somewhere."

"A suspicious-looking character?"

"Yes, sir. Rough customer, I'm afraid. Broad, hefty bloke with a bald head. He threw a flower-pot at me."

"He—what?"

The policeman snorted. "Well, sir, it might have dropped off a window-ledge, but I know better. Shall I have another look round the back garden?"

"John!" said Marcia. She was beginning to recover her nerve; her lips were parted and her brown eyes shone. "You know, I'm afraid he means Uncle Henry."

The policeman turned round sharply. "You don't mean you mean the man, ma'am?"

"Did he have spectacles and a top-hat on?" demanded Sanders. "Of course we know him. He's my uncle. Damn it all, constable, this is going too far! He's a little eccentric, but when it comes to harrying him round like a criminal—"

Some remnant of anger smoothed itself out of the law's forehead.

"Very sorry if I've made a mistake, sir," he said stiffly, "but I've got my duty to do. You must understand that. I'll have to make a report of this, in any case. And I'm afraid he's smashed the daylights out of your cucumber-frames. I chased him across them, and he went through. I almost got him once, because his hat fell off and he stopped to pick it up. If he is your uncle he could have saved a lot of trouble just by answering my questions. And you might tell him he'll get into more trouble one day if he keeps on swearing at people the way he swore at me. *Good* night, sir."

Sanders, with the wrong key in his hand, took a few more steps towards the front door. The policeman remained where he was.

"Good night, constable."

The policeman remained where he was.

Never in his life had Sanders passed a longer series of seconds. He reached the front door, and lifted the key.

"Don't you think, my dear," he said to Marcia, as though struck by an afterthought, "we'd better go round to the back and find Uncle Henry? He's probably in his studio, and—"

"Hadn't you better open the door first, sir?" said the constable, very quietly.

Sanders turned his back, and fitted against the lock a key several sizes too large for it. What he found when he touched the door was like a sounding of the trumpets of hope, and relieved the nausea which had been creeping over him.

The door was unlocked. He turned the knob, pushed it open, and looked round coldly.

"Satisfied, constable?"

"Good night, sir."

Taking Marcia by the hand, he drew her inside and closed the door. There was a stuffy and musty odor in the hall, as he had noticed when he was there with the chief inspector that morning. A faint edge of light came through the frilled curtains of the side-windows, showing the unfinished sketch on the wall. A throaty clock was ticking somewhere in the silence. The floor-boards seemed more than usually creaky.

"That's torn it," whispered Marcia. "Aren't you going to turn on any lights? Won't he think it's awfully queer if we come in here and no lights go up?"

Sanders peered out through the side-window. "We can't risk it yet. We *think* Mrs. Sinclair is at Scotland Yard; but suppose she's still in the house? And what about the maid?"

He felt her shiver.

"You know, I—I don't like this," she said.

"Well, you wanted to come."

"Oh, I'll carry on. But what do we do now? And what did you want with that horrible fly-paper?"

"We've got to find H.M. I said we'd meet him at the back of the house at midnight. We weren't supposed to stir until then, until he could find out how the land lies. But, with that policeman watching us, there was nothing else we could do. The fly-paper was to put against a window and break the glass without noise; the pieces of glass stick to it. We don't need it now. Let's get through the house and out at the back. But, before we do, I want to show you something."

The boards in the hall still creaked. He took her as quietly as he could to the front parlor where that morning he and Masters had seen Mrs. Sinclair and Sir Dennis Blystone. The long windows were not covered, except by lace curtains through which a good deal of light penetrated. A fire had almost smouldered out in the grate. The room was full of heavy hangings and bric-a-brac, with the gaunt shadow of a grand piano cutting off the half-light from the window. On a mat on top of the piano, where he remembered them, stood a cut-glass pitcher full of water, and some tumblers. They had changing lights in the gloom. The clock in the hall ticked throatily.

"Is that policeman still outside?" Sanders muttered.

She crept over to the window, and jerked back.

"Yes! He's standing out on the pavement, looking straight at this room—"

"Good. Now watch."

. "What on earth are you doing?" she whispered. "You look different, somehow, in here. What are you doing?"

"I am going to show you," said Sanders, "the real meaning of the quicklime and the phosphorus."

From his pocket he took the small vial of whitish powder, calcium oxide or quicklime, which he had bought that afternoon. Keeping close to the edge of one window, he drew back the lace curtain slightly, opened the vial, and sprinkled a wide trail of its contents along the window-sill. Then, putting a little water into a tumbler, he began cautiously to sprinkle the water on the lime. . . .

There was a pungent odor, the sort of odor you might smell at a marble-cutting works, and something appeared to be happening under the curtain. A thin veil seemed to rise along the glass, and the room darkened.

"Now the other window," he said. The room darkened still more, and he was afraid she was going to scream.

"It's all right," he assured her fiercely. "But you see what's happened? Both windows are now completely 'frosted,' sealed up and whitened out much tighter and darker than though there'd been a real frost. But anybody outside—like that policeman—notices no difference. All he knows is that he can't see into the room. The curtains are not drawn; but still he can't see in. And, unless you showed a very bright light in here, the room would seem to be empty . . ."

From another pocket he carefully drew out a second vial, which he had wrapped in a wool sheath. A faint yellowish-green glow appeared in the room, with such stealthy effect that it seemed to alter the look of faces and furniture. The vial contained phosphorus. Sanders held it up.

"Got it now?" he whispered. "It's the superburglar's electric torch. I read all about it today. There's quite enough light to see by—notice? But the light doesn't jump up and flash round dangerously, like an electric torch. Now suppose I were a burglar. The windows are frosted. You can't see this little light through them. I could rob this room under the very nose of a policeman standing and staring at the window; and he would never know there was anybody in an uncurtained room facing the street. The quicklime and the phosphorus are simply part of the tool-kit of an up-to-date housebreaker."

That small, changing, yellow-green glow distorted all things. It made Marcia's face unfamiliar as Sanders looked at it; and he supposed it must have the same effect on his own. As he stood by the piano, the marsh-light brought out different hues in the cut-glass pitcher and in the wood of the piano.

"But—" the girl cried, and lowered her voice. "They were

91

found in Mrs. Sinclair's handbag. You can't think *she* is a burglar, can you?"

"No, not at all. Don't you remember: that's what has been puzzling Masters and everyone else? He and H.M. argued about it. He could explain the meaning of the articles; but he couldn't see how they applied to her. It was the big snag. But they don't belong to her: they belong to someone very closely connected with her. And you'll spot it straight away when you think of the connection between Mrs. Sinclair and—"

This time Marcia did cry out. He had been holding the vial higher, so that the soft-glowing core fell across the bearskin hearth-rug to the other side of the fireplace. First they made out the shape of a wing chair, and then the shape of someone sitting in it and looking at them.

At his ease in the chair, seeming even older and more wicked-faced as he nodded at them, sat Ferguson.

CHAPTER ELEVEN

THE soft glow remained steady. Sanders felt strung up but oddly clear-headed. On the patterned wallpaper in the corner behind Ferguson hung a schoolroom sketch by (if it were genuine) Picasso. And Sanders knew now why Ferguson had looked so oddly familiar, and what Ferguson resembled. Ferguson resembled a somewhat crusty schoolmaster, sitting back with his birch across his knee. There were even inkstains on Ferguson's fingers.

Only it was not a birch which lay across Ferguson's knee, with his hand fingering it. It was a thick-barreled and silvered-steel pistol of a design Sanders had never seen before.

A coal dropped with a rattle in the grate, and Ferguson spoke while his ink-stained forefinger moved on the trigger of the pistol.

"Well," he said in his harsh, common-sense voice. "Well."

"I told you not to get yourself mixed up in this," he added.

Then he went on in the tone of a schoolmaster when some pupil has begun to argue about the grade on an examination paper.

"To begin with, don't talk nonsense, young man. Your friend the policeman may be outside. But you won't whistle for him, young man. If you do I'll put a bullet in you. And don't say the shot would give me away, because it wouldn't.

This is an air-pistol. Just to show you I don't mean to stand any nonsense from you, I'll let you have one for good measure."

He hardly seemed to lift the mechanism on his knee. Though Sanders saw that his hand jerked as though with a kick, he heard no more than the snap of a trigger and a thud somewhat deeper than that produced by the report of a boy's air-rifle. Blended with it, a part of the same unreality, Sanders felt a sharp push as of someone knocking past his left shoulder, and a brisk pinch in the left arm above the elbow. Nothing more. Perhaps the noises were intensified in his own brain.

But Ferguson's face was altering a little before his eyes. He glanced down. There was a tear in the sleeve of his coat, exposing the lining and horsehair of the fabric, which was blotted out. The arm began to feel hot and wet, as though it were crawling. Possibly a few seconds after the shot, something stung the arm like fire, and Sanders felt that it was somehow beginning to swell up.

Even yet he could not realize that he had got a bullet there. But he was feeling more than a little queasy.

"There's a newspaper over the arm of the chair beside you," said Ferguson. "No; don't lower that light; use your left hand. Reach down and get that newspaper, and spread it out under you. Stand on it. I don't want you getting blood on the carpet. Do as I tell you."

The whole arm burnt like fire now, and seemed to go on swelling. He moved it with difficulty. Then he found himself standing on the newspaper.

"Have you got it all clear?" asked Ferguson, "or shall I give the young woman some of it?"

"No." said Sanders. "If you've got to plug away at somebody, plug away at me."

"Right. I will," said Ferguson—and fired again.

This time Sanders did not know or seem to care whether he had been hit. What he could not reconcile was the petulant, sour calmness of Ferguson's words with the snaky, calm movements of his trigger-finger.

"You've got to learn," said Ferguson, "that some things in this world are serious. I told you. But, oh, no. You knew it all. You and this young woman were just too big for your breeches. You were the big I Am. All right; now you'll take the consequences. Do just as I tell you. Hand me that vial of phosphorus. Take up that newspaper in your right hand and hold it under your arm. Yes, it'll hurt a little; but I could have put it in a place that would have hurt a bloody sight more. If you spill anything on the carpet—mind that

93

paper—I'll give you another. Now walk ahead of me, both of you."

He might have been a schoolmaster dryly sizzling the hide of a ten-year-old pupil who had tried his patience beyond endurance. It was this which began to induce in Sanders a wild and light-headed rage. But Sanders could do nothing, and he knew it.

Marcia, though she was very white, walked quietly. At the end of the room was a door which Ferguson told Sanders to open. Past this they went through a passage, and into a little room where Ferguson had evidently been making himself comfortable.

A lamp with a newspaper round the shade burned on a table near the fire. Heavy shutters were on the windows, backed with thick rep curtains to exclude every chink of light. The room had a stone-flagged floor, with a few tubs and a mangle stacked into one corner; it smelt of centuries' washing. But a padded chair was drawn up before a bright fire. On the table stood a glass of hot milk; a plate of cold beef, with bread and a cruet-stand, had been pushed to one side. Ferguson sat down in the padded chair. Sanders observed that he was wearing carpet-slippers, and had a fountain-pen in his breast pocket.

"Sit down over there," he told them, "and keep off the carpet."

"When you're hanged," said Marcia, "I'll come and dance in front of the jail."

Sanders thought she was going to cry. Ferguson regarded her without animosity.

"Shut your mouth, young woman," he said. "I've got nothing to say to you. You've played the fool and you'll take what is coming to you. That's all I can see in the matter." He looked towards Sanders. "But I have got something to say to you."

Sanders's arm was a mass of pain and his head had begun to ache violently; but he tried to steady his eyesight. With the pistol in his left hand, Ferguson sipped at the glass of hot milk. The steamy smell of washing was thick in the room.

"Here, take this," added Ferguson, tossing across a napkin, "and twist it round. Pull that wash-tub over. I don't want you fainting on me. You're soft enough as it is, Mr. Too-Big-For-Your-Breeches. Now tell me a few things. So you know who I am and what I am, do you?"

"Yes."

"Well, who am I and what am I?"

Sanders steadied himself. "Your name is Peter Ferguson, and Haye had enough on you to hang you. By profession

94

you're a cat-burglar, and you're almost worn out. I may be too big for my breeches, but I'm a doctor, and I'll tell you this: you're not as old as you look, not by ten years. Your real age is about forty-five."

Again he steadied himself, focusing his eyesight.

"That is part of the game, your elderly looks and your clerkly looks. Most people think of a burglar as being a young tough. If they came across you in an office you were robbing, they would find an elderly man with glasses, and a clerk's wrist-bands, and his coat off, and a pen behind his ear. It's one of the best disguises ever invented."

Ferguson did not comment; he sipped his milk.

"And they wouldn't suspect you of being a cat-burglar," Sanders went on dully. "They wouldn't think you were agile enough. But a person's only got to look at your walk to see that. That was how you got out of the building last night. The chief inspector said there was a drain-pipe on the rear wall of the building; but that it was too far away from the window for any normal man ever to have reached it. He was quite right, of course. But a cat-burglar could have made it without difficulty. That's you."

Ferguson glanced sideways. Very little expression passed over his face. His ink-stained forefinger scratched on the glass he was holding up.

"Now that surprises me. You're right," he acknowledged. "A little more intelligent than your breeches too, aren't you? Do the police know this?"

"Certainly they know it. Masters and Sir Henry Merrivale guessed it this afternoon, when they realized you and Mrs. Sinclair were connected, and that the quicklime and the phosphorus really belonged to you. Besides, you were ass enough to leave a pair of spectacles behind when you got away. That showed that your age and general debility weren't what you pretended. If you had really needed those spectacles, if you were accustomed to wearing them, you would no more have left them behind than you would have left your trousers. What's more, you were fool enough to leave a fingerprint on the lens. If you're known to Scotland Yard, as I suspect, they know all about you by now."

He spoke calmly, fitting together evidence in his own careful way, though he felt inane and rather foolish. All things came to him in sharp sounds and colors. Best of all he remembered the oily snap and thud of the pistol like the noise of someone beating a carpet; and the pistol was looking steadily at him from Ferguson's chair. Then the steamy smell of the wash-house got into his nostrils, and wouldn't get out.

But something he said had stirred Ferguson. Ferguson's eye had a more curious gleam.

"The police don't know me, young man. What's this about my being connected with Mrs. Sinclair?"

Silence.

"Are you going to speak when you're spoken to? Or haven't I made it quite clear that I'm standing no nonsense?"

"No," said Sanders. "You've had things too much your own way so far. I know you're giving me hell, and I suppose I must be under a kind of anaesthesia; but you've had two shots already, and they don't hurt much, so why should I be afraid of you? I don't like you, and I don't like your manners. The point is, what are you going to do after you've finished making a target of me?"

Ferguson, like a deity, did not bother to comment or argue. He merely lifted his wrist again.

Even when there were footsteps outside the door to the passage, his eyes hardly flickered. He moved himself a little so that he could cover the door. With a mutter of hard breathing, Sir Henry Merrivale pushed open the door and ducked his ancient top-hat under the lintel. H.M.'s face looked lowering and rather dull of intelligence.

"Evenin', son," he said. "That'll be quite enough of that."

There was a silence. Ferguson's wrist moved.

"Get over there beside him," Ferguson said.

H.M. obeyed orders. Waddling over between Marcia and Sanders, he pulled out a kitchen-chair and wheezed down on it. His top-hat was on the back of his head, and the corners of his mouth were pulled down as though he were smelling a bad breakfast-egg. His overcoat was open; a corporation adorned with a gold watch-chain projected from it. After a brief comprehensive glance at Sanders, he settled back and twiddled his thumbs. He did not say anything. It seemed all the more ominous because he did not say anything.

"Oh, yes," said Ferguson, as though recalling. "I know who you are. You're the Whitehall comic that everyone laughs at. Are you also under the impression that I don't mean business? I suppose it was you were running about the back garden tonight."

H.M. nodded. He seemed interested in studying Ferguson's face.

"That's right, son. Y'see, I thought it might be wise to have the coppers a bit interested in this house tonight—especially as I thought you were probably inside. Believe me, if these two young 'uns had obeyed my orders and met me in the back garden, there might have been a little less shootin'. You're a fine, brave feller, you are. I admire you."

Ferguson considered him, for the first time with a pale and skeptical smile. The veins seemed to be heightening in his forehead.

"We'll attend to you in a minute," he said. "In the meantime—talk."

"Sure," agreed H.M. "I'm like the doctor here. I want to know where you stand. You can't keep on puttin' bullets into people and then turn 'em out into the street and say; 'Now you've had your spanking; go home.' Unless you mean to kill somebody?"

"I don't kill," said Ferguson. "I never have and I never will. That's a fool's trick. I haven't decided what I'm going to do with you yet; but I *could* turn you over to the police you're so fond of. You're housebreakers."

"Uh-huh. You could do that. But there are two reasons why you won't."

"Talk," said Ferguson.

"Well, I was just sittin' and thinkin' . . ."

"Talk."

"All right, son. The first reason is that in theory you're supposed to be dead. You're Mrs. Sinclair's husband, who 'died' in Biarritz a year ago. And she collected a packet of insurance out of that fake."

"Talk."

"Y'see, we had a bit of an idea you two were connected. The doctor was tellin' you about it a while ago. Masters and I wondered what the connection was. Then we were talkin' this evenin' to Sergeant Pollard, who collected a lot of information about Mrs. Sinclair today. Her late husband was a certain Peter Sinclair who 'died' during an epidemic of some kind in Biarritz in 1936. The only thing anybody seemed to remember about him was that he had been an elderly gent who staggered everybody's wits by his thunderin' agility on a tennis court. Now, we already knew you were a highly skilled cat-burglar. Y'see, we've had some information now from both Bernard Schumann and the French police. So, with regard to Mrs. Sinclair's late husband, I looked at Masters and I said, 'Could it be?' And he looked at me and he said, 'We'll find out.'—And we have. Son, the game is smackin' well up. Honest it is."

Ferguson sat back in the padded chair. A nerve was beginning to twitch beside his eyelid.

"It would be interestin'," H.M. pursued woodenly, "to sort of sketch out your career and Mrs. Sinclair's, if I had time. Because at various times both of you have worked out some awful clever pieces of crookedness. What I'm wonderin' is whether you worked together or separately."

97

"You may keep on wondering," said Ferguson. "In the meantime, what else do you know? I want some more facts. 'If you had time?' Time! You've got all the time in the world."

"I know, son," said H.M. "But you haven't."

"Are you going to talk," said Ferguson, "or must I give you a little medicine? Perhaps it would do you some good."

"Oh, look here! Don't be a howlin' ass! You megalomaniac fathead, what I'm tryin' to tell you—"

Ferguson fired point-blank. As in a nightmare Sanders heard the familiar snap and thud, as though he were conscious of every oily spring that moved inside the mechanism. Unconsciously he leaned sideways, more towards the wash-tub which was beginning to be stained in that steamy kitchen. But he heard another sound blending with it; and he saw the bullet-hole jump up black in the wall some inches from H.M.'s head. Marcia Blystone gave out a whispering kind of cry. She would not last much longer. H.M.'s expression did not change.

"You missed," he said.

"Too bad," snapped Ferguson excitedly. "That means we must try again. If—"

"I wouldn't," said H.M., shaking his head. "You can blow me to glory if you keep on tryin' and if your hand stays steady, which it won't. But that wouldn't be wise. Somebody's done the dirty on you, son. There was poison in that hot milk you've been drinkin'. And, unless you stop playin' the fool and let me give you an antidote, you'll be dead yourself in ten minutes."

There was a pause of such bursting quality that even the noise of the fire seemed intensified. Dr. Sanders glanced up quickly. He saw Ferguson's eye, and understood. The symptoms of atropine poisoning were coming on with such dissolving rapidity that this time a certain person had evidently taken no chances on the size of the dose.

The silence was broken by Ferguson's sour amusement.

"We're very clever, aren't we?" he said. "We're all too clever for our breeches, it appears. Don't try it on, Merrivale. I never was one to be taken in by bluff. Now go on talking."

H.M.'s little eyes opened. "You don't think I'm bluffin', do you? Can't you feel your own symptoms?"

"I'm quite comfortable, thank you," the other told him. One of his carpet-slippers had come loose and slid across the floor; he retrieved it by feeling about with his foot. "But you're not. And you'll be a sight more uncomfortable by the time I've finished. What else do you know?"

It was very hot in the room. The sweat was starting out on H.M.'s forehead.

"Give me that gun! Curse it all, do you want to sit there and commit suicide with two doctors in the room?"

"I must just risk that. I warn you, Merrivale: stop this nonsense and answer my questions. How do you know that—"

H.M. surged to his feet.

"Come on, son. Let me have that gun."

"All right. Watch the little birdie," said Ferguson. He raised the air-pistol and steadied his wrist on the arm of the chair for good aim.

CHAPTER TWELVE

IN THE bare little waiting-room at New Scotland Yard, Mrs. Bonita Sinclair sat with every polite indication of patience. But at intervals she would glance at her small wrist-watch, and then up at the clock, as though wondering if occasionally there would be a difference in them. Both at the moment said that it was five minutes to midnight.

From across the room, Detective-Sergeant Pollard watched her. Pollard's private admiration was not lessened, even if it was now mingled with admiration of another kind.

Mrs. Sinclair wore black, from black woolly coat to black hat with the brim turned up in front. Her legs were crossed; and, as she leaned back in the chair, her long body had a grace which made her seem to be sitting upright in a throne. Her face, with its round chin and small mouth, was in complete repose. The blue-black eyes never met Pollard's; they moved round the room, up and down and into corners, with incurious blankness.

But this seemed to be wearing thin. She smiled at Pollard from under her eyelids. And Pollard, off guard, was indiscreet enough to return it. Then she spoke.

"May I—is one allowed to smoke?"

"Certainly, Mrs. Sinclair. Have one of these."

The big building was full of echoes, and both their voices seemed to come back with some loudness at such an hour. Pollard wondered whether he could be overheard by Masters in the next room. He hastened to offer her a cigarette. He even lighted it for her: a process which would be eyed by Masters with disapproval.

"Thank you so much," she said, with a smile and a little jerk of her head.

Pollard blew out the match and stood at a loss. Finally he compromised by pitching it backward in the general direction of the grate behind him, and succeeded in landing it on the waistcoat of Chief Inspector Masters, who opened the door at that moment.

"Will you come in now, ma'am," stated Masters. His eye said to Pollard that he was to come along; but that they would discuss that match later. A light was burning over Masters's desk. On that desk three messages, all from the French police, lay under the blotter. Indicating a chair for her, Masters contemplated her with boiled-eyed politeness.

"I was just telling the sergeant," said Mrs. Sinclair, evoking an atmosphere of communal friendliness, "that I cannot understand why you asked me to come here at such an hour." She gave herself a little shake as she settled in the chair. "I understand you even have my poor maid here. I'm terrified, really. You're not going to keep me up all night, or give me the third-degree, or anything, are you?"

"No, ma'am."

"Then—?"

"First of all, ma'am, I must tell you that it is your privilege, if you wish it, to have a solicitor here when you answer my questions."

At these ominous words, she first hesitated over her cigarette, and then regarded him with a perplexed smile.

"But, really, Mr. Masters, how could I get a solicitor at this time of the night? Wouldn't it be simpler if we waited until tomorrow morning, and then we could all come here together?"

Masters was wooden. "If you insist, ma'am. At the same time I've got some very serious news for you, which you may prefer to hear now."

He waited.

"What news?" she asked in a slightly different voice.

"Do you know, Mrs. Sinclair, that if certain persons care to press the charges, you can serve a long prison-sentence for extortion?"

It is an unpleasant word. She held out her cigarette levelly, one long finger hesitating to tap the ash; her breast rose and fell as though she were sleeping.

"But—truly, I don't understand."

"I'll be frank with you, Mrs. Sinclair," said Masters, leaning forward with the air of one who makes a fair business proposition. "I know how your game is worked. Every experienced copper in the business knows the basis of it. Though I'll say this for you: nobody so far has developed it, or enlarged it, or put so many twists in it, as you have. Eh?"

He leaned back with satisfaction.

"It's a new angle to the art-business, which very few people ever heard of. It's about famous pictures. *I* don't know anything myself; but I've got it all from the people who do know. We'll omit real names, ma'am, though I've got a list of 'em here."

This time Masters tapped his notes, spacing each word.

"Let's say, for instance, that in sixteen-something the Italian artist Thingummy paints a picture that everybody likes. It's a hit, as you might say. He's famous, and his work's famous, and this picture is, too. Well, then everybody wants it. His home town wants it. The national picture-galleries all over Europe want it. The Duke of Something wants it for his private house. And so on. All good payers: eh? So who's going to get it?

"Now, Sir Edward Lytle tells me," said Masters with satisfaction, "that even these great artist-blokes weren't above grabbing up a few extra guilders, or whatever they used for money then. They were on to a good thing, and they knew it. They didn't want to offend anybody either. So, between the Duke of Something and the Prince of Something else, what does this artist do? Why, he paints the same picture twice and sometimes three and four times over. And he sells it to all of 'em as the original Thingummy that they can boast about to the neighbors. There's no deception—except in a manner of speaking—because it really is the real thing, painted by the chap himself. Sir Edward says it's happened time and time again: only for Lord's sake to keep it quiet."

Curiously, Mrs. Sinclair seemed to breathe easier. Her candid eyes opened.

"But what on earth has this to do with me?" she cried.

The chief inspector stopped her.

"Just listen, *if* you please. What happens then? A hundred years, a couple of hundred years go by," said Masters broadly, like one who controls the thunder. "The Thingummies get scattered. Usually one stays—in a public gallery, mostly—and is known as the original. It's accepted. Nobody suspects it. With all the million copies floating about, nobody thinks of looking for another original, even if he finds it. Any more than I think that the Soul's Awakening we've got on the wall at home—"

Mrs. Sinclair shuddered.

"—is the original Soul's Awakening, painted by whoever-

101

it-was. But, according to Sir Edward, the world's flooded with these originals stuck away. Now, then."

Masters got down to business.

"Suppose it's somebody's business to look for these originals; and find 'em. Say it's you. Right you are: what do you do?

"Several things. You go to a millionaire private collector. You say, 'Would you care to buy the original Venus at the Bath?' The collector says, 'In a pig's eye, madam; the original Venus at the Bath is in the national gallery at Leipzig,' —or wherever it is. I'm just inventing names, you understand?"

"Yes. I gathered that," Mrs. Sinclair told him briefly.

Masters edged his chair closer.

"Just so, ma'am. Well, then you say, 'Believe me, this is the Venus at the Bath. If you doubt it, get your tame expert in and see.' Of course, you've got nothing to lose by the closest examination. It's found to be genuine. Collector wild to buy. 'I'll sell,' you say; 'but keep this quiet, or there'll be trouble with the Leipzig gallery when they find out what they've really got.' The inference is that the Leipzig gallery's been sold a pup; but you don't *say* so. Being a collector, Sir Edward says, and queer as blazes in that respect, the chap usually rubs his hands together as pleased as Punch, and keeps quiet. He's got what he wants. You've paid maybe ten pounds for that Venus. You sell it for a couple of thousand. And, even if there is trouble, what you've done is legal."

Privately, Sergeant Pollard thought that he would never again enter an art-gallery without an uneasy feeling of wonder when he looked at the pictures. What Mrs. Sinclair was thinking he could not tell.

"I'm not sure I follow you," she remarked. "If all this is legal, why are you talking to me about extortion and—?"

"And blackmail," said Masters. "That's not all, ma'am. Not by a long chalk. If it stopped there, it'd only be a bit of neat jiggery-pokery, always providing you kept on the right side of the law of fraud.

"Where it gets ugly is when you come to deal with the big public or private galleries. They've got a famous picture. A spanker, one that cost maybe twenty thousand pounds, and that half the world comes to see. It's the draw of the town, like the Blackpool illuminations. Now, what would happen if someone let out that there were several others of it too?

"It's a commercial matter, ma'am. A thing is valuable because it's unique, like a freak. Otherwise the bottom drops out of the market: only reasonable. So you (let's say) go to the Something Museum. You show them the duplicate of one of their prize exhibits. They're already in a ticklish position. They've already poured out plenty of money for the prize exhibit, maybe more than the directors wanted to pay or the public thought it was worth. 'Now,' you say, 'would you like to buy this duplicate and stow it away like sensible people—or shall I take it elsewhere?' That, Mrs. Sinclair, is what I call extortion.

"Then there's the little matter of unfinished pictures. That picks up some loose cash between the big killings. Sir Edward Lytle told me about it long ago. When any well-known painter dies, he usually leaves a heap of unfinished sketches and canvases. The smart crook gets there first and buys up what he wants. If he's got a smart forger with him, that picture can be completed so well that experts swear it's genuine. And it is genuine, mostly. That's your racket, Mrs. Sinclair: you never sell anything except genuine stuff."

In his most urbane fashion Masters settled back. But he looked at her grimly.

For a short time she did not reply. It was dark in the room except for the light over the chief inspector's desk, which brought out every move in her sensitive face. She was looking downwards at her clasped hands, so that her eyelids seemed waxy, and they could see her breathe. For a moment she had the air of a woman about to throw herself trustfully on Masters's mercy.

"Those things," she said, "are so terribly difficult to prove." She looked up.

"Forgive my stupidity in these matters. But, in order to prove fraud in the case of the unfinished pictures, you would have to show that the picture had been guaranteed in writing as an untouched original. Regarding the other matter, isn't it a field for specialized knowledge, really? Isn't specialized knowledge valuable in itself, and to be commended?"

"That's as may be. What I'm getting at—"

"An art-gallery," said Mrs. Sinclair, "could not prosecute without publicity. And isn't publicity the very thing they are trying to avoid? Then they must prove under what terms the picture was offered to them, mustn't they? I only ask. It seems that the worst you can say to me, Mr. Masters, the very dreadful worst, is that everything I sell is genuine."

"Not quite the worst. No."

She was impatient. "I suppose it's flattery, really. I ought to appreciate your thinking I have enough intelligence to work out all those ways to—"

"Not altogether yours, ma'am," interposed Masters, in a

quick and yet quiet tone. "I daresay a good part of it came from your late husband, Mr. Peter Ferguson."

Mrs. Sinclair went white. It was an abrupt and startling turn: Sergeant Pollard would not have imagined that her face could look like that.

"I'd just like to give you a few facts about him," Masters went on comfortably. "This evening I got a letter by special messenger from Mr. Bernard Schumann, his former employer. I've also got a long cable from the French police.

"His real name is Peter Ferguson. He's only forty-two years old, as you probably know. He's the son of a Scotch clergyman. He got a science degree at Aberdeen. Good at all kinds of gadgets, anything involving the use of his hands. Expert gymnast. Has had all sorts of jobs, including acting: played old men's parts at twenty-five. Employed by Mr. Schumann, first at Cairo office in manufacturing imitation papyruses—no fake there; the stuff was advertised as imitation—and later in London office. Robbed his employer. Escaped to Continent. That's Mr. Schumann's statement.

"Now, the information of the French police. Ferguson known to have associated with men who had been sentenced for burglary. Used aliases of Peter Sinclair and Peter Macdonald: keeping the Scotch touch. Suspected of being concerned in a series of burglaries, best Continental-scientific style, where quicklime was used to steam windows. Disappeared; believed abroad or dead. But on June 11, 1935, in Nice, a certain Peter Sinclair married a certain Bonita Fisher. That's you. Address given as 314 Boulevard des Cygnes.

"Mr. Schumann's letter enclosed a snapshot of Ferguson. We radioed it to the French police. Snapshot identified by Madame Du—never mind—by concierge at that address as being Sinclair. In other words, your husband. Final information! 'Sinclair' is supposed to have died at Biarritz in May, 1936. He died during that smallpox scare which the authorities hushed up so carefully. That's why nobody seemed to know much about his death; they don't want such things known at pleasure resorts. Body buried more or less secretly, in charge of old servant. Doctor issued death certificate without seeing body. Hah! But Ferguson didn't die. He's in London now. Right at this minute, ma'am, the French police are getting an exhumation order. They'll find the coffin empty. And you collected the insurance. That's fraud, and a fraud that can be proved."

Masters tossed his memoranda on the desk.

What effect the chief inspector expected Pollard did not know. But not in the least, Pollard imagined, the effect his words made. Mrs. Sinclair lay back in the chair, and uttered a

104

kind of shuddering sigh of relief. It seemed too honest to be theatrical; the relief that went over her face was like pallor.

"Thank God," she said.

Masters jumped up.

"May I ask, Mrs. Sinclair, what you're saying that for?"

She kept her eyes closed. "Will you believe me," she asked, "if I tell you the truth?"

"Well, ma'am, you might try me. I'll get it sooner or later."

"Please don't say that. I know you always think I'm not telling the truth, and I can't imagine why. Yes, yes, yes! He is my husband. And he is not dead. But I swear to you," she told him quietly, "I did not know that until last week. I—the truth is that when I thought he was dead I was glad."

"Notebook, Bob," said Masters briefly.

She sat up and nodded her head curiously, with a fixed look. Pollard thought he had seen that expression on the face of a woman about to impart some quiet confidence over a bridge-table.

"No, let me tell you. What I cannot imagine is why or how I ever came to marry him. But he—swanked so, that it took me in."

"Oh, ah. I see."

"You don't see. What you cannot seem to understand is that he had a way with him, at first. What impressed me most, I think, was his complete self-assurance: he seemed to know exactly what he wanted, and he was determined to get it. You couldn't move him. The trouble was that in spite of all his will-power and talk he never did get it. It made him furious. Then I found out that for all his boasting he wasn't a rich man. With all his smattering of knowledge he wasn't really good at anything, except perhaps tennis and gymnastics. But that only made my friends laugh. What is more, that—that man wanted to live off me. Off *me*."

With a voice so clear and musical as Bonita Sinclair's, it was impossible for her to approach anything like a yelp. But the last two words suggested it, while her round eyes were fixed on Masters and she seemed to be pouring out her difficulties at last. Sergeant Pollard felt that the chief inspector was suppressing a smile.

"Most unusual, ma'am," said Masters grimly. "Was his knowledge of art-fake, the trade he'd learned at Mr. Schumann's, of any help to you?"

Confidences were checked for the moment.

"You will please not say that," she flashed at him. "It is wrong and foolish and slanderous. I have a certain work

105

to do. It calls for specialized knowledge, as I told you. That is all."

"Is it?"

"But I began to suspect that Peter Ferguson was—yes, I will say it: a criminal, probably. And, really, that was the last straw! Almost any sort of person is accepted on the Riviera; but, as a husband, that acrobatic mummy was already impossible. I kept him under cover as much as possible. If I didn't he would manage to insult my friends."

Masters was impatient.

"Now, now! Let's come back to the point, Mrs. Ferguson, and face the facts. You thought you were getting a good catch in him. You were wrong. So you both took the best way out, and you helped him to 'die' for the insurance."

She spread out her hands.

"But I didn't! I keep repeating that. I knew absolutely nothing about it, except that I was glad when I heard he was dead. I was not even there at the time. I was traveling in Italy with some friends; you should be able to establish that. When I was summoned back, everything was over. He and the servant must have managed the whole death and burial between them."

After going so far as to stare at her, Masters adopted an air of persuasiveness. "Now, listen to me. We can't get any further if you insist on talking like that. You don't suppose he managed a mock death and burial for fun, do you? Lummy, you don't think he walked in afterwards and collected his own insurance from the company?"

"No."

"Then how was it going to benefit him? I'm afraid, Mrs. Sinclair, that it won't do much good just to say you weren't on the spot at the time. If you didn't make any inquiries, and simply put in a claim for the insurance—"

"But that is what I am patiently trying to tell you. I did not get any insurance. I didn't even put in a claim for it."

Again Masters rose very slowly from the chair. His eyes looked congested, and he made a motion in the air as though he were trying to soothe some person other than himself.

"So how did it benefit me?" asked Bonita Sinclair.

"I am informed on credible authority," said Masters, with the pompousness which indicated a dangerous state of mind, "that Ferguson, or Sinclair, took out a large policy in your favor."

"Isn't that gossip? You couldn't have got that from the police."

"I am informed that it was common knowledge in Biarritz—"

She was looking tired now. She lifted her hand and appealed to him.

"Please, please. You may as well hear what really happened," she insisted. "And then I should like to go home. Yes, of course he *told* everybody he had a large policy, and that he used to keep the premiums paid a year in advance. But I never believed it, naturally. I thought it was simply a part of his usual talk. I never thought of it again."

"Well?"

"Last week," she answered simply, "I came home from the opera on Monday night, and found Peter Sinclair sitting in my drawing-room in his carpet-slippers."

There was a pause.

"That is the plain, simple, horrible truth. Everything had been so nice, Mr. Masters. I thought I was rid of him. I usually have rather a happy life; and that was the only part of it which had not been happy. But here he was. He said he had come for his share of the money.

"Then the truth came out. He had not lied to me. He really had taken out an insurance policy, for fifteen thousand pounds, at the Paris office of the London Pari-Annual. He left it in a safe-deposit box in Biarritz, where he thought I knew all about it. And it's still there. The premiums really had been paid far in advance: so nobody at the company inquired about it and nobody had received notification of his 'death.'

"Don't you see the wicked, *wicked*—" (Pollard wished she would not stress the word)—"thing he had done? He did not dare take me into his plan, because I should not have agreed to such a thing. He set a trap for me, because I refused to support him. He insured his life and managed a mock death. He believed I would attempt to collect the insurance, as I certainly should have. If the company refused to pay, or made any trouble, he would have vanished and I should have had to bear all the blame. If the company paid, he appeared after a suitable interval to—to blackmail me. And I should not have dared to give him away."

She paused, nodding somberly, and added two things:

"That is Peter Ferguson to the life."

And:

"I did not feel much like laughing. There was too much money involved. But I almost laughed at the way he looked when he learned how it had all come unstuck. Because there had been no fuss, he thought I had collected the money. But all the time he has been eating acorn-husks and dream-

107

ing about it, the policy has been lying unclaimed in Biarritz. We just sat and looked at each other—the dirty mummy."

Her own words seemed to have induced in her a kind of hypnosis. She shook this off, seeming to brighten in one respect and grow fearful in another.

"Urr!" said Masters.

But he kept an impassive face.

"Just so, Mrs. Sinclair. Ferguson himself said we were dealing with the cleverest group of crooks in Europe. And we are."

"I've told you everything," she murmured, disregarding this and lifting her eyes again. "You can see now, can't you, that I didn't stand to gain anything by this horrible mock death? You can see I wasn't concerned in any fraud?"

"But maybe in worse things, you know. Where is Ferguson now?"

"At my house."

"Oh, ah? Been there all the time, has he?"

"But what else could I do? What else could I say to you? He's been threatening all sorts of things. Not that he could say anything about me, really." She hesitated as the telephone rang on Masters's desk, and her voice trailed off as he answered it. She still kept murmuring disjointed words which Pollard could not catch; but Masters's eye never left her while he listened to the telephone. "It's about me!" she cried. "It's about me, isn't it?"

With an air of great deliberation Masters replaced the receiver.

"Tell me," he said smoothly. "Your husband's life-insurance premiums had been paid a year in advance?"

"Yes."

"Just so. And when does that policy expire, do you know?"

"In—in May of this year, I think Peter said."

"Fifteen thousand pounds," said Masters. "And a month to go. You may collect that policy after all. Ferguson's dead now, right enough."

CHAPTER THIRTEEN

IN HIS own bed at home, Dr. Sanders was haunted by elusive dreams. They did not alarm him or trouble him unduly. Half the time he seemed to be analyzing something or working at a puzzle, and he was giving careful consideration to what he ought to do.

At the back of his mind he knew that he was safely at home in bed. There were waking moments when his arm throbbed dully, when he became conscious of a cool breeze through the open windows, and of the ticking of his watch on the table beside the bed. But these things became intertwisted with the figures of sleep. His dreams had some connection with a kitchen or a wash-house. He or someone else was bending low and moving across a stone-flagged floor. A piece of sticky fly-paper was concerned in it.

There was a fire, too. Someone was lying at the foot of a padded chair, whose seat had come loose. Under the seat of the chair there were castaway newspapers, and Marcia Blystone was leaning over the back of it while Sanders and Sir Henry Merrivale·bent over the figure on the floor. Most of all his dreams concerned the end of the night, where they grew into reality. Two bullets had been extracted from his left arm by a surgeon in Cheyne Walk; the bone had been broken, but broken cleanly; and the arm was now padded into a splint. Afterwards he had seen Marcia Blystone put into a taxi, and he remembered—whether in dream or in reality—that her arms had been round his neck.

Distinctly and unromantically, though, he recalled a voice in the background. It was the voice of Sir Henry Merrivale. It was irritable. It threatened them both with a swift kick in the pants if they did not shut up and go home.

He fell asleep comfortably.

When Sanders opened his eyes again, it was in the sunlight of a noble spring morning. The trees outside the windows of his flat seemed to have turned green overnight. Despite the state of his arm, he had an extraordinary feeling of well-being—a feeling which had nothing to do with the presence of H.M. and Chief Inspector Masters, who were standing at the foot of the bed.

"Morning, son," growled H.M. "How are you feelin' now? We just sort of dropped in." For some reason H.M. seemed stuffed and embarrassed. He glowered. "Have a cigar!" he added, with an air of inspiration.

It was perhaps not a very good suggestion. But Sanders accepted the cigar, while trying to collect his wits.

"Ferguson," he said. And all the events of the night returned to him.

"Ah, sir," the chief inspector greeted him heartily. "Good morning, good morning, good morning! Everything all right?"

"A bit stiff. Otherwise fine."

He examined the cigar, shifting himself on his pillows.

"What Sir Henry is trying to say," pursued Masters, "and what he can't get past his teeth for the life of him, is—thanks. You dished that chap Ferguson just in time, doctor. Yes, it was a neat idea. If you had tried to tackle him openly, he could have broken you across his knee—to say nothing of his gun. But to take him sideways and slap that piece of flypaper over his face! Not bad, doctor. Not bad."

"Not too bad," said H.M.

Sanders stared at the windows, whose curtains were being ruffled by a warm breeze. So, in a sense, was he. The flypaper had been of some service after all, even if he had not used it in burgling the house. He remembered Ferguson writhing on the stone-flagged floor at the foot of the chair, his face caught in that sticky surface like a larger fly, and the pistol knocked across the room when Ferguson became blind.

No, it had not been any part of a dream. The chair was there, its seat disarranged when Ferguson fell. Marcia was sitting huddled in it, while H.M. went out in search of a telephone.

"Sir Henry," the chief inspector went on, "insists on calling the fellow a megalomaniac, whatever that may be. I've got a shorter word. There were eight bullets in that Kreuger air-pistol of his, and he'd only fired four of 'em when you snaffled him. Sir Henry also wishes to say—"

"I can do my own talkin', can't I?" demanded H.M.

"Well, sir, I only—"

"I can do my own talkin'," said H.M. "What I want to say, son, is this. Last night, in the excitement of the aftermath, I seem to remember havin' at some point introduced the subject of, with regard to you and the wench, a kick in the pants. Now in all fairness I got to admit that maybe I spoke a bit hastily. But, oh, my eye! Of all the revoltin' slush I ever did hear, the expressions of affection and esteem poured out by Dennis Blystone's daughter towards you were unquestionably the slushiest and most revoltin'. I further wish to say—"

It was H.M.'s "parliamentary" style. Sanders made noises.

"I—er—don't remember it," he said. "Did Miss Blystone get home all right?"

"Uh-huh. So far as I know."

"And Ferguson? Have you got your witness?"

H.M.'s expression grew somber.

"No, son," he said. "Ferguson's dead."

He took out a cigar. "If the silly dummy had let us attend to him, he'd have pulled through. But it was too late. And

110

he talked about people wantin' to be the big I-Am! He committed suicide just as sure as someone else intended to commit murder when another whack of atropine was shoved into his glass. Your landlady's bringin' up your breakfast, son. Yes, you can get up if you insist, provided you stay in your room and keep quiet for today. In the meantime, we all ought to do a little serious sittin' and thinkin'.''

During breakfast, while H.M. smoked furiously and Masters paced about the room, the chief inspector informed them of developments at Scotland Yard on the previous night.

"But that's as may be," he concluded. "What I want to know is what in blazes went on at Mrs. Sinclair's house last night." He turned to H.M. "Apparently, sir, you arranged a burglary without saying anything to me about it. Very well: we'll say no more about that—"

"Thanke'e," growled H.M.

"—but what were you up to? What did you see or find when you got there? Ferguson was our chief witness. And no sooner do we find him than somebody polishes him off. So what went on?"

H.M. considered.

"Well . . . now. I rather thought Ferguson might be hidin' away at Mrs. Sinclair's. It was the logical place to look for him. But if I told you about it, I was afraid you'd bring a squad of coppers (as I seem to remember you've done before) and Ferguson would have sheered away like the man on the flyin' trapeze. So I thought I'd take a hand in the game my-self. Why not? I ask you, why not? Burn me, nobody is goin' to say *I* got a corporation! Look at that. Hard as ir—"

Masters looked at him with enlightenment. "I see, sir. That was the real reason, wasn't it? Just in order to prove you were an active old beggar," the chief inspector fumed, "and hadn't got a corporation (which, if you'll excuse my saying so, is as plain as the dome of St. Paul's), you deliberately—"

"All right, all right," said H.M., making querulous gestures. "I'm to blame. I'm always to blame, except at the end of a case. Then you shove your infernal bouquets at me and say you knew I had the trumps up my sleeve all the time. Looky here, Masters. Two of our friends, the doctor here and Denny Blystone's daughter, insisted on searchin' the house. I thought it would be interestin' to see what happened. But I didn't want them to run the possible risk of meetin' Ferguson there. So I thought I'd better get there first, and mooch round a bit, and find out if Ferguson really was inside. That's why I made 'em swear to meet me in the back garden at a specific time. Everything would'a been all right if one of your coppers hadn't spotted me."

"And you threw a flower-pot at him. That was fine, sir. Why did you have to go chucking flower-pots all over the place?"

"I was bein' crafty," said H.M.

"Crafty, my foot. You simply got mad because he spotted you, and—"

"I tell you I was bein' crafty," roared H.M. "It's not very complicated, is it? The best way to find out whether Ferguson was in the house, and make him give some sign of his presence, was to cause a first-class, three-ring row. And it was, too. That copper and I went across the cucumber-frames like a couple of dancin' bears, corporation or no. The trouble was that the blighter insisted on stickin' to the trail. I couldn't get rid of him. So I had to take refuge—"

"In the house?"

"In the house. Sure. What else could I do? My pal Shrimp Calloway had given me an excellent bunch of skeleton keys. I was goin' to hand 'em to Dr. Sanders, because," said H.M. apologetically, "I wasn't sure he knew the technique quite so well. *I* wasn't goin' to get mixed up in the burglary myself. But I repeat: what else could I do? I got in. That was why the front door was unlocked when my two amateurs got there."

Masters looked gloomy.

"Well, sir, maybe you know what you're doing. I say *maybe*. But the point is, what about this poisoned milk? What was going on inside the place?"

"Poisoner at work," said H.M. briefly.

The chief inspector whistled. He got out his notebook. "You don't mean you saw—?"

"I'm afraid so," grunted H.M. "At risk of callin' down thunders for my cloth-headedness again, I'm afraid so. Lemme tell you. As soon as I got inside the place, I made straight for the back door. Y'see, I wanted to get in a, position to get out into the back garden before my amateurs arrived. The whole house was dark. I still didn't know whether Ferguson was lurkin' or not. As a matter of fact, he was. I was passin' the hall door of that little back room when a light went on inside."

"And then? What did you do?"

"I got into the cupboard under the stairs. And if anybody makes any smart remarks—! No? All right. Anyhow, I could see across to the door of the little room. It was open two or three inches; I could see the chair and table by the fire, with the lamp. There was a sound of movin' about, and I heard Ferguson talkin' to somebody."

"How did you know it was Ferguson?"

"I saw him, that's how. The sweep stuck his head out into the hall and looked round. His pictures are pretty distinctive, son. He and his companion (whoever it was) had evidently been standin' in there in the dark, lookin' through the window and watchin' my little performance in the garden. Well, he stuck his head out into the hall, and he had that air-pistol in his hand. He went up and down the hall, sniffing at things, and tried the front and back doors. I could'a reached out and wrung his ruddy little neck off, but there was somebody else in the little room. And that person was most uncommonly active while Ferguson was out in the hall."

"You didn't see the other person?"

"I saw his hand," said H.M.

"Just that," he added doggedly. "In a brownish kind of glove. I told you—if you got any ears—that the door was open a few inches. I could see the table by the fire, and the lamp with the newspaper round the shade, and the plate of cold beef, and t'e glass of milk. I should think the hot milk had just been made; it was still steamin'. The devil of it is, son, that my glasses aren't made for long sight. I saw some blurry brown gloves jump out and do a kind of war-dance over the milk. They seemed pretty nervous. And they were foolin' about with a medicine-dropper. They squirted the medicine-dropper into the glass, and almost upset the whole shoot. Then they sort of brushed and moved about, as though they were a butler settin' a table."

"But didn't you even see a sleeve?"

"No. The light was too dim, and they were just on the edge of it. Brown gloves. They gave me the creeps, Masters, I'll swear they did. Like being alive."

His cigar had gone out. He turned it over in his fingers, and blinked at it.

"Well. As soon as they heard Ferguson's footsteps comin' back, one of the gloves jerked back out of sight. The other hovered round over the glass for a second, as if it was wonderin' whether it had forgotten something. It hesitated no end, till the last minute. Picture of a poisoner at work. Just before Ferguson got to the door, *it* jerked back.

"I heard Ferguson say, 'They seem to have gone, whoever they were; but you'd better get out of here.'"

"Didn't the other person say anything to that?"

"No. Then Ferguson turned out the light. It was blacker than Cerberus in that place. I heard more confused footsteps. I thought, 'That's done it. I've got him now, both Ferguson

113

and the murderer.' I was just wonderin' what to do and the best way to do it, when I heard another kind of noise. When I realized what it was, I nearly busted out of my cupboard like the monk of Siberia. You know what it was? It was shutters bein' closed. That sacred son of a vulture, Ferguson, had let the murderer out through one of those full-length windows—"

"But you should have realized, Sir Henry—!"

"Sure. Crow. Strut like anything. There it was. I knew it next second, because Ferguson turned on the light. He seemed to be walkin' up and down for a minute, pleased as billy-o. Next he reached under the seat of the chair, and fished up some sheets of paper. Then he sat down by the lamp, and got out a fountain-pen, and started to write. He'd evidently been writin' before that. When he mooched past me in the hall with his air pistol, there was fresh ink on his fingers."

Sanders nodded, with a coldly vivid recollection of that ink-stained forefinger curving round the trigger of the gun, or scratching at a poisoned glass of milk.

"Go on, sir," prompted Masters.

"Not much else. Bah! He didn't write much. He'd no more than got hold of his pen when there was another rumpus at the front of the house, outside." H.M. nodded towards the invalid. "It was my two amateurs arguin' with the persistent policeman. They must'a met him smack in front of Mrs. Sinclair's door—"

"We did," said Sanders feelingly.

"Ferguson got up, and shoved away his writin' again, and turned out the light. I thought that was my cue to get out the back door and meet my amateurs in the garden—as arranged. Burn me, how should I know they would be maneuvered into comin' slap into the house by the front door? I only tumbled to it when I was out in the garden, and heard voices comin' through the shutters from the little room. So back I came, and sort of stepped in. You know what happened. I was extremely bucked to find that Ferguson had guzzled over half of his tasty cup. What a night!"

Masters got up. He stumped over to the window, and stood looking down into the street.

"Fire away," growled H.M. "Say it. Say I lost both Ferguson *and* the murderer."

"So you did, sir. It's the truth. All the same—"

"You see a silver linin'?"

"N-no. That's to say, not exactly. But some facts." Masters grinned crookedly as he turned round. "That pair of gloves was the murderer, right enough. We found the medicine-

114

dropper you were talking about. It was thrown away behind one of the wash-tubs, with atropine in it. And five grains of the stuff in Ferguson's milk. But you see what this tends to? What time did you see the visitor there?"

"H'm, yes. Yes. The pair of gloves left the house at midnight, just before my amateurs got there—"

"Which eliminates Mrs. Sinclair," said Masters. His amusement faded, and he scowled. "I'm getting to the point where I don't seem to mind these blasted setbacks so much. Gone! Our best suspect. She had every reason to wish that her husband was dead. She touches a fifteen-thousand-pound insurance policy—"

"I doubt it, son. Considerin' all the funny business involved in the history of that policy, I rather doubt whether she'll ever touch a penny."

"In any case, she was sitting in my office at midnight. And there you are, sir. She couldn't be your pair of gloves. She's got an alibi as big as a house."

They considered this for a time. H.M. continued to roll his dead cigar in his fingers.

"Then what's the next course?" he demanded. "You got any leads, new or otherwise?"

"I should think that would be pretty clear, sir. Eh? I shall be interested," said Masters in his most pontifical manner, "to find out just where the others, aside from Mrs. Sinclair, were at midnight last night. And as for Felix Haye? Oh, yes. Point number one: the private inquiry agents—"

H.M. sat up. "Inquiry agents? What inquiry agents?"

"You know all about it. When Haye had the bottle of Ewkeshaw's ale sent to him, with another dose of our friend's poison in it, he told the solicitors to put the matter in the hands of a firm of private detectives. They did. I had a message from Drake this morning. *And* they chose a good one: the Everwide. Drake, Rogers & Drake are in another temper. In addition to stealing the five boxes, our murderer also pinched some securities belonging to them. In any case, they've had word from the Everwide that the Everwide has picked up some information about the bottle of ale. That interests me. That's point number one."

"Uh-huh. And what's point number two?"

"Judith Adams."

"Judith Adams?"

Masters drew a deep breath through his nostrils. "Something very queer there, Sir Henry. Very queer. She's the fifth name on Haye's list of five people who might do him in. But who in blazes *is* she? Nobody has ever heard of her. I've wired Haye's aunt in Cumberland; the aunt doesn't know. I've had Bob Pollard tackle half the people who knew Haye; they don't know. But she must be somewhere close at hand, or Haye wouldn't have included her as a source of danger. I mean to find her. I tell you, Sir Henry, there's some hanky-panky of a different kind connected with that name. If there is such a person as Judith Adams, why doesn't anybody know her? There's not a Judith connected with the whole case."

Ordinarily Dr. Sanders had complete control of his facial muscles. Ordinarily he would not have blinked an eyelid at the recollection that came to him. But, at the recollection of where he had heard that name mentioned, he sent his coffee-cup rattling across its saucer.

Masters was looking at him.

"That's torn it," said H.M., with a gusty sigh. "I was wonderin' how long it would be before somebody dropped to it. Yes, son, there is a Judith connected with the case. Sir Dennis Blystone's wife."

CHAPTER FOURTEEN

"OH?" said Masters, with sustained quietness. His suspicious eye moved from Sanders to H.M. "I remember Sir Dennis is a friend of yours, and that the young lady's certainly a friend of Dr. Sanders. How long have you been keeping this back?"

"Nonsense!" Sanders burst out. "You don't think that Lady Blystone—"

"I thought you were to be trusted, doctor. How long have you been keeping this back?"

Sanders was considering the past with such concentration that he almost forgot to reply.

"Nonsense!" he repeated. "I wasn't keeping anything back. I only heard the name, or met her at all, for the first time last night. And I'm not certain what her name is anyway. She and Sir Dennis were in the hall when I went round to pick up Marcia at their house. She was rather upset—"

"She was, was she?" said Masters, getting out his note-book again.

"—wait! About Marcia being 'taken to Scotland Yard.' They both were, for that matter. Sir Dennis addressed her as 'Judy.' That may not mean anything. You don't want to be misled by a coincidence in names. What you want to find out is whether her maiden name really was Judith Adams."

116

The chief inspector turned with grim inquiry to H.M. "Ho ho," said the latter. "So I'm the villain of the piece again, hey? I'm usually cloth-headed and always crooked. I throw flower-pots at your coppers. I lose your murderer and polish off your chief witness. When I can't obstruct the juggernaut o' justice in any other way, I goose the machinery by keepin' back information. Well, I don't know what her maiden name was. It's no good glarin' at me, Masters. I don't know. But it ought to be easy to find out."

"It ought," agreed Masters grimly. "Was Lady Blystone acquainted with Haye?"

"I tell you, son, I don't know!"

The chief inspector looked quickly at Sanders. "One thing, though," he pointed out, "we can settle now. A matter of alibis. Now, doctor, you say that you met Miss Blystone at her home last night; and then you both went on to Mrs. Sinclair's. Sir Henry says you two arrived there at just on midnight. Meantime, the visitor with brown gloves—the murderer—had been talking to Ferguson in the back room at Mrs. Sinclair's. Eh?"

H.M. grunted agreement.

"Just so. And presumably the visitor had been there for some little time? For some minutes, anyhow?"

"Yes, I think we can say that," admitted H.M., peering up over his spectacles.

"Good! But Dr. Sanders had just come on from Sir Dennis's, where he saw both Sir Dennis and Lady Blystone. *If* that's the case—well, it's unlikely that Lady Blystone, say, could have dashed on ahead to Mrs. Sinclair's, and could have been the brown-gloved visitor who was just leaving the house when Dr. Sanders got there? By that we could eliminate both the Blystones, couldn't we?"

Sanders was not deceived by the helpful urbanity of the chief inspector's approach. He was also annoyed, as H.M. has been, by the cussedness of all circumstances.

"I'm afraid we couldn't," he said. "I called at the Blystones' house at just past eleven o'clock. But we weren't to meet Sir Henry until twelve. Marcia and I spent most of the time driving round in a taxi."

"H'm. So there's an hour unaccounted for. An hour," speculated the chief inspector. He shut up his notebook, becoming brisk and hearty again. "Well, doctor, Sir Henry and I will have to be getting along. We only dropped in to see how you were. You'll be interested to know that I've got two good men on the track of that atropine—who bought it, and where. That's what always trips up the poisoner, you know. Ready, Sir Henry?"

H.M. sat woodenly, looking at a similar aspect of the bed-post.

"You run along, Masters," he said. "I'll see you presently. I got somethin' to say to the doctor."

Masters hesitated. He glanced at the other with powerful suspicion.

"Here! Man to man, now, Sir Henry: are you up to any games? Are you trying to do me in the eye again?"

"Honest to God, son, I'm not."

"Then just tell me this. Can you make one single good constructive suggestion as to what I ought to do?—Yes, yes, I know: aside from the first smart reply you'll think of, I mean?"

H.M. considered.

"Yes, I'll give you two. First, with regard to Haye's murder: a piece of the routine you like. Assign several of your best men, and check up on the movements of Mrs. Sinclair, Blystone, and Schumann for the entire day up to the time they met in Haye's flat at eleven o'clock in the evening. Got that, son? The entire day. I want to know the smallest movement they made, every one of 'em."

"But why? What difference does it make what their movements were before eleven o'clock?"

"Oh, Masters, my son," said H.M. despondently. "If you can't work that out you've got no reason to call me a fathead. Second point, with regard to Ferguson's murder last night: find out what Ferguson was writin' just before he died."

The chief inspector grinned.

"Yes, sir. I'd already thought of that myself. You told me about Ferguson taking some sheets of writing-paper from under the seat of the chair, and putting 'em back again. Unfortunately, as *I* told *you,* we've been all over that room already. We searched everything, including the seat of the chair. As I remember it, there was a sheet of writing-paper there all right, along with some newspapers stuffed away out of sight. But there wasn't any writing on the paper. So we didn't find anything."

"I know," agreed H.M. "Neither did I. That's all, son. Hop it. I'll see you at dinner tonight."

When the chief inspector had gone, H.M. did not speak for a long time. Sanders pushed his breakfast tray to one side and crawled out of bed. Though he felt suddenly weak and light-headed, he steadied himself enough to get a dressing-gown round his shoulders and put on his slippers. Then he took an easy-chair by the window.

Below him was the broad, swept neatness of the Maryle-bone Road, polished with sunlight. Even motor-cars had a glitter, and the noise of traffic seemed more quiet in warm air.

Then he and H.M. looked at each other.

"What," he asked, "did you want to see me about?"

"Haven't you got any idea, son?"

"No."

"I didn't want to see you, exactly," said H.M. "But I wanted to see Marcia Blystone. She's comin' to see you this morning. At least, she most solemnly promised she would last night. It's a funny thing about a woman," he added, abruptly seeming to wander into drowsiness. "You can scare the daylights out of her. She'll be half-faintin' and out of action for a week. Yet at the back of her mind there's something that's always awake and always practical, even if she's hoppin' from ice-floe to ice-floe like Eliza crossin' the river.

"Now, a man's not like that. If he's in scaldin' danger or difficulty he's got eyes and ears for only that one thing. Everything else is washed out. The most money-grabbin' bandit, in the middle of a gun-battle with the coppers, wouldn't spare two seconds to scoop up a fifty-pound note out of the gutter. But a woman would. Her life's like that. All this," added H.M., "is by way of preface. Masters has been talkin' about people who obstruct justice. But of all the people who most consistently, charmin'ly, and earnestly shove justice into the ditch at every turn, your friend Marcia Blystone is the worst."

"How so?"

"She pinched those two sheets of paper Ferguson had been writin'," said H.M. "She pinched 'em out of the chair. Didn't you see her?"

"Hell!" said the other, sitting up. "No, I was thinking about other things. But—"

"Sure. So was I. That's the point I'm makin'. However, it happens to be the case. Just throw your mind back over the lit'le rumpus, and tell me what happened to the chair after Ferguson slid out of it."

"The seat came loose. It was pushed forward about half-way."

"Uh-huh. And what did the gal do?"

"First she leaned over the back of the chair while we were holding Ferguson down, and then she sat down—" he stopped.

Again they looked at each other.

"Something's got to be done about this, son," H.M. pointed out seriously.

"But how could she have known the sheets of paper were there?"

"I don't think she did. She must have seen 'em starin' up at her when the padded seat was forward. Which is what I mean by presence of mind."

Sanders reflected. "There's just one thing I'd rather know, at the moment, than anything else in the whole case. If Sir Dennis Blystone is a criminal, what is his crime?

"You see," he went on, "we've cleared some of the lumber out of the way. We're learning to fit the person to the crime—though you and the chief inspector seem to have known it all along. Through our own adventures and Masters's interview with Mrs. Sinclair at the Yard, we've now got two. Ferguson was a burglar. Mrs. Sinclair is an art-swindler. There remain Bernard Schumann and Sir Dennis Blystone.

"What Schumann's line is I haven't got the slightest idea. Masters has cleared him from any charge of selling fake Egyptian antiques. Sir Dennis made some wild joke about Schumann killing people and selling their bodies as mummies; but, aside from being impractical, it's no more than a joke or Blystone wouldn't have said it. Schumann seems, in the best sense of the term, a gentleman. He somehow does the dirty with alarm-clocks and magnifying-glasses. But, whatever his crimes are, they can't be very serious. He is the calmest and most undisturbed and helpful of the lot.

"With Sir Dennis Blystone it's different. He—am I talking too much?"

H.M. spoke without opening his eyes.

"Not at all, son. Fire away."

"With Blystone, as I say, it's different. The people attached to him take on in various ways whenever they think of it. Lady Blystone nearly has hysterics. Marcia says she'll kill herself or go to Buenos Aires if it ever comes out. The old man himself, in moments of uncertainty when he loses his smooth-speaking dignity, is the uneasiest of any. Now there seems to be something pretty bad behind this. He's a whited sepulcher if I ever saw one. The atmosphere in that house was sinister; it reminded me of the time I went to take a girl out to a dance, and the old man had been drunk, and —anyhow, what sort of unholy crooked activities is he guilty of?"

Sanders stopped, for H.M.'s face was wreathed with fantastic jollity. H.M. chortled, rocking back and forth, with a subdued noise as though he were strangling.

"Exactly," he said.

"What do you mean, exactly?"

"That in itself is interestin'," observed H.M. more soberly. "When women have real guilt and anguish on their minds, they don't talk about it. When they hear the copper walkin'

120

in every footstep, they don't talk about what they'll do if the truth comes out. No, son: they guard high crime with silence or pride. But what sort of crime does make dignified elderly ladies have hysterics, and adolescent daughters twist through any hoop rather than reveal it?"

"Well?"

"A comic crime," said H.M. "A social disgrace. That great surgeon, and justly respected man-about-town, has been in the past nothin' more than a rather successful pickpocket."

To say that the case clattered down round Sanders's ears like falling masonry, to say that the world had to be readjusted and the Marylebone Road come into focus again, would be an understatement. He stared at his companion, who appeared to be quite serious. He made a feeble sort of noise. He concluded by merely listening.

H.M. stuck the cigar in a corner of his mouth, and spoke in an argumentative tone.

"Y'see, son, it's a mistake to think of the pickpocket—and most people do think of him like this—as a seedy little blighter who shuffles past furtively in a dirty collar. Oh, no. Usually the pickpocket is the most quietly distinguished and best-dressed man in the bus or tube. He's got to be. It's a part of his profession. For in that case you don't think anything of it when you are shoved up against him in a crowd, whereas you'd shy away from the shifty feller by instinct. In the same way you never glance twice at the well-dressed stranger who sits readin' his newspaper beside you in the train. You prefer to sit or stand by him rather than a grubby 'un. All this may be painful class-consciousness; but there it is. Ain't it well known, incidentally, that Blystone never uses a taxi when he can travel by bus or Underground?

"Now, all coppers know these points about pickpockets. Masters, of course, spotted Blystone's little hobby as soon as he saw his hands—"

Sanders was groping out of a daze.

"His hands? But he's got very fine hands."

"Sure: in their own way. There's an awful lot of rubbish talked about hands, son. For instance, you've heard people talk about 'the fine sensitive hands of a musician'—meaning the long, slender, delicate kind. You'll disprove that merely by usin' your own eyes. Most musicians have broad, strong hands with square-tipped fingers. So have most surgeons.

"Hans Gross's encyclopedia o' crime points out that the best pickpocket has the first two fingers of his business-hand the same length. *Vide* Blystone. Reason? The pickpocket, y'know, don't grope round in your clothes with all five fingers wrigglin'. You'd spot him in half a tick if he did. He uses his hand like the blades of a scissors: first two fingers together, second two together: slidin' in and liftin' with the space between. So."

H.M. illustrated moving the fingers like a child making a silhouette of a talking donkey on the wall. Again Sanders tried to adjust his mind.

"By the Lord," Sanders muttered, "before we're through with this business you'll have me suspicious of everything and everybody in the world. First it's frosted windows. Then it's pictures in art-galleries. Now it's well-dressed people in buses. If anybody ever writes an account of this case, it ought to be called The Criminals' Handbook. Then those four watches were merely—?"

H.M. nodded.

"Spoils, son. Blystone's spoils from a few old raids. Felix Haye somehow got hold of 'em, probably together with the number of the watch, who owned it, when and where it was taken. Those watches have the most howlin'ly simple explanation of the lot: so simple that nobody seems to have thought of it. As for the dummy arm, which I told you long ago belonged to Blystone—"

"Well, sir?"

H.M. made a sour face. "Copied. Gross tells about a feller who made a mighty good livin' out of those dummy arms. It's used by the well-dressed chap sittin' beside you to divert all suspicion from himself. He's holdin' his newspaper in two hands and readin' it. The neat gloved hand and arm on your side are dummies, while the real hand is usin' its scissor-fingers as it pleases."

The real cause for uneasiness came out.

"But is the man stark mad?" demanded Sanders. "Why should he do that sort of thing? He's one of the best-known surgeons in London—"

"Uh-huh. So, most people think, was Jack the Ripper."

"Yes, but—"

"He can't help it, son. It's a well-known form of kleptomania; see Gross again. Dennis Blystone is well off. He doesn't need watches or money. I sort of think he's got over it now; he's put down the odd spot in his mind and he can almost laugh at what he used to do when he did need the money. How it started I dunno; but I do recall that in our younger days he used to be fond of conjurin' tricks and was awful nimble with his fingers. I expect there used to be times when he did need the money—like all of us. Do you dare say it couldn't happen to you?"

There was a silence.

"But you see now," grunted H.M., "why there was such a

thick atmosphere of a parent recoverin' from a spree. And if little Marcia Blystone has ever seemed to act queer and cussed and unnatural towards things, you can understand it. I tell you, son, I've been as worried as blazes! If this business comes out—"

"It would ruin him."

"Ruin him? Burn me, he'd be laughed off the face of the earth! I don't suppose he's in any danger of bein' prosecuted or servin' a stretch. In that respect his offense is lighter than any of the others. It's merely devilish. But just think of what must'a gone on in his own home, what he and his family thought when they knew Felix Haye had tumbled to it, and then tell me if it's not possibly the most blinkin' serious of all the cases."

"Of all the cases?"

"Sure. He's got everything in the world to lose. Would he commit murder to destroy the evidence?"

Sanders did not know. In his mind rose Blystone's tall and commanding figure, as though the man were about to begin a lecture. Always there was about him that strange air of weakness or hesitation. But chiefly Sanders was thinking of Marcia.

"And she," he said, "stole—or you think she stole—whatever Ferguson was writing last night. The real story of the murder?"

"I dunno, son. It seems very probable."

For some reason Sanders was feeling a trifle queasy in the stomach, much more queasy than he had felt last night.

"I know what you're thinking," he said, when H.M. has been silent for a long time. He could not help facing and considering the facts, even when he did not wish to face them. "Atropine has been used in this case in large quantities. It's not a common poison. On the contrary, it's a medical man's poison: especially a medical man like Blystone, who does head and eye operations. On the other hand—"

H.M. opened one eye. "You're gettin' back into form, you are. On the other hand what?"

"It would be easy for anybody, even without a knowledge of chemistry, to go straight to its source and get all he wanted. I mean that the original herb, *atropa belladonna,* is found in plenty of English hedgerows. Any book on botany would give the murderer a full description of it; those black cherry-sized berries couldn't be missed. If the murderer boiled the leaves and roots, he could extract as much atropine as he needed. Masters's confident talk about 'tracing' the poison is pretty thin. Besides, until you can show how the poison was introduced into the drinks at Haye's—"

"Oh, that?" said H.M. disconsolately. "I know that."

"And the atropine was not put in by anybody who sneaked in from outside while the drinks were unattended?"

"That's right, son. It wasn't."

Mrs. Bartlemy, Sanders's landlady, was in the offing. They heard her puff along the passage outside, and knock at the door like a steam-hammer. When she put her head in at the door, she was obviously impressed.

"Lady and gentleman here, sir," she announced, as though stating a novel fact. "Sir Dennis Blystone and Miss Blystone."

Sanders got ready for it.

"Ask Sir Dennis and Miss Blystone to come up," he said.

CHAPTER FIFTEEN

"I've come," began Marcia, "to—"

She saw H.M., and stopped abruptly. Behind her in the doorway her father seemed to waver like a figure on wires. Then, while Marcia's eyes went back to Sanders as though in half-defiant inquiry about his health, Sir Dennis Blystone took command of the situation. Clearing his throat, he moved forward. Sanders noted again the straightforward eyes under jutting brows, the neatness of cuff and tailoring.

"Merrivale!" he said, striding over to shake hands. His handsome face showed real pleasure, and his walk was springy. "Hel-lo, Henry! It's good to see you again. I haven't run across you in a donkey's years. How are you?"

"Hello, Denny," said H.M. rather sheepishly, and glared at the floor. "Keepin' pretty well, thanks."

"Fit as ever, you old horse?"

"Uh-huh. I'm reducin'."

There was a long pause. Then Blystone, after a hesitation, turned to Sanders. His manner was more quiet, but just as sincere.

"Dr. Sanders," he said in a low voice, "I hope you will forgive my coming here. Let me be frank. I think you were very foolish to lead my daughter into the nonsensical and dangerous pranks you two played last night, though I have a suspicion it was Marcia who did most of the leading. In any case, I have been able to keep it from her mother." His manner had a shade of paternal humor under its gravity. "But thank God you both came through it safely; that is all we need care about. And that you did come through it safely,

124

I recognize, was due to your courage and determination, which—"

Sanders was embarrassed, hideously embarrassed, more embarrassed than he would have believed possible. His arm throbbed like the blood in his head.

"—at the same time, you must realize that your conduct was unprofessional and, from the point of view of your career, absolutely insane. If this comes to certain ears, you must be aware of the result. You had no authority to do what you did. You are not, of course, a practicing physician; but if you'll allow me to advise you—"

Whereupon Sanders blurted it out.

"Let's clear the air," he said. "In another minute we'll all be standing here like a lot of Schumann's mummies. Sir Dennis, we've heard all about the four watches and the pocket-picking. We also think Miss Blystone had better give the chief inspector that manuscript she took from Ferguson's chair last night. After that, everything's fine—" he spoke in one sentence—"and there's no harm done and there's whisky in that cupboard so let's all pour ourselves a drink and make ourselves comfortable."

"Oh," said Blystone.

That was all.

"What a devil of a rotten diplomat I am," observed Sanders. "Anyhow, there it is."

Blystone stroked his cheek with those curious two fingers. For a second Sanders thought he was going to make a speech, or become kindly and persuasive. But he did none of these things. He spoke in a quiet voice, though his eyes seemed to be deeper in his head.

"No, thanks," he said mechanically. "I don't care for whisky. As you say, there it is. I—I'm afraid I'm no good to anybody."

It was the beginning of a somewhat painful speech. In this case H.M. was not sympathetic.

"Oh, for cat's sake!" he roared. "Don't take on like that. Out of pure cussed self-pity you'll have your own kid weepin' and convince yourself you're a fallen tower of poetic magnitude. Well, you're not. All that's worryin' you is a social convention. 'They eat and drink and scheme and plod, And go to church on Sunday. And many are afraid of God, But more of Mrs. Grundy.' That's you, son. Pinchin' watches! Cor! if you got any sense you'll pinch somebody's watch at the next dinner you go to, and hold it up, and talk about it freely as an amusin' hobby. Do you know how to laugh? Then use it on yourself. Lots of respectable people are amateur conjurers."

Blystone, roused out of himself, looked up sharply.

"You don't think—?" he demanded.

"Why not?" said H.M. "Pinchin' watches! Cor!"

During this time Sanders had been watching Marcia. It was as though another sort of girl emerged, and showed honest human nature all over her face. The expression is inexact and not particularly fine writing; but that was how Sanders thought of it. She stared at H.M.

"You know," she cried, "you're not bad! You really are a tonic."

"I'm the old man," said H.M. with dignity. "You trust me and everything will be all right, in spite of what Masters tells you."

She turned to Blystone.

"He's absolutely right! Laugh. Laugh all over your face. Then it doesn't really matter if you do go about with that hussy in Cheyne Walk—"

"Marcia!" said Blystone. He seemed shocked.

"There you go again," groaned H.M. "Standin' on your sacred rights as head of the lares and penates, and bankin' up the old hearth-fires of home. Horseradish. She's twenty-one, ain't she? Take me, for instance. I've got two daughters. They both think I'm the funniest thing that ever staggered in out of the wet, but you'd be surprised at what a feelin' of peace it brings under the ancestral roof."

"Hang it, Henry, I only said—"

"You take my tip," insisted H.M., now embarked. "Meet a friend of yours this afternoon, lift his wallet, and hand it back to him. He won't run from you screamin'. When people go to conjurin' entertainments and lend the magician a top-hat or a watch, they don't really believe he's goin' to slosh eggs in the top-hat or bust the watch to glory with a hammer. If they did there'd be a gibberin' mob chasing him round the Alhambra after every performance."

"I think," said Blystone, turning to Sanders, "I think I could use a spot of that whisky after all."

H.M. was inexorable.

"No you don't! You sit down there and listen to me. Do you realize, with all your little troubles on your mind, that we're dealin' with a murder? They hang you for it."

"So I've heard," said Blystone gloomily.

He was in better shape, though he still looked dazed. He followed H.M.'s gesture and sat down on the edge of the bed.

"Y'see, my son, you've got yourself mixed up with real criminals this time. They're not foolin'. Two pretty nasty killings have happened. Did you do it?"

"Good Lord, no!"

"Uh-huh. Got any atropine?"

"Yes, but I can account for all of it. Fortunately."

"What were you doin' last night between eleven and twelve o'clock?"

"I went for a walk."

"Yes. You would. Can you prove where you went?"

"I don't know; I hope so."

"Where'd you go?"

"In the direction of Scotland Yard."

"Why?"

"I heard they were detaining Mrs. Sinclair there." He seemed to speak without thinking; afterwards he gave a stealthy but stern glance towards Marcia, who now stood close behind Sanders's chair.

"Where'd you hear that?"

"I—from my wife, I think. Yes. She spoke about it when Dr. Sanders came there pretending to be a detective-inspector—"

"No, I'm hanged if I did!" snapped Sanders. "All I said—"

"Shut up," H.M. told him austerely. His little eye fastened on Blystone again. "Where'd your wife hear it?"

Blystone seemed puzzled.

"Well . . . I hadn't thought of it. Probably from her maid. Her maid knows Mrs. Sinclair's maid; and I also heard that Mrs. Sinclair's maid was taken to the Yard, too. I imagine she was gratified and spread the news. Does it make any difference?"

"What's your wife's maiden name, son?"

"Look here," said Blystone in a fussed voice, "what's all this got to do with it? Her maiden name? Barbara Gore-Reeves."

"Barbara! It's Judith, ain't it? You always used to call her Judy."

"Yes, but she called me Punch," answered Blystone, with an attempt at dignity. He straightened his collar. "It—er—dates from the early years of our marriage. I was young and full of theories, and had strong ideas about how babies should be treated."

"You're not lyin' to me, are you, Denny? The name wasn't Judith Adams?"

The other blinked. "Judith Adams! No, I should think not. It will be quite easy to prove, if you care to come round and ask her. But, I say, Merrivale. A little discretion—you understand? Lady Blystone is a highly strung woman, and not at all well. The last time you were there. Chewing tobacco, you know. She says she can't understand why you, who have one of the oldest baronetcies in the Peerage, and a string of academic degrees after your name, will lower yourself to use slovenly grammar so consistently. Women don't understand it. Sometimes, I admit, neither do I. By the way, where was I? Oh, yes. The name. I can show you her passport as well. But—"

He was interrupted. Marcia moved across in front of him, composedly opening her handbag. Though Sanders had not been able to see her, he sensed a certain excitement.

From the handbag she took two sheets of closely written paper, crumpled up into a ball, and handed them to H.M.

"There it is," she said. "Read it."

H.M. weighed the sheets in his hand.

"Oh," he said. "This is what you pinched out of Ferguson's chair last night. So you're confessin'?"

"Read it, please."

She brushed the other matter aside. As though with a consciousness of duty done, she leaned against the ledge of the window. All worry seemed to have left her, though the reaction of relief was strong. Her brown eyes were shining with that intent expression which Sanders had come to know: it meant that they would shortly hear another theory.

"You were quite right," she declared, "about his having got mixed up with real criminals. Brr! Well, I guessed it. I knew he was the worst of the lot the first time I set eyes on him."

"That who was the worst of the lot?" asked Blystone sharply. "What are you talking about?"

H.M. spread out the sheets on his knee. It was a full minute before he spoke. Sunlight strengthened outside the windows. For the first time Marcia turned to Sanders, very deliberately, and smiled.

"This has torn it," said H.M. "Oh, my eye! This has unquestionably torn it."

"What has torn what? What is it?"

"Merely the full story of Haye's murder," said H.M. in a hollow voice.

Blystone's hands moved out and crossed. He sat rigidly on the edge of the bed; and his straightforward gaze did not waver.

"Mentioning—?" he suggested.

"No. not mentionin' the name of the murderer. Not in so many words, anyhow. Y'see, Ferguson didn't have time. It's headed in fine flowing handwriting, *Statement with Regard to the Murder of Felix Haye, Esq., by Peter Sinclair Ferguson, B.Sc., E.O.M. (Egyptian Order of Merit).* Ferguson was the sort of feller, y'see," he explained apologetically, "who does put degrees after his name. I think he must'a rather prided himself on his literary style, for he's spread himself here. His shadow is still on us. We can't escape him. Shall I read it?"

"Read it," said Blystone, "and hurry up."

It was true. Ferguson's shadow was still there, as palpable as something that hung at the window.

Emulating the example of Felix Ĥaye [read H.M.], I wish to put on paper the name of the person who killed him, and also the highly ingenious method by which the crime was managed.

Unlike Haye, I do not anticipate any danger. But, in the unlikely event of anything happening to me, I feel that the police should have all the information at my disposal.

First a word of personal history. During the years 1926-27 I served as Chief Production Artist to the Anglo-Egyptian Importing Co., Ltd., at their office and warehouse in the Boulevard Kasr El Ali, Cairo. Here were manufactured such articles as scarabs and the mummies of animals, made of glass paste and siliceous clay; larger statues with Antwerp schist to represent black basalt; and papyri of considerable convincingness.

I may mention that my reproduction of a XIXth Dynasty papyrus, presented by us as a token of esteem to H.M. the King of Egypt, earned warm commendation from His Majesty, and resulted in my receiving the Egyptian Order of Merit. I am one of the few who have received this.

The greater part of our valuable stock was in a separate warehouse, where Bernard Schumann had his private office. Bernard Schumann was and is head of the Anglo-Egyptian Importing Company. To avoid income-tax complications he calls himself managing director; but he is sole owner. I am in a position to indict this man for arson and murder.

"Arson and murder," repeated Blystone mechanically.

He was looking rather white. Nobody moved, and there was no noise except the rustling of the sheets as H.M. smoothed them out.

"Arson and murder?" said Sanders. "Schumann?"

"That's right," agreed H.M. without inflection. "Bob Pollard collected the information yesterday that nearly all Schumann's valuable stock had once been wiped out in a fire—completely uninsured stuff, mind you. He got a lot of sympathy for that, because he's known as an honest dealer. Good old Ferguson goes on to explain it."

The fire was planned and executed by Schumann, in order

129

to conceal the murder of his only serious competitor, a genuinely brainy and unscrupulous Moslem named El Hakim, who was putting him out of business. It was all arranged beforehand. Schumann deliberately allowed the insurance on his stock to lapse, as though through forgetfulness.

This was his reasoning. The world will never believe that anybody will deliberately destroy a fortune's worth of his own goods in order to commit any crime whatever. And the only way to commit a perfect murder, said Schumann, is by such a sacrifice. Pour faire l'omelette, said Schumann, il faut casser des oeufs. He thought the omelette was worth it. He is very cold by nature.

He stabbed El Hakim (I do not know with what) in the loft of the warehouse on the afternoon before the night he intended the fire to break out. He arranged it so that when the fire broke out he should be far away, with an alibi.

This is how he did it. The floor of the warehouse was thick with shavings, excelsior, and other combustibles. He added petrol to these. He then obtained the works of an ordinary alarm-clock. As is known, the ringing mechanism of such a clock consists in an arm or clapper which is agitated violently back and forth against the bell until the clockwork runs down.

Bernard Schumann removed the bell from the clock. To the arm or clapper he fastened with wire several large ordinary matches.

The clock was placed in such a position by a large wooden box that, when the alarm went off, the matches would be rasped against a sandpaper surface and catch fire. The box was drenched with petrol, the infernal-machine piled with shavings.

Bernard Schumann, of course, could time the fire to begin at any hour he liked: all he had to do was set the alarm for that hour. In this case it was at ten P.M., when he was sitting on the terrace at Shepheard's. I have seen few more spectacular sights than when that blazing pyre went up to the sky, with Schumann wringing his hands among his friends.

Remains would naturally be found in the ruins. Sooner or later they would be identified as those of El Hakim, since El Hakim would be missing anyway. They were found. It was assumed—as Schumann meant it to be—that El Hakim had tried to ruin his rival, had set fire to the warehouse, and had himself died in the fire. This is called poetic justice, and I must say it looked like it. Schumann received much sympathy. It was a very good idea.

"There," said Dr. Sanders, also in a hollow voice, "is an example of classic understatement to go with any. A very good idea is right."

H.M. nodded seriously.

"Always assumin'," he replied, "that good old Ferguson is tellin' the truth—yes. There's not a flaw in it. The murderer don't try to hide the identity of the body, which is where so many of 'em go off the rails. He never tries to hide anything. They can investigate all they like, and he's still safe. Psychologically it's sound too. As Ferguson says, nobody can believe a man will destroy a fortune's worth of his own property in order to commit any crime whatever."

He scowled.

"Humph. These details are all new. *If* they're true, it comes close to bein' the perfect murder. The only thing that was known before—score up again to Masters and ordinary police experience—is that Schumann's crime was arson."

"You knew that all along?" asked Blystone.

"Sure. That alarm-clock trick is as old as sin and Satan. It's a commonplace. Whenever you find a suspicious character carryin' alarm-clock works *without* the bell attached— as this was—you just keep an eye on him to make sure his game's not arson. When at the same time you've got a magnifyin'-glass in the feller's pocket, you want to look sharper still. For it's not only a magnifyin'-glass. It's also a burning-glass. And that's a device for startin' fires as old as Egypt itself."

Sanders reflected. There had been doubt in H.M.'s voice.

"Yes, but look here, sir! The alarm-clock works in Schumann's pocket couldn't have been the ones he used to start the fire in Cairo. Wouldn't the heat have melted them into an unrecognizable lump of metal?"

"It would," growled H.M. "That's what's botherin' me. Unless (as is quite possible) Schumann is addicted to arson, and was plannin' another stroke. We don't know Felix Haye's bit of information.' We don't know what was in the five boxes."

Marcia folded her arms. She was looking at her father.

"Excuse me," she interposed in a soft voice. "But Ferguson has a few very juicy things to say about Mrs. Sinclair—his wife. His lawfully wedded wife, as I've told my Dad. I didn't know about her being an art-crook, though, until I read that."

"Now, Marcia!—"

"Well, did you know it?"

"This is not your affair, Marcia," retorted Blystone peevishly. "She has done nothing which was not quite legitimate business. Has she, Merrivale? What does Ferguson say about her?"

"Ferguson," said H.M., running his eye down the micro-

131

scopically written sheets, "Ferguson, out of pure meanness of heart, was simply takin' a whack at everybody. If somebody did put him out of the way, he wanted to pull down as many as possible when he tumbled. The only one he don't discourse on, Denny, is you: because he apparently didn't know you. But I'll skim over the relevant parts, up to Haye's murder."

I never had any actual proof against Schumann for the Cairo fire, but he knew I knew. When I wished to return to England, and asked to be made manager of the London office, I received the appointment.

Whenever Bernard Schumann tended to grow sharp or above his place, I had a habit of looking down my nose and saying, "Great Fire of London, 1666." "Great Fire of London, 1666." "Great Fire of London, 1666." It was very effective. I do not think he could hear it in his sleep without feeling he had been betrayed.

But I may remark here that I am a man of wide and diverse interests. I did not like to remain in an office, and did not remain for long. I left for the Continent, taking a sum of money with me. You will be able to guess why Bernard Schumann did not prosecute me.

"Then," said H.M. with ghoulish relish, "we got some remarks on his marriage to Mrs. Sinclair, and their happy life together. In spite of your insistence—" he peered at Marcia— "we'll pass over 'em. For the rest is pure jam. It tells us what we want to know about the night before last."

It was strange how old friends met after many years.

On Monday night of last week, I walked into my wife's house. I had not seen her for nearly a year. I am not sure that she really believed me dead.

Not at all sure. She is a woman of great acumen, and I do not think she could have missed that insurance policy unless she saw a trap in it.

In any event, she welcomed me with open arms, and we spent a very pleasant night—

"That's a damned lie," said Blystone.

"Well, after all, son," returned H.M. meekly, "the woman was his wife."

"But she isn't his wife now. Or, rather, she's his widow."

He suddenly seemed to realize that he was talking in front of his daughter, and corrected himself by saying that it was of no consequence. But under his anger there had been a certain satisfaction and thoughtfulness, as though he looked ahead. H.M. was looking at him steadily.

"Is it any good tellin' you, son, to watch out for your fingers in a different way? This is fire. You're mixin' with some of the cleverest criminal minds in England. Mrs. Bonita Sinclair and Mr. Peter Sinclair Ferguson were pull-baker, pull-devil every second of the time. They tried to put something over on each other with a regularity and smoothness that rather gives the old man gooseflesh." He rubbed his hand across his big bald head. "I've been mixin' my metaphors badly. So I can finish 'em off by sayin' this: You're fightin' out of your weight. All right, all right! Don't yell. I'll wind this up."

It was plain, therefore, that she had a use for me. And she had.

Let me say right here that I never had the honor of meeting Mr. Felix Haye. I do not know who he was. I do not know why he should have been interested in me, or why he should have thought I wanted to kill him, or where he got the quicklime and phosphorus I once used in certain activities of mine. The man was a fool.

Buy my wife told me about him. Someone, it seemed, had been trying to kill Haye with a bottle of poisoned ale.

Shortly—I do not know how she learned this—Haye meant to call a meeting of those who might be responsible. This presumptuous fool had somehow and for some reason collected dangerous evidence against several persons. She did not know how many. She also believed that he had hidden it away, or was going to hide it away. She said the persons included me, but I believed her to be lying. My wife was very frightened.

This was what she proposed to me:

I should attend the meeting, unknown to Haye. This would not be difficult. I learned with surprise that Haye's flat was above my old office. I know that building as I know the Moslems' Koran, which has always appealed to me as the most inspired religion.

I should wait in Bernard Schumann's office. She would leave the door of the flat on the latch when she went in. After allowing a time for the party to settle down in one room, I should then go into the flat and listen.

This Mr. Haye, my wife said, had a rare talent for boasting and spreading himself. She believed that he would either hint at or tell outright the place where he had hidden the things that worried my wife. Even if he refused to talk, she believed she could prod him on to do so.

Let's stop this fancy-fancy talk. I am sick of writing it. My wife needed me because I can crack any crib on earth.

133

There: you've got it now. That was my purpose in being there. Haye was going to talk, and I was going to hear it. As soon as I heard what he had done with the stuff—in my wife's case it was two letters written by her, guaranteeing the genuineness of a fake Rubens and a fake Van Dyck, which could have sent her up the river for five years—I would be ready to get out and act. Unless Haye had the stuff in some place like the Bank of England, I could get it while he was still talking about it. That's no lie. I mean it.

This is what she wanted me to do. I said I would do it for a thousand pounds. We finally compromised at seven-fifty.

I waited until they were all upstairs in Haye's flat, and then I got into Bernard Schumann's office with my twirlers. I liked that. I like pretending, and if any one came in I was going to pretend to work there. I was not afraid of meeting Schumann. Even if I did meet him, I was all ready with "Great Fire of London, 1666."

But I did not meet Schumann. I went upstairs to the flat at ten minutes past eleven. They were all in the kitchen. This fool Haye was imitating a baby, to judge by the sounds.

I got into the bedroom, where I could look through into the sitting-room. Just after I got in there, who should I see but Bernard Schumann. He walked out of the kitchen carrying a tray with a cocktail shaker, some glasses and a tumbler on it. He put them on a little table and went back to the kitchen, where Haye was going on like a baby.

If you think that anybody put poison into that cocktail-shaker or the tumbler or the glasses while they were standing there unattended, you are wrong. Nobody did. I was watching.

In a few minutes all the people came back from the kitchen. Haye told them to sit round the table. Then he gave them hell, in a silky kind of way. He started, "Friends, Romans, countrymen," and generally made a fool of himself. I thought he was soft. He talked so soft that I could not make out what he was talking about, or what it was he had on each of them. But he said he had left the stuff with his solicitors, Drake, Rogers & Drake, and that was all I needed to know. They seemed to be getting wild and drunk on just one drink. At the time I could not understand it.

H.M. raised his eyes and studied Blystone.

"So," he observed in a flat tone. "Haye did tell you what he had on his mind, hey? He didn't just crack jokes before the atropine worked?"

Blystone, whose mind seemed to be turned inwards, roused himself again. Evidently he did not know how to deal with this. After drawing in his chin for weighty utterance, he hesitated and looked extremely foolish.

"Yes. Haye said a few things," he admitted.

134

"What things?"

"It is difficult to say," answered Blystone weightily. "He could not talk straight. He did not talk straight, in any event. In the first place he tried to be—what is the word I want?—elliptical. In the second place the atropine was working. What between the atropine and Haye's Henry-Jamesian tendency never to say a straight thing straight out without some underlying pun or joke or double-meaning, the result was confused. I am afraid I was listening only to what concerned me. But—"

"But?"

"Do you believe this swine Ferguson is telling the truth?"

"Sure. About this part of it, anyway."

"Then how was the atropine put into the drinks?" demanded Blystone, leaning forward like a lecturer over a rostrum. All his mind and soul seemed concentrated in the question. "I'll swear that Bonny—Mrs. Sinclair—didn't do it. It's been worrying me. I watched her."

"How closely?" asked Marcia, and made a puffing sort of noise which indicated contempt. She looked fiery with annoyance.

"I watched the others too," said Blystone. "And they didn't. The thing is absolutely impossible."

I waited to see if Haye would say anything more, but he only raved. That tall ass with the distinguished manner was singing, "Pull for the shore, sailor." I watched the wardrobe too, which made me get out.

Then I went down to Bernard Schumann's office and got the telephone-directory to find out the address of Drake, Rogers & Drake. I did not know them. It took a long time, because there are nearly three columns of Drakes in the directory.

In the meantime, it got all quiet upstairs. I did not like that. Just when I had found the address, and was preparing to go and see about it, there was a noise from upstairs. I had just turned the light out, fortunately. Someone came down the stairs from Haye's flat, and passed Bernard Schumann's office, and walked down the next flight of stairs.

I followed. It was dark on the stairs. The person went down to the ground floor, and started unbolting and unchaining the back door of the building. This person got it open and went out. I followed. When this person went out through an alley, and into the street again, I saw who it was—as plain as day.

You will be surprised when I tell you.

This person started walking, very fast, down Great Russell Street in the direction of Southampton Row. That was the direction I was going anyway, so I followed. From Southampton Row this person turned into Theobald's Road, and I had an idea this person must be making for Gray's Inn, as I was.

I was right. He was going to the solicitors' office. He (or it might have been a she: what do you think? I say that for convenience) went down a little court behind the building. Then the person climbed up a fire-escape.

This happened at fifteen minutes past twelve. The person went to a certain window, and seemed to be turning back the catch of the window with a knife. Then the person went through the window, and came out two minutes later, and got away.

I always know what to do. I always have. But I was not sure here. I was supposed to do what my wife was paying me for. It seemed that somebody had done it already. I was not worried, because I had the goods on this person profitably afterwards, so I did not attempt to stop this person. But I thought I had better make sure this person had cleaned out the evidence in the lawyers' offices, especially as he might not have cleaned out all of it.

I went up the fire-escape myself.

It was all right. A box painted with Haye's name was lying on the floor with its lock broken—a difficult job. There was nothing in it. I went all through the offices, making sure nothing had been overlooked. I always do the job right. Then I thought I had better get back to Great Russell Street.

It was half-past twelve when I left. A night-watchman saw me and started a row, so I had to duck. This delayed me. It takes nearly fifteen minutes to walk from Gray's Inn to that place in Great Russell Street, and I was delayed too. It was ten minutes to one before I got back.

The damned back door, by which I and this other person had left the building, was now bolted on the inside again.

I had not expected this. I did not understand it.

Even if I could not get into the building this way, getting in was easy for me. (See my history above.) I went up the rainpipe at the back of the building, and got through the window of Bernard Schumann's office.

It was a dirty business, because climbing up like that gets you all over dirt. When I reached the office I had to brush myself and wash my hands. What worried me was what had happened in the flat above, which I did not know at the time.

I had no sooner finished washing my hands when I heard people coming up the stairs. By this time I knew that there was something dirty and wrong in the business. I thought I had better find out what was what. So I played the part of Bernard Schumann's clerk, and went out and met that flighty girl and the young doctor.

"Uh-huh. There's not much more," said H.M., examining the back of the last sheet, "and the rest of it you know anyway. We know now why Ferguson wasn't afraid to give his own name and throw his weight about as Schumann's clerk: he thought Schumann would never give him away. And he had to say something, and give some explanation of what he was doin' there, because when the murder was discovered he wanted to find out what in the blazin' Tophet had happened. It was only when he did learn, after inspectin' the drugged dummies in the flat upstairs, that he decided to disappear." H.M. blinked at Sanders. "It's a sad thing, y'know, but Ferguson really didn't know what had happened until you told him."

"And then—?" said Sanders.

"Well, his practical soul was upset. He was human enough to inquire after his wife. But he was so thoroughly put on edge by the bewilderin' variety of the hocus-pocus that he talked a bit indiscreetly before you and the wench. He must have regretted that afterwards. But he was always regrettin' things. He never quite made a success of crime, somehow."

H.M. weighed the manuscript in his hand. He seemed to be assessing a character.

"This is all very well," snapped Blystone, "but it *tells* nothing. You seemed to promise great revelations from all that maundering. For a second there I thought the truth was coming out. Ferguson tried to be a bit too tantalizing. He never said or even indicated who the murderer really is, or how the atropine was administered—"

"Oh, yes, he did," said H.M.

Again Blystone's hand went to his cheek. Marcia, Sanders noticed, kept a look of blank composure.

"I'm not jokin', son," insisted H.M., holding up the sheets. "It's all here, if you read it properly. Truth sort of groans between the lines. It can't very well be missed."

He peered round with sour amusement.

"What's the bettin'? All riddles have now been solved, except the gentle minor riddles of who killed Haye and how was the merry party drugged? We got a neat list. Peter Ferguson—burglar. Bonita Sinclair—art-swindler. Dennis Blystone—pickpocket Bernard Schumann—arsonist. Bernard Schumann in particular interests me. 'Great Fire of London, 1666, Great Fire of London, 1666.' Rememberin' what I do of Ferguson, I should think Ferguson had a way of makin' them words a knocking nightmare. But the party's not exactly complete until it's plain, in spite of Haye's craftiness, who Judith Adams is. She's awful elusive, son. She's real but

137

elusive. Nobody so far has been able to hazard a guess about her."

"Nonsense," said Blystone.

"Eh?"

"I said nonsense," repeated Blystone curtly. He seemed interested but puzzled. "I started to tell you once before; but, as usual, you cut me off. There's no mystery about that. I know quite well who Judith Adams is. She is—"

CHAPTER SIXTEEN

SERGEANT POLLARD received the information about Judith Adams only a few minutes after he entered Felix Haye's flat.

He had spent a not very profitable morning. Chief Inspector Masters had returned from seeing Dr. Sanders at eleven o'clock, and instructed Pollard, at Sir Henry Merrivale's insistence, to begin checking up on the movements of the various people concerned for the entire day of Haye's murder.

And Pollard began, of course, with Bonita Sinclair. The face and figure of that brilliant little so-and-so remained in his mind. After interviewing her at her house in Cheyne Walk—she was in tears and a dangerous kind of negligee— he followed a tortuous trail from dressmaker to restaurant. But he satisfactorily accounted for every minute of her time up to eleven o'clock on the night of Haye's death.

Sir Dennis Blystone came next. Sir Dennis was not at his office in Harley Street; the secretary informed Pollard that he had gone to see Dr. Sanders. However, between the secretary, Lady Blystone, and two maids, he also accounted for Sir Dennis's movements up to the time he had left to pick up Mrs. Sinclair in Cheyne Walk.

By Lady Blystone he was not impressed. She was a tall woman with hard hair and drooping mouth, who did much more questioning than he did. She wanted to know all about him, including what school he had gone to. Though she thawed somewhat at the reply, and offered him a biscuit as though he were a parrot, she did not like the police. Lady Blystone was particularly nasty about a certain Detective-Inspector Sanders, who she said had come roaring into the house last night and bullied everybody into submission. Pollard did not enlighten her. He merely said something about a policeman's lot.

138

"If I were the old man," he said to himself when he left the house, "I should—" And he fell to thinking of Bonita Sinclair again.

From Harley Street it was not a great distance to Bernard Schumann's office. Pollard not only wanted to see Schumann; he also had to question the caretaker about possible visitors to Haye's flat upstairs, and to pick up that poisoned bottle of ale before somebody accidentally or deliberately lifted it.

After getting something to eat at a snack bar, he drew a blank in Great Russell Street. The Anglo-Egyptian Importing Company was open. But a courteous and soft-voiced Egyptian, making much use of gesture, informed him that Mr. Schumann was remaining at home that day. Mr. Schumann was not well. Mr. Schumann, in fact, had not even been at the office on the day of the crime.

Pollard went upstairs.

It was getting on towards three in the afternoon; and the sergeant was warm and irritated, with a full-blown case of spring fever coming on. The sunlight poured into Haye's flat, making it almost light, though the paneled hall remained dusky. Here under the roof it was very warm and very oppressive and very quiet. You could smell the dust.

After some rummaging in the kitchen cupboards, he found the bottle of ale. Then he wandered into the living-room. The noises of the town were muted and sealed up here. The atmosphere was drowsy.

Pollard sat down and lit a cigarette.

Again he contemplated with interest the bright-painted murals of the nymphs on either side of the fireplace. One of the nymphs, he thought, looked a little like Bonita Sinclair. The more he considered it the more like Bonita Sinclair she looked, and he made some imaginary anatomical comparisons. The woman might be crooked (mentally, that is; not otherwise), but they now knew she was not a murderess. Not by a jugful! He could give her an alibi himself. She had been at Scotland Yard when Ferguson was poisoned. After all, what had the woman done? Used her specialized knowledge to good effect, but what of it?

Pollard got up and wandered towards the bedroom, wondering in what capacity Bonita had known Felix Haye. The bedroom was very large and had only one small window. It contained an enormous bed and an enormous wardrobe. A cavalry saber stood in one corner. There was one of Haye's shirts still hanging over the back of a chair, and a pair of castaway socks flung under the bed. A photograph of a famous conjurer hung proudly over the mantelpiece; it

139

was autographed, "To my good friend Felix Haye," and was the *chef-d'œuvre* of the room.

Back in the living room again, Pollard found himself looking at the shelf of bright-jacketed books.

He wondered idly what Haye's literary tastes had been, and began to glance over the titles. Several books of puzzles of a simpler kind: Haye had not the intelligence or imagination for the hard ones. *One Hundred Parlor Tricks You Can Do. Jokes and Sayings for All Occasions. The Life of the Party,* another joke-book. A volume of very pungent limericks, published in Paris: Haye's face and presence seemed to look out of the collection. Novels. *Barney of the Bar-X. The Sheriff of Whistling Gulch. Alua, Virgin of the South Seas.* Several collections of intimate memoirs of the great, their pages gleefully underscored wherever some noted person had been proved to be shady or dishonest in any way. And—

Pollard's gaze grew fixed and staring.

JUDITH ADAMS

The name jumped up in white lettering on a red background. It was the name of the author of a book.

For several seconds, in that hot and quiet room, he stood staring at it. Pollard's scalp stirred with heat or revelation. Then he reached out and took down the book.

Its title was *The Lair of the Dragon,* and at first glance he thought it was a thriller. On the title page was written in bold handwriting, "I can use you, Judith." He compared the writing with the annotations in the other books. After some sentence in the memoirs such as, "At the time the celebrated Lord Dash-Blank was conducting his campaign for temperance, it is well known that he was drunk every night," Haye had put in comments like, "Ha ha," or, "I wish I had known this."

The handwriting was the same.

He began to turn over the pages of the book. It was not a novel. So far as he could make out, it was a quite straightforward collection of mythological lore surrounding dragons and similar monsters. Pollard looked at the name of the publisher, and swore with triumph. The publisher was Goffit. And he knew Tommy Edwards of Goffit very well.

The telephone here in the flat was out of order. Muttering to himself, and reflecting that this was going to give the chief inspector one in the eye, Pollard hurried downstairs. He obtained permission from the Egyptian to use Schumann's telephone, and rang up the publisher.

"That you, Tom? Bob Pollard here. I say, Tom: you've got an author on your list named Judith Adams. I want to know something about her. Now, wait! I know you're not supposed to give information about your authors, but this is police business and I've got to have it."

"I don't mind telling you about this one," said Edwards mildly. He seemed interested. "What's the old girl been up to?"

Pollard, remembering Masters's stern eye, was cautious.

"Well, of course, we don't know that she's been up to anything, exactly—"

"I bet she hasn't," said the voice with conviction. "She's dead."

"She's *what?*"

"D-e-a-d. You know. And buried."

"But when did she die?"

"About eighteen-ninety-three. Have you been reading the *Dragon*? It's a re-issue. The book's been dead for years, but what with all this Loch-Ness-monster business, I thought it might catch on. Look here, what's up?"

Pollard blinked at the telephone. He became aware that the courteous Egyptian was listening. If Judith Adams had died in eighteen-ninety-three, Felix Haye must at that time have been all of six or seven years old.

"Wait! Has she got any children, someone like that, of the same name?"

"If she has," said the voice, "it's going to be a first-class scandal even now. Judith Adams was a spinster of a particularly pure and frosty sort. Daughter of a clergyman up in Cumberland somewhere. Died full of years and good works, and all that sort of thing. Read the book: you'll catch it from the style. The description of Siegfried's fight with the dragon is written on stilts so tall that we had to sling out about half of it."

"Do you know whether Judith Adams, or anyone related to her, was in any way connected with a man named Felix Haye?"

The voice whistled. "Wow! Are you on that case? I don't know, but I can find out for you. Ring me back in about an hour, will you?"

"Right," said Pollard. "Thanks."

He put up the receiver, and reflected again. There were noises in the office; and in the front office with which it connected, where Schumann's other assistant was at work. The Egyptian was walking about softly with a ledger in his hand.

141

He stopped by the door, and spoke softly to the man in the front office. He spoke casually in French, as though he were reading from the ledger.

"Il ne comprend pas, ce sale flic. C'est rigolo, hein?"

Pollard came out of his thoughts with a jerk. But he did not turn round. Unfortunately, the Egyptian made no other comment of relevance. All he murmured, in a soft and sing-song voice was:

"Invoice, one blue canopic jar, porcelain, ibis head—"

Pollard got up.

"I thank you for the use of the telephone," he said in French. "What is it that the *sale flic* does not understand, thou *sale* son of the desert?"

The glossy black head lifted from the ledger; the dapper man looked at him sideways, concluded, "—sixty-five pounds, ten shillings, and sixpence"; and then smiled broadly.

"Monsieur must not misunderstand," he replied in French. "I was joking. Perhaps I do wrong to be amused when the police fail to solve a case. But I meant no harm. As for being a son of the desert, I may remind monsieur that I am half Spanish. That is why I smile."

Pollard could get nothing out of him. The other was out from under every question: it was like lunging at a fencer. After some minutes of blistering invectives—it seemed less like browbeating a witness if you mauled him in French—Pollard was forced to retire. Gloomily he thought he had better finish up his business by going to Hampstead and seeing Schumann. The caretaker proved to be out, and he could ask no questions there.

Going out in the Underground, he racked his brains and his notebook. He leafed through Judith Adams's book, wondering alternately how Judith Adams figured in this and how Bernard Schumann's staff figured in it with relation to Judith Adams.

Of Schumann himself he was not inclined to be suspicious. Chief Inspector Masters had said very little about the man, though he had dispatched to the police in Cairo a cable which Pollard did not see. In all probability Schumann was some mild form of swindler, or had made some slip of no great seriousness. Pollard was sure he had neither the courage nor the malice for any real devilry.

The shadows were lengthening when he reached the house on the edge of Hampstead Heath. Pollard, so immersed in the case that he had no time to think of personal matters, suddenly realized the odd figure he must cut with a half-bottle of ale stuck in one pocket and a book in the other, like Omar Khayyam. He went up to the gray stone house and knocked. The place, he thought, must he damnably damp with all these trees so close to it.

Bernard Schumann himself opened the door.

"Oh, yes," he said, when Pollard had introduced himself. Schumann's eye went first to the bottle of ale, and then to the book. There was about him a watchfulness which rather amused the sergant. Schumann's pale blue eyes looked washed out. Pollard noted again the contrast between his delicate hands and the coarse texture of his hair, as though someone had painted it with whitewash.

"I must do my own errands today," Schumann told him. "My housekeeper and my cook are both out. Will you walk into my parlor?" he added, with grave courtesy but the hint of a smile.

The house was very quiet, and nearly as stuffy as Haye's flat. The afternoon light had turned dull; Pollard stumbled over a profusion of furniture in the hall. Some wax flowers got in his way, and then an umbrella-stand. Schumann walked ahead, creaking in stiff slippers.

"My haunt," he explained, opening the door of a big room on the right. It was an overcrowded drawing-room with a great mummy-case in the corner, and horsehair furniture. Pollard noticed the brass bowl on a tripod near the mummy case.

His host indicated a chair at one side of the fireplace— where, despite the warmth of the day, a coal fire was burning.

"Well, sergeant?" he prompted. His fine face was clouded. "I learn from the newspapers that you have found Peter Ferguson, under unusual circumstances. There were not many details given. May I ask if he was poisoned?"

"I'm afraid so, sir."

"I am sorry." Schumann glanced sideways at the fire. He did not look ill. Except for the slippers, he was fully dressed; and his clothes had a catlike neatness. "He was a very able man, though sometimes difficult to get on with. Have you any idea who—er—?"

"A clue has been discovered, sir."

"Oh? May I ask the nature of—?"

"At the moment, sir, I'd rather not discuss it," said Pollard. He spoke in that perfunctorily sinister and stuffed manner which Masters had drilled into him. Actually he rather pitied the old buffer. Schumann looked as though it would strain his strength to lift a paper-weight.

Schumann was looking at him steadily.

"I'd like," pursued the sergeant, "to put some questions to you. What were you doing on the day before yesterday, the day Mr. Haye was murdered?"

143

"Doing? I am afraid I do not understand. Why do you wish to know that?"

Pollard did not know himself. It was a part of his instructions. So he merely looked sinister.

"Just give me an account of your movements, if you will, from the morning until eleven o'clock at night.

The other shaded his eyes with his hand. "Let me see. Come, that is easy! In all the excitement I had forgotten. I was entertaining some very dear friends of mine, Lord and Lady Thurnley—"

"Not the historian?" asked Pollard. Here was a very eminent and respectable witness.

"Yes," said Schumann, evidently surprised that the other should know this. "They live in Durham (you may be aware?) and are not often in London. I called for them at their hotel—Almond's—at ten o'clock in the morning. We spent the morning at the Guildhall Library, and came back to the hotel for lunch. At lunch a telephone message came through for me. It was from poor Haye, asking me to come to a party at his flat that evening. I said that I was entertaining the Thurnleys, and could not possibly do so."

"Yes, sir?"

"Haye told me that another guest, Mrs. Sinclair, had made the same excuse. He said therefore that he was arranging the party for eleven o'clock at night, and he would not take no·for an answer."

"But you didn't really want to go to the party, did you?"

Schumann's eyes, though they remained fixed on the sergeant, seemed to grow far away.

"The answer to that is that I did go. But that is to anticipate. You wished to know my movements during the day. I was with Lord and Lady Thurnley the entire time. In the afternoon we went to a matinee, and then to an exhibition at Burlington House. After tea we returned here. They dined with me here. At about twenty minutes past ten they left here in a taxi and returned to their hotel. A little while after they had gone, I rang up for another taxi, and was driven straight to Haye's flat: where I arrived, as I think I have already said to the chief inspector, at a quarter to eleven. Haye was there, and met me. Up to the time of the Thurnleys' departure, I am sure they will be willing to testify to all this. They are still at their hotel."

"Did you mention Mr. Haye's party to them, sir?"

"No."

He did not elaborate or explain.

"Does that answer your questions, sergeant?"

Pollard considered. He wondered whether he ought to

mention to Schumann the fact that they knew all about those five boxes, and that Haye held evidence over each of his guests. No, better not: definitely not. This was the sort of heavy thunder which ought to be left to Masters, and the chief inspector would have his hide if he departed in any way from his instructions. On the other hand, one aspect of it he was determined to approach.

"Mr. Schumann, how well did you know Mr. Haye?"

"Casually, only casually. I met him some years ago, in Cairo."

"In Cairo?"

"Yes, I believe so. It was—er—a time of some distress and misfortune to me."

Here Pollard had an impression that the other was studying him, his pale blue eye growing fixed. And the sergeant remembered. That was where the fire had nearly wiped out Schumann's uninsured stock. Well, that was nothing against the man; he could not blame the old buffer for looking a bit queer and fed up.

"Yes, we learned about that, sir. You were very unfortunate. I thought myself it was too bad the alarm wasn't sounded sooner."

There was a pause. Schumann spoke in a curious voice.

"Did you, indeed? And does the chief inspector also think it was too bad?"

Pollard smiled. "Well, I haven't exactly discussed it with him. But what I wanted to ask you was this. Did Mr. Haye ever mention to you a woman called Judith Adams?"

His host seemed to reflect. Beside his chair by the dying fire there was a small round table on which stood a cigarette-box, a box of matches, and a paper-knife. Schumann picked up the paper-knife and pressed its point against the arm of the chair.

"I beg your pardon? Judith Adams? Judith Adams? Not that I recall. I never heard of her."

"Mr. Haye didn't mention her name even on the night of the party?"

"No. I should be interested to know, sergeant, why you say *even*."

Pollard examined his notebook.

"All in good time, sir. But if the name of Judith Adams isn't known to you, it seems to be known to your staff."

"My staff?"

"Yes. You have two assistants, one of them an Egyptian—"

"Well? I honestly do not follow all this."

"Judith Adams wrote a certain book," explained Pollard, "which seems to have a direct bearing on this case. I found it this afternoon in Mr. Haye's flat; even the chief inspector hasn't seen it or heard of it yet."

"You have a form of attack, my friend, which I find singularly curious. What is all this about a book? I don't understand. A book about what?"

"Monsters," said Pollard.

Twilight was gathering outside the bay-windows. It was a muddy twilight, dingy and heavy like the room itself. The fire was burning low, under a heavy crust of ash; and only a little illumination was thrown up on Schumann's face. Yet despite the fire and the earlier warmth of the day, this room remained chilly.

Schumann's pale blue eye remained fixed.

He cleared his throat slightly.

"Monsters?" he repeated. "Criminals, you mean?"

"No, no. I mean real—that is, mythological monsters. Dragons and the like. Now, sir, there's reason to believe that the name of Judith Adams is connected with one of the persons Mr. Haye suspected of trying to murder him."

"Mr. Haye suspected someone of trying to murder him?"

Pollard was non-committal.

"Whoever did murder him was no novice," he answered, feeling the bottle of ale in his pocket. "But that's not the point I'm after at the moment. When I found that book, *The Lair of the Dragon*, I went downstairs to your office and rang up the publisher. We had a talk about the book. When we had finished, your Egyptian assistant was amused, and said in French, under his breath, that the dirty copper did not understand. What did he mean by that?"

"I have not the remotest idea," said Schumann, holding the paper-knife upright in two fingers on the arm of the chair. "Is that the book you have there? May I see it?"

"In just a minute, sir. But it had some meaning to your assistants; and, consequently, I suggest it must have some meaning to you."

"You are very hopeful, young man. Dragons! What on earth has the subject of dragons got to do with this?"

"Just try to think, sir," urged Pollard. "There's a connection somewhere. I admit I don't know what it is. All I know is that the dragon was a mythical animal who was supposed to breathe fire. Beyond that, nothing."

CHAPTER SEVENTEEN

SCHUMANN's hand tightened round the paper-knife.

"Quite," he agreed, clearing his throat once more. "But I can't help you either. I can only assume that it must have been one of Haye's heavy-handed jokes."

Regretfully snapping the band round his notebook, Pollard put it away. He got up.

"Then that's that, Mr. Schumann. Sorry to have taken up so much of your time. If you'll excuse me—"

"No, no, no," interrupted Schumann. "The matter is much too interesting. You must not go yet. Not just yet. You must sit down and have a drink. I really insist."

"Sorry, sir, but—"

"It is possible that I can give you some information."

Pollard looked at him quickly.

"About?"

"What would it be about but Felix Haye's death? It is not often that I get an opportunity to talk to such an intelligent young man. For instance, a young man who knows Lord Thurnley as a historian rather than as our representative in Egypt some years ago; and is probably conversant with his work on the Tudors and—"

"Look here, sir, have you got anything to tell me?"

"That is right," said Schumann. "Sit down again." He drew a long and quiet breath; his face, like that of an ascetic clergyman, grew politely blank again. "If I have seemed not altogether helpful in this matter, you must remember that I am not well and that these things distress me. If you ever suffer from diabetes, as I trust you never will, you will be able to understand. You see, I am not over-subtle like you youngsters. These persistent references to conflagrations you may find very amusing; but it is difficult for me to accept them as a literary exercise."

"Confla—" said Pollard. "You don't mean Lord Thurnley's book about the Great Fire of London in 1666?"

Schumann's nostrils seemed to widen, which gave an effect as though he were smiling.

"You really must have a drink," he said. He stretched out his hand to a bell beside the fireplace, and then drew it back. "I had forgotten. There is nobody to call; we are all alone here."

His slippers creaked as he crossed the room. The sideboard

was in the embrasure of the bay-window: Schumann stood with his back to the visitor, moving bottles and opening drawers. Lace curtains, horsehair chairs, occasional tables, all were being blurred out like the mummy-case in dusk. If a fire ever did start here, Pollard thought, it would sweep this dust-trap in ten minutes.

The slippers creaked again. Schumann returned with two glasses of sherry, one of which he handed to his guest. Then he resumed his seat on the opposite side of the fireplace.

Yes, definitely there was something wrong. Pollard frowned.

"Look here, sir, *have* you got anything to tell me?"

"A great deal, both about dragons and about fires. But, before I do, there is some information I insist on having in return."

"Sorry," said Pollard, and got up.

His host did not move.

"Sergeant, you are being foolish. If you reflect for just one second you will realize that. What I offer you may be the solution of everything you wish to know. What, as opposed to that, do you risk? Two minutes of your valuable time, and one or two facts which in twenty-four hours will be published in the newspapers for everyone to read. You are a bad hand at a bargain, my friend, if you refuse to trade on those terms."

Pollard nodded. Putting down his glass of sherry on the mantel-shelf, he waited.

"Good," said Schumann. "I have only one question. When the chief inspector was here yesterday, he suggested that all of our group, our now-famous group, were accused of being criminals. Of what particular crime am I accused?"

Sharply through the quiet house, the noise of the front-door knocker rapped and rapped again.

Though Bernard Schumann sat quite still, his expression altered a little. Pollard thought that he shivered.

"I suppose," he remarked slowly, "I shall have to answer that."

"It might be just as well, sir."

The knocker kept on banging. Again Schumann's slippers creaked as he got up and moved out into the hall. When he returned, Pollard understood a part of the reason for that insistent and disquieting rapping. The man who accompanied Schumann was Chief Inspector Humphrey Masters.

"Ah, sir," he greeted Schumann affably. His eye wandered in an unobtrusive manner round the room. "Just happened to be passing, and—oh, hullo, Bob."

He met Pollard with an impression of surprise which the

148

sergeant thought was a little overdone. Meanwhile, Schumann again stood very still by the door. An alertness seemed
to have come over him, a sort of wiry and nervous inspiration
which mingled with the already tangled motives and emo-
tions in this room.

"Yes, sir," said Pollard. "Following my instructions, I—"
Masters cut him off.

"Just so. Mind if I sit down?" he asked Schumann genially.

"Not at all. Make yourself comfortable."

The chief inspector wandered over to the fireplace. Spreading out his hands before the fire, he glanced at the glass of
sherry on the mantel-shelf.

"I hope I wasn't intruding," he went on. "Fact is, sir, I
knew you had a guest. I saw you pouring out two glasses.
Through the window, you know. But—here, tut, tut! Don't
tell me you've gone and offered the sergeant a drink?"

He looked round with an inquiring frown.

"Is it forbidden, my friend?"

"It is, sir. Absolutely forbidden," lied Masters cheerfully,
"to anybody below the rank of inspector. However, if you
don't mind my saying so, I could do with a bit of a warmer
at this time of day. Do you mind if I take this on?"

"Let me get you some brandy."

Masters reached out and laid a hand on the other's frail
arm as he turned.

"Wouldn't think of it, sir! Waste a good glass of sherry?
Not if you had my salary you wouldn't. I'll just have this one."

Picking up the glass, he walked over and settled himself
comfortably on the sofa. He lifted the glass.

"Your very good health, sir."

Schumann did not move.

"Yours, chief inspector," he said.

Struck with another thought, Masters frowned and put the
glass down on the table beside him.

"Look here, Bob, what are you doing out here anyway?
You've come out here behind my back, my lad. What have
you been talking to Mr. Schumann about?"

It was Schumann who answered. "Chiefly about dragons,"
he said. He creaked back to his own place at the fireside,
and waited with an air of courteous if high-strung atten-
tiveness. "Can you explain anything about it, chief inspector?"

"Dragons?" repeated Masters. He did not appear surprised.

"It's Judith Adams," said Pollard. "I've found out who
she is—or was, rather. I discovered her book in Haye's flat."

"Oh, ah!" said Masters, enlightened. "You mean the old
lady who wrote the book about fire-breathing monsters?
Sorry to take the wind out of your sails, Bob, but I am afraid

149

I know all about it. Sir Henry rang me up about it. A whole lot of information, Sir Henry had. Yes, a whole lot. Sir Dennis Blystone told him about the book. And there were other things too."

He looked sideways at Schumann.

"Did you know, Mr. Schumann, that Peter Ferguson left a statement before he died?"

"I did not know it. But I am not at all surprised to hear it."

"Would it interest you to know, sir, that some very serious accusations were made against you? Of course, I daresay you can give me a satisfactory explanation of them. But—"

Schumann shaded his eyes with his hand, but he spoke with great clarity.

"Yes. I have been very patiently waiting to hear them for some time. A most ingenious game of cat-and-mouse has been played with me this afternoon. The sergeant plays it even better than you do, though he intimated that he was the only one who knew the facts."

Masters glanced sharply at his subordinate. Pollard wanted to make an elaborate parody of a Hebraic shrug; but he conveyed his perplexity to the chief inspector. Pollard now guessed the significance of that damning glass of sherry at Masters's elbow. He supposed that he should have guessed it long before: but who would have suspected the old buffer of a trick like that? Even as he felt that he might have been close to a bad kind of death, still Schumann had gone up a good deal in his estimation.

Masters played with the stem of the sherry-glass; and Schumann's arms had begun to shake on the arms of the chair.

"You were saying, sir?" Masters prompted.

"I was saying that you had better not waste your time. Out with it, man! Just before you came in, I had made a bargain with Sergeant Pollard that I would give him some important information about this case if he at last—at long last—told me what I was accused of."

The chief inspector dropped his bluff and amiable manner.

"What would you say, sir, if I told you it was murder?"

"That is the question of a policeman all over. I made the bargain on the grounds that I should get a straight answer. *Do* you say it is murder? We cannot get anywhere until I know."

"Yes, sir, I do say that."

"Murder." Schumann removed his hand from his eyes and regarded Masters in a puzzled away. "And is *that* all?"

"Have you committed many worse crimes?"

"Nonsense. Anything else?"

"Yes, there is."

"Specifically?"

"Specifically, sir, that on a certain night in the year 1927 you willfully set fire to the warehouse of the Anglo-Egyptian Importing Company in Cairo, by means of an alarm-clock mechanism to start the fire; and that in destroying the warehouse with its contents you also destroyed the body of a man named El Hakim, whom you had killed. Now, I'll be frank with you. I guessed this fire-raising business. When I heard about that grand blaze of yours in Cairo, I sent a cable to the police there. When I heard about the murder of El Hakim this afternoon, I sent another cable. There'll be an answer to it very shortly. In the meantime—"

"In the meantime?"

"Shall I drink this sherry?" asked Masters, pointing to the glass.

"By all means. I thought you wanted it."

"I'll say this for you, Mr. Schumann. You're a cool one and no mistake. So you think it would be quite safe for me to drink poison?"

Their host leaned back, as though someone were forcing his head. Drawn out of some obscure musing, he seemed to be trying to assimilate a new and strange idea.

Then he put up his hand and knocked his knuckles against his forehead.

"God in heaven," he said. "You blithering ass. Do I understand—you don't mean you think there is poison in that sherry?"

"I can only tell you that I'm going to have it analyzed just as quick as I can. And I'll be very much surprised, Mr. Schumann, if I don't find it's loaded with atropine. What's your answer to that?"

"This is my answer," said Schumann courteously.

His movement was so swift, so much at variance with every other gesture he had ever made, that Masters had no time either to intervene or even to think. He reached across, flicked up the glass, and drained its contents at a gulp.

Then Schumann sat back coughing and apologizing at once.

"That," he explained, with a suspicious kind of twinkle in his eye, "is an insult to my hospitality which I cannot allow."

He got out a handkerchief and coughed again. Masters, less ruddy of face, was on his feet.

"So that's the game." Masters snarled. "All right, Bob. Telephone in the hall. Hop to it. Nearest hospital; emergency case. That stuff doesn't work very fast. We've *got* him now. We've got him so dead to rights—"

151

Schumann lifted his hand.

"Inspector Masters," he said formally. "May I ask you to stop talking like a shilling shocker and listen to me for just one moment? Sergeant Pollard: stay where you are.

"You think this is a case of suicide. 'The scorpion, surrounded, destroys himself.' You now propose to summon an ambulance (a process with which, I admit, you should by this time be familiar): to stir up a hospital; and for the second time in three days to submit me to the application of a stomach-pump. No, thank you. I have been through that pleasant experience before. I object to it at any time, and I particularly object to it when it is unnecessary. If you try any such lunatic measure as that, I will institute proceedings against you and make a fool of you for every person in England to laugh at. And I will go out of here fighting, in order to make the matter worse when I do take proceedings. Now, I warn you."

Masters stared.

"Do as you're told, Bob," he said. "This is Ferguson all over again, only with a reverse twist that makes me—urr!"

"Stay where you are, Sergeant," Schumann instructed him coolly. "Before you make a fool of yourself, Masters, let me make an alternative suggestion. Dr. Burns, my personal physician, lives only two houses up the road. If you rang him, on an ordinary pretext of seeing after my health, he could get here ten times faster than any ambulance. Let him examine me. If there is the slightest trace of poison inside me, you will save me for the gallows more quickly. If not, you will be saved the biggest mistake of your career, for I warn you I can cut up very rough when I try."

"What shall I do, sir?" demanded Pollard. "I think he's telling the truth. What shall it be?"

"Gawdlummy," said Masters, "I wish I knew. Socrates never drank the shamrock quite the easy way he polished off that sherry. Nobody ever did. But we can't afford to take chan— no, stop a bit! What's the name and address and telephone-number of that Dr. Burns?"

Schumann told him.

"Hop to it, Bob. If there is such a person, and if he'll come over, ring for him. There'll be the devil to pay if we whack this bloke under the chin and cart him off, and it turns out there's nothing wrong with him. But if you can't get that doctor or anyone else there, you know what to do."

He took quick little pigeon-toed steps up and down the room, regarding Schumann malevolently. Schumann himself now picked up the other glass of sherry, the one he had poured for himself, and drank that too.

152

"Just to clear everything up," he explained.

Masters permitted himself some wicked language.

"I feel impelled," Schumann went on, "to drink out of the decanter on the sideboard and taste the contents of all the other bottles as well. You have given me a very bad time this afternoon, one of the worst quarters-of-an-hour I have ever spent. To be frank about it, I should like to put the knife in your gizzard and twist hard."

He turned his wrist in the air, meditatively.

"But, aside from the fact that I do not want to be roaring drunk when Dr. Burns arrives, I should like to explain the matter to you. In the meantime, my friend—"

"Well, sir?"

"Will you tell me where you got this insane notion of yours? Will you explain to me why I should wish to kill myself or anybody else?"

"We can't get around facts, you know."

"I am not trying to get around facts. I am trying to find out what they are. What am I supposed to have done?"

Masters came over and looked down at him significantly.

"First, there's a little matter of arson—"

"I beg your pardon, there is not. Even supposing this nonsensical charge were true? Even supposing you had some evidence to support it? Where does the arson come in? Arson is the willful and malicious destruction by fire of public property or property belonging to someone else. In Cairo the articles destroyed were a warehouse and some property of which I was the sole owner. No other building or property was damaged. This chair, for instance, belongs to me. I must not touch any chair belonging to you. But I can take my own chair into the back garden and destroy it with fire or any other means I choose. You don't dispute that?"

"No," said Masters grimly. "But there's a little question of a murder as well—"

Sergeant Pollard returned to the room. "Dr. Burns is coming straightaway," he reported.

He looked curiously at Schumann, who appeared to be still a trifle shaky but enjoying himself.

"I am accused (I think?) of murdering a certain Nizam El Hakim before or during that fire. Now, I can give you the best of reasons why I did not kill Nizam El Hakim."

"Well, sir?"

"Because," said Schumann, "Nizam El Hakim is not dead. Sergeant Pollard was talking to him this afternoon."

Masters has afterwards had several remarks to make about this case. He has said that he seldom before met an affair in which every time he opened a door, asked a question, or

153

merely turned round, he got a new and more painful jolt under the short-ribs.

But the chief inspector did not appreciate this one as much as Pollard appreciated it.

"You don't mean that Egyptian fellow in your office?"

"I do," responded Schumann calmly. "Did you ask him anything about himself, including his name? I venture to think not. To be more accurate, he is half Egyptian and half Spanish, but—"

"Yes, but why was he laughing so much?" insisted Pollard.

"I imagine it depends on what you said in his presence."

"Nothing about you, I'll swear."

"Never mind all this," interposed an exasperated chief inspector. "What *about* this man El Hakim?"

"It is time," said Schumann, "to dispose of an ugly and absolutely nonsensical report which was circulated at the time of the fire. The fire I admit: that is, I admit the fact of its having occurred." A shadow of the old uneasiness was back on his face. "El Hakim at that time was in the same business as myself, though in a much smaller way, and in bad financial straits.

"Well, gentlemen, on the night of the fire El Hakim disappeared. Actually he had run away to Port Said to escape his creditors. But, on top of the fire, it was reported that the skeleton or at least many bones of a human body had been recovered from the ruins. The first wild rumor was that El Hakim had fired the place and been killed in doing so. The next and wilder rumor—" his fingers clenched—"was that I had somehow been concerned in it. I suppose you got this information from Ferguson?"

"There's no harm in saying we did, sir."

"Yes," agreed Schumann, with an unusual malevolence in his eyes. "Ferguson insisted on playing detective to such an extent that I had to send him back here to my English office—"

"Why should you have minded his playing detective?"

"It was a confounded nuisance, as I think you must admit."

"I mean," said Masters, "you could always have sacked him."

"That's neither here nor there. Do you wish to hear my story? Very well.

"Of course there were bones found in the ruins! They were bones in a perfect state of preservation for two thousand years: in other words, those of a very fine Theban mummy of the XXIst Dynasty. The mummies of the Theban epoch, as you may know, are so perfect when unwrapped

154

that the flesh yields to the touch and the limbs may be moved without breaking."

He smiled.

"If I ever do commit a murder, gentlemen (which is unlikely), I shall do so in a house where there is known to be a mummy of that sort. Then if the house burns down afterwards, few doctors on earth will be able to swear that the remains of my victim may not just as well be those of a harmless King of Egypt . . . You said something, chief inspector?"

Masters scowled.

"I said, sir," he answered with powerful restraint, "that if before this case is over I hear of just one more ingenious way to commit a crime—just one more—I'll go out and commit one myself. Hurrum! Was all this proved?"

"Absolutely. The police proved beyond question that the remains were those of a mummy. A statement to that effect was issued. But unfortunately there is in such a place no worldwide press that reaches everyone. Even the reappearance of the alleged corpse in Cairo six months later, stony broke and repentant, did not altogether stifle the rumor. Out of sheer self-defense I was compelled to take Nizam El Hakim into my own employ, and flaunt him. But he is a good man; and he has been with me ever since. Of course Ferguson knew the actual facts quite well. The conceited idiot was only making trouble: as usual. You need not accept my statement. If you have cabled to Cairo, you will hear about it shortly. At the moment, I think that knock at the door must be Dr. Burns arriving."

Masters and Pollard looked at each other.

Five minutes later a somewhat annoyed G.P., who had come rushing from tea in order to circumvent a wholly imaginary case of atropine poisoning, was saying some realistic things to Schumann about the intelligence of the police.

And Masters and Pollard stood in the gloomy hall and looked at each other again.

"All right, my lad," growled the former. "You needn't rub it in. But I could have sworn I saw him hocussing that sherry, so what else could I think? If he's telling the truth about this Cairo business—"

"I think we know he's telling the truth, sir."

"Then what's the fellow guilty of? What evidence did Haye have against him?" Masters reflected. "It's arson in some way. There's no doubt of that. He's a—whatd'yecallit?—"

"Pyromaniac? Firebug?" supplied Pollard. "Yes, sir, I think that's so. But does even a pyromaniac make a bonfire of all his possessions and dance round it? In any case, I should think he's out of the picture as far as murder is concerned. For it seems he's got some information to give us. By the way, what were you doing out here this afternoon?"

Masters frowned.

"To ask him about just that. Also, to tell him that Sir Henry Merrivale wants everybody concerned in the case to come to Haye's flat tonight for a little demonstration—"

"You mean—?" Pollard whistled.

"Never you mind what I mean, my lad," said the chief inspector ominously. "I'll do the 'meaning.' Let me know what you've found out today." He listened with heavy attention while Pollard sketched it out. "So you got on to the publishers, eh? That's Goffit of Bloomsbury Street, just round the corner from Haye's place?"

"Yes, sir. The point is, I don't see how that Judith Adams book can have any relation to Schumann, under the circumstances. That's the trouble. If it referred to Schumann, why should Haye have included in his list of suspects *both* the names of Bernard Schumann and Judith Adams? It must refer to somebody else. It's got to."

"Never mind your theories. What else did the publishers say?"

Pollard swore. "Hold on! Tommy Edwards was going to see if he could find out anything for me. I promised to ring him back in an hour, and I seem to have forgotten it. It must be nearer two hours now. I hope he's still at the office."

Again he went in some haste to the telephone, and it was now Masters who said some pungent and realistic things about duty. Masters said he would not have a subordinate of his making mistakes like that. Masters said a good police officer never made mistakes. Masters said that if he (Pollard) failed to catch Edwards at the office—

Fortunately, he did catch Edwards at the office.

"My pal," said Edwards bitterly, in no better frame of mind than the chief inspector. "I've been sitting by this phone waiting to give you the real, true low-down, straight from the horse's mouth—"

"Sorry, Tom. What's the news?"

The telephone was mollified.

"Well, to begin with, there's not much more known about Judith Adams personally than I told you. Her literary executor is a nephew, a clergyman in Stockton-on-Tees, who can't very well be mixed up in this affair. But I have established a connection between Judith Adams and somebody who may be mixed up in the case."

"*What?* Who is it?"

"Steady, now. I got it from old G.G.—Grotius Goffit—

himself. About a month ago a fellow came into the office, looking very secret and mysterious, and asked to see the head of the firm on important business concerning one of our authors. G.G. saw the fellow himself. The old man was as worried as blazes, wondering which of 'em was in jail again. He—"

"Never mind that: go on."

"I am. Well, the secret business turned out to be the fact that this fellow wanted to buy a book. He said he lived near by, and had seen the announcement of Judith Adams's book, and wanted to buy one. He said his father had worked for Miss Judith in the north; and he had known her well as a young man, and so on. G.G. was so relieved that he gave the fellow a copy and shooed him out. The fellow departed saying thanks, faith and begob."

"Why faith and begob?"

"That's the point. Because he's an Irishman: named Riley or Riordan, G.G. thinks. Anyway, he said he was the caretaker at number 012 Great Russell Street round the corner; and that's where your friend Haye was murdered. Now as I was saying—"

For what seemed a long time Pollard stared at unresponsive carbon, which was still talking.

"Are you listening to me?" asked the voice.

"Eh?"

"Bob," said the voice impressively, "I have a theory."

CHAPTER EIGHTEEN

AT NINE O'CLOCK that night, when the lamps of Great Russell Street were again glowing and there was a hint of rain in the air, a policeman on his meditative round noticed a two-seater car drawn up at the curb in front of a house he had good reason to know.

From this car issued sounds which seemed to indicate a debate or a scuffle. The policeman approached.

"Now, then!" he said.

In the car, at the wheel, sat a remarkably good-looking girl with brown hair and brown eyes. Beside her was a serious-faced young man of thirty or so, with a raincoat draped over an arm in bandages and splints, and a hat pushed forward over his nose as though by rakish feminine arrangement.

"It's all right, constable," said Dr. Sanders. "We are only agreeing."

"We are going to be married," Marcia Blystone informed him. "Whee!"

"I see," said the constable. "Well, you can't take longer than twenty minutes, sir."

Sanders poked his head out of and round the car as the policeman went on. "Now I wonder," he said, "whether there was any ulterior meaning in that remark?"

"No, you don't," Marcia informed him. "You jolly well don't dodge away from the subject like that. I tell you, you should *not* be out of the house tonight. You should not be out with that arm of yours. The night air will be bad for it—"

"That, my sweet, is an absurd scientific fallacy. If you will stop to consider the factors involved—"

"Well, I don't care; I *know* it's bad for you. Really you shouldn't have come out: I don't care whether H.M. wants us to be there or not. And don't think you will have any opportunity to be heroic tonight, either, because you won't."

"I wish," he said, "I wish you would cut out all this talk about heroics. I have never been heroic. I have never wished to be heroic except," he admitted honestly, "that I once wanted to be a member of the Secret Service and chase people in foreign hotels—"

"Did you?" she asked eagerly. "So did I." They had been discovering a succession of these same interests all afternoon.

"—when I was eighteen or nineteen, which is to say the emotional age of most of my life. I have sometimes thought it would be a fine thing to have knife wounds and show scars. I have never received a wound from a knife (except during an operation for appendicitis, which is not a scar that can be shown to everybody); but I have got a couple of bullet-wounds, and at the moment I cannot regard them as anything but a damned nuisance."

"Darling," said Marcia, "you're being positively brilliant!"

He was not sure of this. But he did know that he was so exceedingly pleased with things in general that if it were not for his logical habit of mind he would have been talking wildly.

"As a result," he continued, "this talk about heroics, while secretly very flattering, is utter rubbish. I don't want to indulge in heroics. They give me a pain when I see them in the movies, and there was never a part I was less suited for."

"So you're beginning to disillusion me already, are you?"

"I am not trying to disillusion you. Now there's a very good example. There's a very good example of your trick of ap-

158

proaching a subject obliquely, and somehow confusing the issue like a conjurer or a theological writer—"

She removed his hat, and creased it in the proper way after her previous effort to get the effect of Napoleon by creasing it sideways. Then she fitted it back in a position which was very nearly as uncomfortable, and made him look like a dissipated journalist. She studied the artistic effect while he continued to lecture. Then, instinctively, they both looked up the dark façade of the building to the lighted windows at the top.

"If," she said abruptly, "we're both so anxious to go up to Haye's flat, why don't we *go* up?"

"Because," he admitted, "there's likely to be an emotional dust-up; and you don't relish it any more than I do."

She admitted it. Four persons besides themselves and the investigators were to be in Haye's flat that night: Schumann, Sir Dennis Blystone, Mrs. Sinclair—and Lady Blystone.

From what Sanders could gather, the last-named person had consented to be there only under pressure. Her position had been simple: She Would Not Meet That Woman In Public. She was serene about it; she did not deny the existence of Mrs. Sinclair, and expressed her intention of having a talk with Mrs. Sinclair in the future; but she would not meet that woman In Public. Bonita Sinclair's views had not been heard. Sanders was inclined to wonder about them.

Two other persons were supposed to attend: Timothy Riordan, the caretaker of the building; and (to Sanders's surprise) an Egyptian who worked in the Anglo-Egyptian office. The reason for the presence of the caretaker he discovered when he and Marcia went upstairs.

Dim lights now burned on the landings of the building, to light the company's way up. He and Marcia were the first of the outside guests to arrive. When they reached Haye's flat, they found a police-conference in progress in the drawing-room.

There was about it an air of definiteness and quiet which Sanders did not like. The refectory table was piled with papers. People moved slowly and talked slowly. In one corner sat H.M., smoking a cigar and reading *The Lair of the Dragon*. Sergeant Pollard moved round the table, with another man—evidently a police officer—whom Sanders did not recognize. Chief Inspector Masters was at the head of the table, questioning Riordan the caretaker. It was plain, Sanders thought, that the newcomers were interrupting something.

The chief inspector looked up sharply.

159

"Sorry," he said. "Aren't you a bit early? We hadn't finished—"

"Nonsense," rumbled H.M. without lifting his eyes from the book. "Let 'em come in. They'd better be prepared for a part o' this. Stand over there, you two, and be quiet."

Sanders liked it less and less. He and Marcia moved over against the wall as though they were waiting for the beginning of a spelling-match. Masters turned to the caretaker.

"Now, I want you to go over, so that the sergeant can take it down, what you've told Sir Henry. That book Sir Henry's reading—you loaned it to Mr. Haye?"

Riordan was far from the comic character of music-halls. He looked stolid and rather secretive. His age might have been sixty: he had close-cropped brownish hair and a face that itself looked close-cropped and grained with work. His darkish-colored hands he held with the edges of the palms against his stomach, the fingers crooked upwards, as though he were waiting to catch a ball there. Each idea he seemed to turn over in his mind, secretly, before he spoke. Then he spoke with a parliamentary, not to say Delphic, grimness and roll.

At the moment he merely nodded with dignity.

"You tell us you knew Miss Judith Adams in the north?"

"That I did. An educated traveled lady, that spoke foreign languages so it was a pleasure to hear, and my father her coachman."

"Where did you learn about this book?"

"It was in an illustrated paper I read of it. About the grand writer that was dead, and it was the lady herself. Many things in that book was told to her by my father himself, though not in such fine language."

"Why did you want to buy the book?"

"If," said Riordan slowly, "I may not read the lady's book—"

He began to bristle so slowly that it was several seconds before you realized any anger. Masters stopped him.

"None of that! How did you come to lend Mr. Haye the book?"

"Didn't I put it on my table for people to see? Didn't the gentleman see it?"

The purpose of this Sanders did not see. Sir Dennis Blystone had been able to tell them that "Judith Adams" was merely the name of an author whose book about fabled monsters seemed to have engrossed Haye. All day they had argued as to the meaning of it. It couldn't have any reference to Timothy Riordan himself? Nonsense! Yet he remem-

160

bered Marcia's earlier suspicions about the caretaker, and wondered.

"Now, then," pursued Masters. "About the night Felix Haye died. When did you last see him alive?"

"Awbejasus!" cried the caretaker impatiently. "Haven't I told you all that? Yesterday to the sergeant—"

"Yes. You have: all except one thing you didn't mention before. None of that, cocky. When did you last see Haye alive?"

"It might have been past six o'clock, when he went out in his evening-dress to get his dinner."

"Did he say anything to you then?"

"He did, as he was going out. He said, would I be good enough to clean up his rooms, as it was grand people he was meeting that night."

"Did you do it?"

"I did. Haven't I told you?"

"You've got a key to this flat?"

"I have."

"Wait half a tick, son," interposed H.M. "Better let me handle this."

H.M. came lumbering over to the table. Putting his cigar down on the edge, he leaned his fists on the table and peered at Riordan over his spectacles.

"I tell you what, son. If you're so blamed anxious not to talk, let me do the talkin', and you just correct me if I go wrong. Just nod or grunt: I'll understand. You came in here to tidy up the place. Now, Haye had been drinkin' before he went out to dinner, hadn't he?"

A nod.

"Yes. Cocktails, son?"

Another nod.

"Yes. You washed out the shaker, put away the bottles, and cleaned off the drainboard. But you didn't finish tidyin' up this flat. Look in that bedroom, for instance: there's still clothes lying all over the place where Haye finished dressin'. Why didn't you finish tidying up? You wouldn't tell us, but I'll tell you.

"It was because you saw plenty of drink in the kitchen, includin' a fetching bottle of whisky. A lot of people have remarked on your powers of sleepin' through awful racket and commotion on the night of the murder, and not being roused till the coppers dragged you out. That was the reason. You took down that bottle of whisky and sat here in the flat drinkin' until you were afraid Haye might be due back. So, since the bottle was pretty much depleted anyway, you took it along with you and went downstairs to the basement.

161

That was shortly before Haye got back here himself, round about twenty minutes to eleven."

There was a silence.

"And what if I did?" blazed the other.

"Nothin' at all," said H.M. mildly. "It's something any of us might have done. But now comes the important part, and I want the truth. The truth: got it? *Did you come up from the basement again at any time—at any time, mind—before the coppers woke you up?*"

Everyone in the room looked stoical; yet everyone, Sanders felt, was holding his breath for the answer. They seemed to see the case poised on a thin edge.

("But what is it?" whispered Marcia, close against Sanders's ear. "They look like hangmen! But what difference does it make?")

The caretaker himself looked impressed and therefore suspicious. He said:

"And how should I know?"

"Try to think, son."

"And why should I?"

"All right, son. Of course, if you were too drunk to walk—"

"Ah, bedad, and who was too drunk to walk?" shouted the other suddenly. "I mind it well. It was a matter of a door banging in the middle of the night."

"What door, son?"

"The back door of the building, that somebody had left wide open. I got up and bolted and chained it about a quarter past twelve."

Round that ring of faces went a flicker, a loosening of breath, which said that they had heard what they wanted.

"That's all, son," said H.M. "You can go."

When he had stalked out, Chief Inspector Masters began to gather up the papers on the table with an almost violent satisfaction.

"Got the bounder," breathed Masters. "Murderer sewed up tight as a drum, if I know anything about it. Now—"

He glanced towards Marcia Blystone and Dr. Sanders, and cleared his throat.

"—suppose, sir, we adjourn to the other room and have a bit of a conference?" said Masters, checking himself. "Bob! You and Wright pick up that chap from the Everwide Detective Agency, the one I told you about, and follow Sir Henry's instructions. Off you go; but hurry back here. Will you come with me a moment, Sir Henry?"

He was very brisk, was the chief inspector. H.M., who seemed worried, had barely time to gobble a word of greeting to the two new arrivals before Masters shepherded him into the bedroom and closed the door.

But he missed more interesting visitors. Bonita Sinclair, Lady Blystone, and Sir Dennis Blystone were coming up the stairs into the hall of the flat.

It had something of the effect of a procession. Afterwards Sanders remembered all things with that clarity which seems to come in the middle of the night. The flat carpeted throughout in brown. The rich shell of a room with murals and wall-lamps. The hall more dingily paneled, with the fur wraps of the women moving against it. The unnecessary violence with which Blystone put down an umbrella in the umbrella-stand. Even the mutter of traffic in the street, and the faint hum of the refrigerator from the kitchen.

"All right," whispered Marcia. "Here we go."

But still Sanders noticed the order of the procession. First Bonita Sinclair, with Lady Blystone following her. Was there anything in this? For he was staggered by the complete amity which seemed to exist between the two women.

They heard Lady Blystone—yes, Marcia's mother—say in a bright tone:

"What do we do with our things, Punch, my dear? I've never been here before, you know."

"Bedroom," muttered Blystone hastily. "I'lltakeum."

Divested of her fur coat, which by some miscalculation she flung back over Blystone's face and head, she marched into the living-room with a hard assurance and brightness like the glaze of false teeth. Mrs. Sinclair followed more slowly. Behind them Blystone groped blind with his head among the coats.

Sanders did not know whether it was an allegorical group, but he was uneasy. Lady Blystone marched up to them. She must have been enlightened as to the fact that he was not Detective-Inspector Sanders of the Criminal Investigation Department, for she studied him with one comprehensive glance.

"Your hair wants straightening, Marcia," she said automatically. "Dr. Sanders, isn't it. My husband told me who you were this evening. How do you do." She spoke without question-marks. "Oh, Mrs. Sinclair! Will you come here, please. I don't know whether you two have met. This is my little daughter Marcia."

She reached out and patted the little daughter on the head, a process which nearly brought about an explosion.

"How do you do?" said Marcia. "This is my future husband. We're going to be married."

(And this is a hell of a time, thought Sanders, to bring *that* up. But, conscientious as ever, he tabulated in his mind

163

such items as the figures of his income and his other qualifications, in case they got down to business about it.)

"Are you indeed, my dear," said Lady Blystone absently. She looked over her shoulder, thinking of other things. "Dennis, do come along! Sometimes you're so slow. Don't you find my husband slow, Mrs. Sinclair?"

"Not in the least," said the other.

Though she gave Marcia a smile, she was much more grave than Lady Blystone. Lady Blystone herself was riding only a trained procession-horse, suitable for reviews and other stately occasions, but the horse appeared to have got the bit in its teeth. Sanders saw why. She was genuinely happy.

"Marcia, I almost forgot to tell you," she went on. "I am afraid you will have to get along without us for a while. Your father and I are going to take a cruise, a nice long cruise, possibly a world cruise. We decided it tonight."

"You didn't!" cried Marcia. "That's wonderful!"

"Indeed we did, my dear. Your father wondered whether the police might try to stop us, or something of the sort, because of this dreadful affair; but he is sure they won't, and in any case he has too much influence. We shall be sailing next week, and we shall be away for nearly six months."

"Good," said Marcia. "In that case, you will be back just in time for the wedding."

"The what, my dear?"

"The wedding. *My* wedding. In case you didn't catch it, I am going to marry Dr. Sanders here."

"Nonsense!"

Sanders got out his pocket-diary, in which he had penciled a few notes.

"I had hoped," he said, "to go into this at some better time, but you may as well know it now. Marcia and I are going to be married at Marylebone Registry Office in the first week of September. I'm afraid there is not much that can be done about it. However, I think you ought to know——"

He talked for about a minute and a half, shut up the diary, and put it in his pocket. Then they looked each other in the eye. For a moment he thought she was going to break into lamentations; yet something in this businesslike way of doing things seemed to appeal to her. She resumed her air of hard brightness, a little moist now.

"Well, my dear," she said to Marcia, "if you insist on getting married I suppose I cannot stop you: after we have gone into all the facts, of course. I will discuss it with you later. In any case, your father and I cannot be expected to alter *our* plans——"

164

"Of course not! I only wanted to mention that I was getting married, that's all."

Lady Blystone appeared to be of two minds how to take this, but any other confusion of emotion was swallowed up in something else.

"Next week," she repeated. She turned with great politeness. "Have you ever been on a world cruise, Mrs. Sinclair?"

"Never," smiled Bonita.

"I daresay you have been much too occupied, of course. I am sure my husband and I will enjoy every minute of this one."

"I'm sure you will."

Something seemed to be coming unstuck here, or going not according to pattern.

"Your husband, Mrs. Sinclair—you *are* married now, aren't you?"

"No," said Bonita quietly. "My husband died last night. I can't pretend that I am very sorry about it; but he is dead and someone murdered him. That's really why we are here, isn't it? If you can feel very triumphant over a victory of that sort, please enjoy yourself."

There was a silence. John Sanders liked the woman. He liked her against every rule laid down, against every possible hypocrisy or turn of crooked dealing, simply because she said that and seemed to mean it. Then, in the quiet, he became aware that the room was filling up.

Out of the door to the bedroom came Sir Henry Merrivale, Chief Inspector Masters, and Sir Dennis Blystone. Out of the door to the hall came Bernard Schumann and a glossy-haired, stoop-shouldered, sallow-faced man who Sanders supposed must be the Egyptian assistant.

"*Voici le cadavre*," the last-named whispered, chuckling and tapping his chest. "*La tête de morte, c'est moi. Je prendrai ma place au pied de la table.*"

Schumann, who was formally dressed like Blystone, pressed his hat against his chest and nodded.

"I hope we are not late?" he observed. "This is my assistant, Mr. El—that is, whose name some of us discussed this afternoon."

"No, son, you're not late," said H.M. "We were just goin' to begin."

He lumbered to the head of the table, and put down *The Lair of the Dragon* on it with a thump. His only sign of worry was that he kept tapping the side of his cigar to dislodge imaginary ash.

"Sit down, everybody."

Everybody followed his instructions except Masters, who

remained with his back to the fireplace. It was Sir Dennis Blystone who broached the subject.

"Well, Henry, you see we're here. Am I right in assuming that you have been doing some more of what you used to call sittin' and thinkin', and that this is the result?"

"In a way," said H.M.

He seemed to discover with dull surprise that his cigar had gone out. It was Schumann, near his right hand, who leaned across with a lighter and snapped on the flame.

"We have not been introduced," Schumann remarked gravely, "but I think I know who you are. Let this serve as an introduction."

"Thanke'e, son," said H.M.

Smoke curled up in the bright room. H.M., distending his jaws with a concentrated and hideous pantomime face, blew a few rings. On either side of his bald head there were the remains of grayish hair, which he had now ruffled out over his ears. The book on the table showed the bright printing of its title in front of him.

"I was just wonderin'," said H.M., "where to begin. I know now. In the course of this business we've dug out quite a few secrets about people. We've pried into boxes and opened lives. But there's one secret we haven't even discussed yet, though it's at the root of the whole affair. I mean, friends and enemies, the secret of Felix Haye."

CHAPTER NINETEEN

"IT's 'not," pursued H.M., crossing his legs to make himself comfortable, "a very deep secret. It's a matter of character, and most of you know it. Think of Haye's actions. Read his books. Muse over his words. And you'll know what the feller really was.

"He wasn't a blackmailer. He wasn't a criminal of any kind. He hadn't a penny to gain, or a cause to further, or a wrong to right. I doubt if he even acted out of malice. Felix Haye was just what he pretended to be: a quite straight business-man with an undeveloped mind, includin' his sense of humor, and a certain hobby. I tell you what he was: he was a debunker.

"Now, I don't in general object to people who go about feverishly provin' that people are not what they seem. There's a lot of stuffin' that needs to be removed from shirts, and a good spring-cleaning wanted in the home of the humbugs. If a solemn lie is used to cheat an honest man, or sell some useless claptrap, or made into a chantin' hymn of 'service' for profit, or even held over a kid as a threat—then, say I, blow it higher than Boney's kite.

"If you're doin' it because you hate quackery and humbug, you couldn't do a better thing. Heaven will reward you and the gold cokernut is yours. But if you're doin' it merely for pleasure—

"That, d'ye see, is why some people can't let the dead alone. The dead are pretty harmless, as a rule. We're in no danger of bein' invaded by Julius Caesar. Gladstone will never stand for parliament any more. Dickens hasn't got a new novel on the spring list. They can all sort of rest in greatness and do a great deal of good in the grave, provided our modern Juvenals will let 'em. But there are some people who enjoy above all things, for its own sake, to hear that General X was a coward and Lady Y a dipsomaniac. Felix Haye was one of 'em.

"And the reason? Here, I say! Do any of you remember, as kids, the first time you ever heard a female relative swear? Or the first time you ever saw your stately great-uncle kissin' the housemaid behind the door? Or heard some plain speaking about certain members of your family? I bet it startled the ears off you. I know it did me. It did most of us. We never believed they thought of things like that. Most of us, a' course, grow out of that. Things get adjusted, and we come to accept necessary humbug *lento risu*.

"But Felix Haye never did grow out of it. He went further. It became a hobby with him, a source of joy and delight, to dig out the low-down on people he knew. Then he would slyly and subtly taunt 'em with it, to see how they acted. He didn't think he meant 'em any harm. He wasn't going to give 'em away publicly. It was only Young Felix's hobby."

H.M. paused.

"What he wanted, of course, was great or highly placed people. That would have been nuts to him. Only, unfortunately, he didn't know any. He was only a business man in good circumstances with a more or less restricted acquaintance. So he had to be content with the most distinguished persons he did know. Meanin'—"

Raising his finger, H.M. moved it round to indicate the quiet group before him.

Bernard Schumann spoke thoughtfully. "I see. That was what I could not understand. I nearly went mad trying to find out the fellow's motive. I could not imagine why he should be so interested in me. He hardly knew me."

"He didn't know Peter Ferguson at all," said H.M., "except

167

that Peter F. was a very dangerous feller. He learned about Peter F. through Ferguson's wife, but he was awful interested. Now," added H.M. suddenly, "I'm goin' to talk plain slander. How Haye learned all he knew is a secret that'll die with him, and it don't concern our present problem. But he did learn certain things. I first want to tell you—all of you— that there's not now a shred of evidence against any of you for your little peccadilloes. So don't jump up and shout blue thunder at me just because Chief Inspector Masters is standin' over there lookin' sinister. He can't do anything. Consequently—"

Sir Dennis Blystone got up from his chair. Both Sanders and Marcia had been watching him. He had been sitting with his hand on his wife's arm, now and then patting it in an absent way: evidently to Lady Blystone's mingled distaste and satisfaction. There was a grave, thoughtful look on his face as he rose.

He walked straight up to Masters.

"Chief Inspector."

"Sir?"

"Allow me to return your notebook," said Blystone, handing it over. "I got it out of your pocket while I was putting the coats in the bedroom."

"Dennis!" screamed Lady Blystone. She caught herself up then, and remained rigid.

"I must say, sir," snapped Masters, "that this doesn't seem to be the time for any of your funny—"

"Not at all," said Blystone. They saw that he was chuckling. "I am only practising a course recommended by my friend Henry Merrivale. You behold an expert amateur conjurer who will henceforth have a good time in social circles." He added: "God, what a relief! It means nothing at all. I don't care if you publish it tomorrow in the *Daily Mail*. Eh, Judy?"

"Dennis, you fool! You utter—"

"Shut up," said H.M. quietly.

For the first time Lady Blystone consented to look at him. "Really, Sir Henry, don't you think that is going further than even you ordinarily do?"

"Shut up," roared H.M.

For a second Sanders thought he was going to throw *The Lair of the Dragon* at her. And Sanders understood why: H.M.'s feeling was relief. He had seen H.M. carry on in just that way in court at the conclusion of the Answell Case, when the crisis was over and the verdict returned.

But the creepy sensation which had begun to go through Dr. Sanders was produced by another cause. They were all waiting. There was a murderer in this room, and he had not the slightest idea who it was.

He felt Marcia's arm link through his as H.M. turned back.

"Uh-huh. Anybody else like to make a little confession? You can see it's good for the soul."

H.M. glanced at Mrs. Sinclair, who was contemplating him from under her eyelids. Bonita Sinclair had never looked more innocent, or more generally inexplicable. As though to annoy Lady Blystone, she had crossed her knees with far greater disclosure than her innocent air seemed to know.

"Not I, thank you," she answered. And she smiled. "You will have certain persons thinking me far worse than I really am—that I am a murderer, for instance—and I wish I could confess. But what can I say? I work for my living. I sell pictures."

Lady Blystone looked at her.

"I sell pictures," repeated Bonita Sinclair. "If I have any other profession, it has been sanctioned in the past by many great ladies, and policemen are interested in it only when off duty. The woman who does not succeed in it as a wife has my sympathy. That's all. I have committed no crime."

"Hold on!" H.M. intervened sharply, as Lady Blystone made a movement. H.M. pointed to her. "We might as well clean this up here and now. Any charges of poisoning against this gal, any rumors or general hocus-pocus, are a washout. The French police are clear about that. The Italian at Monte Carlo, the one so much fuss has been made about, died of appendicitis. There never has been any real charge of murder against her. She was at Scotland Yard when Ferguson died—"

"Thank you, Sir Henry," the woman said. "So you told me when I met you this afternoon at my house. Then why go over it again?"

"You'll see. No: the only thing Haye had against you was two letters dealin' with a fake Rubens and a fake Van Dyck, guaranteein' their genuineness—"

"That *is* slander."

"Sure," agreed H.M. meekly. "But I got to mention it." He turned to Schumann. "As you say, son, we haven't met; but I know who you are too. Would you like to tell me what Haye had against you in the nature of evidence of arson?"

The room grew very quiet. Masters shuffled his feet on the gritty hearthstone, as though getting ready for a race, while Bernard Schumann looked impatient.

"Confound it all!" said Schumann, clenching his fingers. "I am getting tired of this nonsensical charge. The chief inspector there came to me this afternoon and repeated it, with the added refreshment of murder. I was supposed to have

169

set fire to my own warehouse and killed Mr. Nizam El Hakim—"

It was a staggering enough surprise to Sanders, who had heard nothing of this development, when Schumann indicated the smiling Egyptian.

"—whom I now present in very good health indeed."

"Enchanté," bowed El Hakim, as though he were being introduced.

"I do not," said Schumann, "ask for an apology. That would be too much to hope for. But I do ask that you will have the decency to shut up. You don't accuse me of setting fire to my own warehouse, I suppose?"

H.M. shook his head disconsolately. He examined the cigar in his fingers.

"No, son. Not at all."

"Then—?"

"As a matter of fact," said H.M., pointing the cigar at Nizam El Hakim, "I think *he* set fire to it."

Dr. Sanders had never before watched the interesting and even disturbing spectacle of a dark-skinned person growing pale. He saw it now in the case of El Hakim. The Egyptian jumped up and began to pour out a falsetto of bad French with such rapidity that Sanders lost him after the first sentence. Then, after one comprehensive wave of his arms, he stopped like a clockwork toy. Then he ran out of the room; they heard him bang out.

H.M. held up his hand.

"Mind," he insisted carefully. "I can't prove it. It's rank slander. But I was sittin' and thinkin', and I thought there might have been more truth in the popular rumor than we realized. I think El Hakim fired your warehouse and ran away to Port Said. And I think you very strongly suspected it. Unfortunately, when he came back to Cairo, out of sheer self-defense you had to take him into your employ.

"For it's possible he knows what Haye knew: that you yourself are addicted to arson for the pure hell of it. You've had an awful time, son, and I'm a bit sorry for you. Those alarm-clock works in your pocket, *un*-damaged by fire, had nothin' to do with the blaze in Cairo. They're the relic of one of your arson-pranks that didn't work or only partly worked: and Haye had the goods on you. The point's this: At the moment I don't give a curse what fires you started, where you started 'em, or anything about it. It's entirely outside our problem—which is murder."

Schumann was more excited than he had ever been before.

"You do not care?"

"That's what I said, son."

"Then why bother me—us—with this cat-and-mouse game? You have the answer," retorted Schumann, controlling himself, "to what you called your problem. This afternoon, just as I promised, I gave Chief Inspector Masters important information. Important! I am glad you realize it. I told him who the murderer is."

"You don't mean you know?" cried Bonita Sinclair.

"Madam, of course I know. The murderer is—"

"Steady," said H.M.

Once, on a fair-day in the country, Dr. Sanders had been inveigled into a contraption called the Giant Whirlabout. A series of flimsy-looking seats, each at the end of a long chain, began to revolve more and more rapidly until the victims were being hurled round in the air parallel with the ground. It prompted the thought, "Look here, what happens if the chain should break?" Sanders had a similar feeling now. The whirlabout was moving faster, and he wondered whether anybody could stop it.

"Steady be hanged," retorted Schumann with unconscious aptitude. "I have given you the information. Then why should you sit there and bedevil nearly all of us except the real murderer with questions about our pasts? Sir, I know what I know. I shall be prepared to swear to it in court—"

"Sure," agreed H.M. patiently. "That's the point. That's the whole point. That's why I'm askin' you all this. You blazin' fatheads, don't you realize that this case will have to come to trial?"

He then gave up his meekness and roared.

"It's simple, ain't it? If the murderer's caught, there'll be a trial. And you're *witnesses*. Don't you understand that? What do you think has been worryin' me all along? You talk about hushin' things up! Suppose I got a friend. Suppose I want to prevent truth bein' dragged out of him in open court—the truth being that he's been a pickpocket? And do you think it won't come out? Ho ho! Counsel for the defense will be all over you. So just you make sure there isn't any real evidence to—"

"Now, now!" Masters interrupted warningly. "We can't—"

"Shut up, Masters," said H.M. He snorted, and then grew more mild. "As a matter of fact, I'm not worried now on that score. This friend of mine is cured. He's busted the bogey and learned how to laugh. He won't mind. His daughter's busted the bogey by fallin' in love. But—"

Sir Dennis Blystone interposed.

"Suppose," Blystone said in an even tone, "the murderer is never caught?"

A slight quiver went round the table, as though they were sitting at a spiritualistic seance.

"Oh, my son," said H.M. "The murderer—are you all listening?—is tied up in a sack. That's the sad part of it. The murderer was actually tied up in a sack before either Haye or Ferguson was murdered. Want to know why? Because the Everwide Inquiry Agency, that firm of private snoopers, have found out who bought atropine and who sent the poisoned bottle to Haye. Evidence. Cor! I couldn't have stopped the thing from comin' out if I'd wanted to. And now with Bernard Schumann's ev—"

"What ridiculous nonsense is all this?" demanded Lady Blystone.

"Still," interposed Bonita Sinclair in a soft voice, "there is a flaw in the case even so, isn't there? I only ask. I—I know something of law, you see. In order to convict anyone, you would have to show how atropine was put in all our drinks here the night before last, wouldn't you?"

"Yes," said H.M.

"And we are all willing to swear it was impossible for any of us to have poisoned the drinks. Has it been shown how the murderer could have done that?"

"No," said H.M. "But that's what I'm goin' to show you right now."

He pushed himself up from the table.

"We've got here," he pursued, flinging the stump of his cigar into the fireplace, "most of the people who were here on the night of the murder, with a few additions. So we'll reconstruct a bit. You, ma'am, are goin' to mix another batch of cocktails, with the others watching you. Denny is goin' to have another highball. Mr. Schumann is goin' to carry the drinks in here. As for me, *I'll undertake to poison 'em.* Watch me closely, ladies and gents, and see if you can tell how I do it. Fair enough?"

"Yes, that is fair," agreed Schumann, who seemed savagely perplexed. "But—"

"We've heard a good deal in this case," snapped H.M., "about ingenious ways of committin' crimes. Let's have a concludin' one, a true one, to round off the business; and the best of the lot at that. But, before we do, there's one question I'd like to ask."

He glowered at Sir Dennis Blystone.

"You, Denny. You used to be a teetotaler. Your daughter says you very seldom drink nowadays. You yourself said you don't like whisky (for which I pity you) yesterday in Dr. Sanders's flat. Uh-huh. Then how did you come to call for a rye-whisky highball at Haye's party?"

Blystone looked at him sharply. "There are two reasons. First, I rather like rye. Second, it's not commonly served at parties. If I consistently call for rye and ginger-ale, and none is available, I am not pressed to take other drinks when I don't feel like having any at all."

"Oh? Then it's a general stunt of yours? And Haye was ready with his rye? It was well-known?"

"I should think so."

"All right," said H.M. "Get started. Masters will play the part of Haye. Just to show you there's no jiggery-pokery in the mix-up and scramble round the kitchen sink, I'll stay right here where I can't touch the drinks as yet. Out to the kitchen, now."

The next few minutes were among the longest that Sanders remembered. Under the brisk voice and brisk manner of the chief inspector, Mrs. Sinclair, Sir Dennis, and Schumann were shepherded out into the hall and thence to the kitchen. Lady Blystone sat quietly, her head high; she seemed to be thinking of something else. And Marcia plucked at Sanders's sleeve as he was starting for the kitchen.

"No, we don't," she said fiercely, nodding towards H.M. "We stay here and watch *him*. He's the one to keep your eye on."

Faintly from the kitchen came the sound of Masters's voice, mixed with the hiss and splash of running water.

"The cocktail-shaker, sir, if you please. I'll rinse it, as Mr. Haye did. Here you are, Mrs. Sinclair. The glasses, now—"

Sanders glanced at his wrist-watch. Even the second hand seemed to crawl. In the kitchen they were squeezing lemons. There was a scraping of bottles and a brisk banging, to the insistent hiss of the hot water.

H.M. stood motionless, and scratched his nose.

Then they heard the rattle of the cocktail-shaker.

"Ready, sir!" called Masters from the other room.

"Do as you did the other night," said H.M. without moving. "Have Mrs. Sinclair taste 'em out of the shaker."

Silence.

"All right?" shouted H.M.

Mrs. Sinclair's voice was clear but suddenly shaky. "The cocktails are quite all right, yes. But you're not *really* going to put anything—"

"Carry on," said H.M.

Under any other circumstances, it might have been ludicrous to see Bernard Schumann come into the living-room with the tray. He looked and seemed to feel like an aged waiter. But he nearly dropped the tray before he put it down on a small table near the long refectory one. On the tray stood the nickeled shaker, four cocktail-glasses, and one filled tumbler.

Still H.M. did not move.

"Go back to the kitchen, son," he said to Schumann, "with the others." He looked at Sanders. "You keep time. Burn me, we'll have this exactly as it was without a bit of deviation! They said, 'between two and three minutes.' Give it two and a half. You others out there!" he roared. "Talk! Somebody imitate a cryin' baby. You hear me?"

After refusals that jarred on the nerves, it was Masters who complied. The resulting noise was hideous enough to be funny; but nobody laughed. Masters had powerful lungs, as Haye must have had. Without seeing him, you might have imagined it to be Haye.

Yet nerves, in that group, were under admirable control. One minute. The noise of the baby was wearing thin, but to Sanders it seemed to drown every smaller noise except the ticking of his watch.

Two minutes. Sanders had never known a time so long. Marcia had her cheek pressed against his sleeve; he could see the curve of her eyelash and feel her breathing against him. Once he thought the watch had stopped. All this time Lady Blystone sat still, and seemed to think of other things.

Two and a—

Sanders made a gesture.

"All right," said H.M.

The intermittent crying of the baby died away. A quiet group, led by a quiet chief inspector, came back into the living-room. Bonita Sinclair was pale, though she smiled mechanically.

"Good," said H.M. "Is it now agreed that all the conditions have been fulfilled? Hey? It's just as it was the other night?"

"Just as it was," said Blystone, putting up a hand to his collar. "Including the fact that you've had the opportunity to drop atro—er—something into something while we were in the kitchen."

"Well, doc?" demanded H.M., looking at Sanders.

"He never went near that tray," declared Sanders, and Marcia nodded confirmation. "Not within six feet of it."

H.M. did go to the tray now. He picked up the tumbler and handed it to Blystone. With a grotesque shake and flourish of the cocktail-shaker, he poured out a whitish-looking cocktail into one of the glasses.

"You mixed these," he said to Mrs. Sinclair. "You ought to know, hey? Right, then. You drink this."

Silence.

174

"I would rather not," said Bonita Sinclair. "I have tasted them once. Mr. Schumann brought them in here afterwards. Let him drink it."

Schumann inclined his head courteously. "I have no objection, madam," he said; "since I know who is in charge of proceedings." He reflected, lifting the glass. "For the second time today, I am going to drink a glass which someone confidently believes to be poisoned. In time these things will become bad for my health, and I shall be—

"*God!*" he said involuntarily.

Schumann sprang back, throwing out his hands as though to push something away. The glass dropped and broke with a crash on the tray. Then Schumann wiped his hand across his mouth.

"Sir Henry, what—?"

"It's all right," H.M. told him with great reassurance. "There's no poison in there, son. Only a little mouth-wash that won't hurt you. I had to make you taste somethin', you see, or you wouldn't 'a' believed me."

Very gingerly Blystone had tilted his highball glass. "It's true. There's something in it, and there wasn't anything in it before. But, Merrivale, *how?* How did you do it? What in the name of—"

"Oh, my eye," roared H.M. "It's not as complicated as all that, is it? Think, son. It's heartbreakin'ly easy. There's two sets of drinks. One is made of gin, the other of whisky. One has ginger-ale in it, the other has Cointreau and lemon-juice. But what's the other thing? The only other thing? The thing that's absolutely necessary to both of 'em if they're to be any good at all?"

"Well?"

"Ice," said H.M.

He sniffed, putting his hands in his pockets and glowering round.

"I thought of it," he went on, "when I heard Masters quote Mrs. Sinclair's tale—about Haye standin' by the electric refrigerator and imitating the baby. Ice, son. Ice out of the tray of cubes, in that little refrigerator in the kitchen. D'ye see now?

"Somebody's prepared it. A colorless liquid (atropine) has been poured into the water of a drawer of ice-cubes, and the drawer is pushed in to freeze. Right. The batch of cocktails is mixed, the highball is mixed. The ice-cubes from the drawer are taken out and shoved into each; the shaker is given a couple of rattles; but it's not quite ready.

"Y'see? Mrs. Sinclair tastes the cocktails. But in that couple of seconds the ice hasn't had time enough to melt suffi-

175

ciently in order to loosen its cargo of atropine into the stuff. The same rule applies to the highball, which Mrs. S. tastes as well. Then the drinks are brought in here, put on the table, and left for two or three minutes. When the group comes into this room, the host picks up the shaker, automatically gives it a couple of rattles (which spread the poison better), and pours out. The machine is now loaded; and the carnage is terrible.

"The murderer knew, as you've told me, that Haye drank only White Lady cocktails. His guests would all be certain to join him, except possibly Denny Blystone. But in that case Blystone would have his favorite rye-whisky and ginger-ale. You're lucky, Denny. If you'd been in the habit of takin' sherry, or Scotch-and-soda, or any one of a dozen drinks that don't require ice, you'd be dead now. The murderer would have had to kill you. But a sweet-tastin' highball is pretty sickening without it. And the ice went in.

"That's why the individual doses of poison were so varied: the murderer, of course, couldn't estimate 'em. That's why the murderer had to kill Haye with a swordstick: he couldn't pick and choose his victim with the poison alone. Afterwards, the murderer simply rinsed out the shaker and refilled it with harmless cocktails. He wanted to distract our attention away from the subject of ice. He wanted us to think—as we did think—that the doses were administered in each individual glass by one of the guests at the party."

Blystone stared at him.

"By one of the guests at—? But we didn't do it! We couldn't have done it. None of us went near that refrigerator. Nobody here had the opportunity to freeze poison into a drawer of ice-cubes!"

"I know that, son," said H.M. somberly.

"Then who is the murderer?"

" 'Judith Adams,' " said H.M.

"Oh, yes," he went on. "I know the real Judith Adams is dead. I mean the crashin' hint that was intended to be conveyed by the name. For the real secret of Felix Haye is the secret of his last joke—his richest, ripest, most cunning joke—his last spasm of punning—his masterpiece. It's betrayed the murderer neatly, as Haye meant it should. Y'see, the name 'Judith Adams' was written on the outside of one of those five boxes. But inside the box, my fatheads, *inside*, there was evidence referrin' to the dirty work of a very different person."

"Ah," breathed Schumann.

"The man's mad," said Blystone wildly. "What would be the point of having one name outside and another inside? It was to be opened in the presence of three solicitors, wasn't it? They would discover the difference, wouldn't they?"

"Exactly," said H.M. "You got it! It would be discovered. But not until all three members of the firm opened it in each other's presence. All three, son. All three. The most iron-bound, gruesomely respectable, Sparton-honest firm of lawyers in all London. And they would discover—"

"You mean that the murderer is—?"

"Yes," said H.M. *"All right, Bob!"*

The door to the bedroom burst open, and rebounded against the wall. With Sergeant Pollard at one side, and plain-clothes P. C. Wright at the other, a prisoner was dragged in. But he seemed less fighting than fainting. The watchers had one glimpse of a rolling walk, and a bunched nose, and staring eyes magnified behind a tottering pince-nez.

For men in good physical condition, Pollard and Wright were having some difficulty with a sedentary murderer—the solicitor, Charles Drake.

CHAPTER TWENTY

IT WAS nearly an hour later, when much of the tumult and the shouting had passed, before H.M. resumed.

"Before I proceed to show you that Charles Drake, junior partner of Drake, Rogers & Drake, was the only person in the whole cursed case who could have killed Felix Haye," said H.M., "I'd better emphasize the extreme devilishness of the device Haye had prepared to snaffle Drake in case Drake was the murderer. You follow it?"

Chief Inspector Masters answered him.

"Yes, sir, I follow it. We've worked it out," said Masters, drawing a deep breath. "But there's one thing I followed too. I've been in the Force for thirty years. I started in K Division—Limehouse—in the days when Limehouse was really tough. I've worked among crooks all my life. But, Lord-lummy, until this case came along, I never saw such a gang of crooks in all my born days! And all swells too."

"Well, what else did you expect, son?" asked H.M., and surveyed the silent group with an air of broadmindedness. He seemed almost paternal about them. "What else did Haye go out for except crooks? He attracted them; or, I ought to say, they attracted him. And what was the prize, the ripe plum, of all his collection? Why, a twister in the most crusted firm of solicitors in London, Drake, Rogers & Drake. Young

Charles Drake (he's fifty-three) has been pinchin' securities entrusted to them in a way that—

"Y' know, if it hadn't been for the unquestioned uprightness and reliability of that firm as a firm, this whole business could never have occurred and the murderer's plan wouldn't have worked. I've told you about old man Drake, Charles's father, who came to me to begin with. He values his integrity, his Creator, and his family in the order named. So does Wilbert Rogers.

"And that's where Haye's scheme was so neat. He entrusts to that firm, to be opened in case of his death, evidence incriminatin' a member of it!—the one place in the world where Charles Drake will never think of lookin' for it. Haye knew that Drake, Rogers & Drake never followed instructions of that kind unless all three of 'em were present to open what had been deposited there. Pandora's box would never have the effect o' that one. Charles Drake would be caught by his own father. And why (thinks Haye) should Charles suspect that innocent little box labeled 'Judith Adams?' The woman's name alone would divert his mind; as, burn me, it diverted ours.

"But Felix Haye wasn't very intelligent, y'know. He underestimated Charles Drake. Badly."

The prisoner had been removed, and he had said not a word the whole time: though Dr. Sanders remembered those large, frightened gray eyes moving behind his pince-nez like rats behind a screen. The only upset had been a sudden and unexpected fit of hysterics on the part of Bonita Sinclair, which had calmed down now.

And, at the chief inspector's words, several persons had sat up.

"I must insist," said Bernard Schumann with some acerbity, "that I object to being called a criminal."

Bonita Sinclair said nothing.

"I am not sure that I do," said Blystone thoughtfully. "But there are other parts of it that interest me more. I still don't see that the name Judith Adams in any way points to Charles Drake. You maintain that Drake is the only person who could have committed the crime; and I don't understand that either. I should be interested to hear the steps of sittin' and thinkin' that went into it."

H.M., with his elbow on the table, rubbed his hands over his temples and stared fishily at *The Lair of the Dragon* for a little time before he answered. Then he took a pencil and a crumpled envelope out of his pocket.

"All right," he growled. "Let's work it out."

"You know the theory of the crime we had already de-

178

cided on, which in essentials—I say essentials—is correct. The guests drank atropine. The murderer stabbed Haye, slipped out of the house, went to Gray's Inn, burgled the office, returned with the loot, and strewed it in people's pockets.

"At the first, and up until last night, I was gropin' blind. I thought the murder and burglary at Drake's office must have been committed by Peter Ferguson, actin' in collusion with his wife, Mrs. Sinclair. Lord love a duck, how simple everything would'a been then! It solved our major problem: how had the drinks been hocused?

"In that case all the answers were simple. Ferguson sneaked in and poisoned the drinks while they were unattended here in the living-room. Afterwards he went out of the house by the back door, unbolting it, went to Gray's Inn, cracked the crib as he could do easily, returned, and re-bolted the door. *He* didn't even need to pay any attention to bolted doors. The feller was a phenomenal cat-burglar, who could have gone up and down a rain-pipe just as he did when he 'vanished.'

"That seemed easy enough. Of course, as I insisted yesterday, there were some thunderin' objections to it—if Ferguson were the murderer, why should he hang about in the building after the crime, and make himself so conspicuous, and bray like an ass, and then disappear? But it was the best theory we had, and seemed the most probable. That was why I lent myself to that very rummy burglary last night.

"But you know what happened. Bang went the whole theory. In front of my own bemused eyes, Ferguson was polished off with atropine—I saw the murderer's hands—at the same time Mrs. Sinclair was sittin' with Masters at Scotland Yard.

"Oi. I repeat: Oi. I was beginnin' to get the breeze up badly. I sort of thought I'd better prepare for a little serious sittin' and thinkin'.

"What had I got then? With Ferguson out of the way, it seemed absolutely proved that the murder of Haye must have been committed by one of the guests at the party. Got that? There was a witness, Marcia Blystone, at the front door. But a guest could easily have come downstairs, got out the back door, gone to Gray's Inn, returned, and bolted the door again. It had to be like that. It had to be, because no outsider—Ferguson out of the picture—could *finally have left* that locked building either (1) leaving the back door bolted and chained behind him, or (2) leaving by the front door without bein' seen by the witness.

"But if we excluded outsiders, back we came to the original

179

question of how the drinks were poisoned. The guests swore it was impossible.

"Then was when I woke up to the refrigerator trick and the frozen atropine.

"So far, easy. We think we've established that the only possible murderers are Mrs. Sinclair, Sir Dennis Blystone, or Bernard Schumann. If we want to be precise, we can add a rank outsider like Riordan the caretaker, who was also in the building. But that's the lot.

"Now, if any of you three—you first three—made the poisoned ice-cubes, when did you do it? You ruddy well didn't do it after you had come here for the party that night! Haye arrived here at twenty minutes to eleven. Schumann arrived some five minutes later; and Mrs. Sinclair and Denny Blystone at close on eleven. Immediately afterwards, the cocktails were mixed. It's impossible that after *getting* here one of these persons walked out into the kitchen, removed the tray of cubes already in the refrigerator, knocked out the old cubes, poured in new water with atropine added, and replaced it—all without bein' noticed by anybody. No, that's out, and it's also out on the grounds that there wouldn't have been time for the new cubes to freeze.

"Uh-huh. So the poisoned cubes were made at some time durin' the day or evenin' previous to fifteen minutes to eleven that night."

Schumann leaned forward, lifting his hand.

"Excuse me; but will the chair allow a question?" he asked. "Is that why the police were so anxious to find out what all of us had been doing *up* to the time we met here that night?"

H.M. nodded.

"Sure. But, d'ye see, I hadn't got very far yet. These were my ideas last night. Sort of mullin' over this, I thought: Here, could we narrow down that time a bit? Could we narrow down the time durin' which the murderer froze the cubes? At some time that day he got in and did it, and—

"Yes, there was a witness who could help. A nice innocent witness: so I thought at the time. The witness was Charles Drake, the helpful lawyer, who gave a statement to Bob Pollard. Charles Drake went to Haye's flat at six o'clock that evenin'. He went there to return (in person, mind you) to return a bottle of ale which had just been sent back from the analytical chemist's. It's not often that the junior partner of a crusted old firm scurries about on errands that could be done by the post or an office-boy. But Drake, level-headed Drake, had already heard over the phone about Haye's proposed party that night, and so he was curious.

180

"What happened when Drake got there? Well, Felix Haye was dressin' to go out to dinner. And Haye had been drinkin' a bit—cocktails, as usual. Haye did what? He went to the bedroom, and went on with his dressin'. In the meantime, Charles Drake went out to the kitchen, where he put down the bottle of ale. Fact is, y'know, he spent some time there—as he said—writin' a warning sign to hang on the bottle. During this interval, Haye was in the bedroom talkin' to him by shouting through the flat.

"But Haye had been drinkin'. Cocktails! Ho? Then there couldn't 'a' been any atropine in the ice he used at that time. And he went out immediately afterwards, with Drake, at some minutes past six. It seemed to me that the hocused cubes must have been made durin' the interval between the time Haye went out to dinner and the time he returned at twenty minutes to eleven.

"So. But bright and early this morning, we got two new bits of evidence: the statement of Peter Sinclair Ferguson, and the persistent puzzle of the 'Judith Adams' nobody could identify.

"I looked at Ferguson's statement, and I groaned with awful fervor. One of my eyes started to unseal. I looked at it again, and the other eye came unstuck too. Now, Ferguson wasn't a lily of truth; but he did touch the facts about Schumann, even if he'd guessed wrong, and he did tell the facts about his wife. There was no reason to doubt his account of the murder of Haye, because his whole conduct was based on it. He was murdered just because he knew what he knew. Unless he was tellin' the truth, his murder becomes meaningless and there are certain cryptic remarks in his statement that have no meanin' whatsoever.

"Cryptic? Burn me, I should think they are! He was being very coy, and leadin' up to the climax of tellin' us who killed Haye. But just listen to what he says. Gimme a copy of that statement, Masters.

"He's describing how he stood in the bedroom of this flat, watching this room through a door standin' a bit open. His statement exactly coincides with all the other facts as we've learned 'em. He tells how all of you sat round this table, and Haye started to give you hell. He quotes Haye's words. He hears that the five rummy boxes are in the offices of Drake, Rogers & Drake, in a larger box with Haye's name painted on it. That's his cue, and he's ready to leave to go and burgle the solicitors' office.

"But directly after that remark comes the followin' surprising and altogether meaningless remark:

"*I watched the wardrobe, too, which made me get out.*

"Now, where's the sense of that? The only wardrobe in this flat is that whackin' great one in the bedroom. Well, that's all right. But why should he watch it? Why should it make him get out?

"Was it possible, my lads, that there was somebody else in the flat, an outsider, hidin' in the wardrobe?

"Follow Ferguson from there. He goes downstairs, looks up the address of Drake's office, and hears someone come hurrying downstairs, and follows. They both go out the back door, leavin' it open. In the street Ferguson sees who the person is, and writes. '*You will be surprised when I tell you.*' Why should we be? All the guests at the flat are already under most dazzlin' suspicion. Next comes some real meat.

"The 'person' goes to the solicitors' offices, climbs up a fire escape, and seems—'seems'—to turn the catch of the window with a knife. He goes in, and comes out in two minutes. Time, twelve fifteen *et seq*.

"I repeat: two minutes. Then Ferguson, a practiced housebreakin' eel, follows and has a look round in the office. Hear Ferguson again: '*A box painted with Haye's name was lying on the floor with its lock broken—a difficult job. There was nothing in it. I went all through the offices . . . It was half-past twelve when I left.*'

"A difficult job, says Ferguson with a whole heap of meaning. And he was right. Was the burglary done at that time, by the 'person' Ferguson had followed from Great Russell Street?

"I'll submit to you, with my hand on my heart, that it's not possible. That 'person' goes into the office, finds the box, succeeds in breakin' it open—a difficult job—takes the contents, and leaves: all in two minutes. And is that all? Not a bit of it. What do we hear this mornin' from Drake, Rogers & Drake? Durin' the same burglary (the same one) some valuable securities belongin' to Haye have been pinched, not out of the same box, but out of the safe. All in two minutes.

"Eyewash. First-class, guaranteed-British eyewash.

"Is Ferguson lyin' about it? Possibly; but, if he is, where is the meanin' in any word he's written and why is he murdered? So far we can check up on his story of the murder, and it tallies. Let's assume for the sake of argument that this is true too, until we can disprove it. Out of Ferguson's statement we get the followin' points:

"*Point One*. The burglary at Drake, Rogers & Drake's was not committed at a quarter past twelve. It was committed at a much earlier time.

"*Point Two*. It was committed by someone with a key to the safe of Drake, Rogers & Drake.

182

"*Point Three.* It was committed by someone who knew Felix Haye had securities in that office, what securities they were and where they were to be found.

"That in itself is enough to give a strange burnin' sensation in the back of the skull. But (again assumin' Ferguson's story to be true) where does that get us, my lads? If the burglary had already been committed, we can't now say that the 'person'—at twelve-fifteen—scooped up the evidence, the four watches, the alarm-clock works, and all the rest of it. We can't say that the 'person' took all this stuff back with him to Great Russell Street, and strewed it in people's pockets. It was gone already.

"Gone, in short, long before a quarter-past twelve. But these articles, d'ye see, had to get into the guests' pockets somehow. They couldn't be put into people's pockets until the guests were unconscious, and the guests weren't unconscious until about ten minutes to twelve. So—

"*The murderer put that stuff in their pockets at the same time he stabbed Haye with the swordstick, between ten minutes to twelve and midnight. His work was then over. Afterwards he left the building, went to Gray's Inn, and took one last look round in the solicitors' offices to make sure nothin' had been overlooked.*

"Then he went—home.

"You see how it falls into line, if it's true? (Still if.) Ferguson's statement suggests an outsider, hidin' in the wardrobe: an outsider whose identity will surprise you: an outsider who took a brief two-minute look in the office, and then nipped off home. Oh? You deny there's a suggestion of an outsider goin' home? Let's look at the statement again.

"After seein' the murderer leave, after investigatin' the solicitors' office himself, Ferguson then goes back to Great Russell Street himself. Here's what he says:

"'The damned back door, by which I and this other person had left the building, was now bolted on the inside again.

"'I had not expected this. I did not understand it.'

"Well, now . . . If the murderer had been a member of Haye's party, an insider, why should Ferguson be surprised at that? For, after all, the murderer would have been inside. No, my lads. It surprised him because he thought the outside murderer had finished work, dusted his hands, and gone home.

"But there, it'd appear, our great big beautiful bloomin' theory collapses. We bounce back on ourselves. Back door bolted: front door watched: outsider phooey. Hey? But it wasn't worryin' me so much as it had before. I had even

183

scrutinized the idea that the gal, Marcia Blystone, might be the murderer or an accomplice of the murderer—"

"Here!" protested Sanders.

"You didn't honestly think that I—?" said Marcia.

"Ho ho," said H.M., with sepulchral noise. "Didn't I, though? As I've pointed out before, you've been the most persistent and enthusiastic obstructer of justice in the whole case. You've never told the truth when a lie would serve as well. You pinched Ferguson's statement out from under my nose, and only gave it back when you found there was nothin' damaging in it. But somehow I couldn't see you havin' a key to the safe of Drake, Rogers & Drake, and I couldn't see you with a knowledge of Haye's financial affairs. Havin' observed you in action during your little spot of burglary at Mrs. Sinclair's, I couldn't see you either as a successful burglar-murderer or a successful accomplice. It wouldn't do.

"It had begun to be plain, though, who might do.

"Good old 'Judith Adams'!" said H.M. with feeling. "Denny Blystone told me about her, and her book on dragons. I could'a cussed. In fact, I did. It wasn't evidence. It wasn't anything except an example of Felix Haye in his vilest punning mood, in the worst humor of *The Life of the Party*. Judith Adams's learned manner, and her taste for languages which even Timothy Riordan remarked on, gave him his information. Oh, my eye."

He pointed his finger malevolently.

"You, Denny. Derivation of the word 'dragon'?"

It was Schumann who answered. "*I* have pointed out that, Sir Henry. From the Latin *draco* meaning a tame snake—"

"A tame snake!" grunted H.M. "Sure. A tame snake. Now listen—" he picked up the book—"to what good old Judith has to say about it: 'The *draco* of the Romans was not the fire-breathing serpent of Christian legend; but a tame, though occasionally venomous, snake which was kept as a pet by the wealthier families. From it is also derived the English word *drake*, meaning a small piece of artillery. But it is notable that in Spanish the Latin *draco* is *el draco,* and was applied in Elizabethan times, during his raids, to Sir Francis Drake.' Bah! There it is. Felix Haye couldn't resist it: either the tame snake, or the small piece of artillery, or the actual repetition of the name. Can't you see him chuckling over that? He wasn't very subtle, I'm afraid. And he died because he wasn't. *El Draco,* Drake—"

"My assistant, Mr. El Hakim," said Schumann, "is half-Spanish, as I have mentioned. Yesterday the sergeant could not understand why he was so amused when the sergeant was arguing bitterly about that book over the telephone. Haye has often referred to Charles Drake under that name."

"Uh-huh. And you," growled H.M., "had to have the trousers scared off you before you'd part with the information.

"Never mind: let's get back to real proof.

"Now, I'd already asked Masters to check up on the movements of Mrs. Sinclair, Denny Blystone, and Bernard Schumann for the entire day of Haye's murder. I was pretty sure the atropine was put into the ice-cubes between six o'clock—when Drake was visitin' here—and twenty minutes to eleven. Could any of 'em have done it? Moreover, could any of em have carried out the real burglary at Drake, Rogers & Drake's place?

"And they couldn't.

"Between this morning and this afternoon, Sergeant Pollard gathered up information which proved Mrs. Sinclair's movements for the entire day, up to the time she came here with Denny Blystone at eleven. His movements were established as well. The same applied to Schumann. Schumann had spent the entire day, until an hour so late as to put him out of it, with dazzlingly unimpeachable witnesses like Lord and Lady Thurnley. They confirmed it. None of those three, then, could have been responsible for the murder and/or burglary. None of 'em came anywhere near this flat or Drake's office.

"But who did come to this flat at six o'clock?

"Charles Drake, and only Drake. Who had a golden opportunity to load the ice-cubes with atropine, while Haye was dressin' in the bedroom? Drake. Who spent a long time in the kitchen? Drake. Who knew every detail of the party that night, when it was to begin, and who was to be there? Drake.

"But tie him even tighter! Felix Haye drank iced but undrugged cocktails at six o'clock. Then he left. Could anybody have come into the flat afterwards and done the dirty besides Drake? I don't mean only Mrs. Sinclair or Denny or Schumann: could *anybody* at all have done it?

"No. Just as he was goin' out, Haye instructed the caretaker, Timothy Riordan, to come upstairs and tidy the flat. Which Timothy Riordan did straight-away. He then, like a true son, proceeded to sit down in the kitchen and get roaring drunk on Haye's whisky. Again like a true son, you weren't goin' to budge him from that bottle. He knew when Haye would get back, and he didn't mean to stir much before then. Even when he did, he took the rest of the bottle along. But, drunk or sober as Timothy was, nobody could have

185

crept into that little kitchen and messed about with the ice while he was there.

"Of course," said H.M. apologetically, "you can say, if you like, that the sinister murderer was Timothy himself, and that *he* poisoned the ice. But I'm afraid you'll find it full of holes. I doubt if even the subject of ice ever entered his head—it's a good thing it didn't, or he'd be a dead man now. I doubt if you can think of Timothy for sixty seconds, thinkin' of the evidence at the same time, and believe he fits into the pattern of guilt any better than Marcia Blystone or, say, Lady Blystone.

"All the same, though, one thing remained as a howlin' objection. If Drake was the murderer, how did that back door get itself bolted and chained? Without that, it'd'a been a clear field all the way through. The answer is both poetic and appropriate. Gin has figured in this case. Rye has figured in this case. Scotch has figured in this case. Timothy was full of Irish; and, when he heard the open back door bangin' at a quarter past twelve, he came up like a loyal son and bolted it.

"Charles Drake's whole course is pretty clear now. Haye had a twist on him, but Haye didn't *show* he had a twist—or tried not to. Haye was a rotten actor. To show it would have spoiled his whole joke. Drake has probably known for months that Haye knew about his crooked work in the firm. How much Haye had on him he wasn't sure. But Drake, bein' a practical man, took practical measures. He sent Haye a bottle of ale loaded with atropine.

"It's a funny thing Drake talked to Pollard like a cynical artist in crime, an artist of ripe experience and thought: and maybe Drake believed he was. Drake knew one thing, anyhow. If you creep into a chemist's in false whiskers, and buy a little bit of poison on some lame excuse, and sign the book with a false name, they'll have you as sure as hangin'. You can go to five different chemists' and get traced five times as easily, as Monte Cristo pointed out years ago. The only way to buy poison invisibly is to buy it in such enormous quantities that nobody ever thinks twice about it. F'r instance, take nicotine: as deadly a poison as there is. You can't buy dabs of it. But there are places in the hop-district of Kent where you can buy a lorry-load of it and roll away with no questions asked. It was the same with Drake's atropine. He set himself up as a 'firm' manufacturing eye-lotions. He bought a ten-ounce bottle of pure atropine from the wholesalers, so much that it couldn't even be thought of as a poison.

"But Haye wasn't havin' the ale. Now, did Haye suspect who had sent that bottle. I got an idea his suspicions were pretty ripe and fresh. Otherwise why did he bring that bottle to his *solicitors,* and have *them*—meanin' Charles—send it to the analytical chemist? He talked a lot about it to Drake. He asked Drake to put a firm of private detectives on the trail. But, all the same, I doubt if Haye suspected him of murder as much as he suspected a medical feller like Blystone or a gal of many husbands like Mrs. Sinclair.

"Then Haye came chargin' round with his five boxes, burstin' with delight over the neat trap he'd prepared for his enemies: both for his other enemies and for Drake, in case there was funny business. Drake saw through him. I'll lay you a fiver to a cold kipper that Drake understood 'Judith Adams,' and opened his own box, very shortly afterwards.

"We dunno what Haye had on him. Drake isn't likely to tell us, d'ye see. But the contents of that box must'a shown that Haye's real knowledge, his other knowledge, must be hair-raisin'. And that was too dangerous. Now Haye certainly had to die.

"Drake waited for the party or board-meetin' that was to come off. Haye undoubtedly had let drop hints about it already, and Drake was gettin' ready. He had to stage a fake burglary and pinch all the boxes, the others as well as his own. I'm inclined to think he lifted all five boxes before the actual day of the 'burglary' and murder. He opened 'em all and found curious articles inside, with full descriptions and histories written by Haye—a tireless annotator—about Blystone, Schumann, and Mr. and Mrs. Peter Sinclair Ferguson.

"Then Drake had his great idea. Suppose, on the occasion of the party, he could manage to dose the lot of 'em with atropine? Not kill 'em! Just make 'em unconscious. Then he could enter the flat in safety. He could make a little search to see if Haye had any more evidence. He could kill Haye with Haye's famous swordstick or even with the saber Haye kept there. Haye would be skewered, and three potential murderers would sit round him unconscious in the room. In their pockets he would put a little evidence. A *little,* that's all. Incongruous and rummy things, like watches and a magnifyin'-glass, that'd be unpleasantly difficult to explain when the tableau was discovered—as he meant it to be discovered.

"Do you follow that? To blow the whole gaff on 'em would be foolish. They might break down under investigation and get too friendly with the coppers. If there were only hints against 'em, they would stick together in the tracks of their crooked pasts; they would tell lies together; they would shield each other. And all three would unconsciously be pullin' together to save the bacon and hide the face of Charles Drake. Not bad.

"One point was uncomfortable. The evidence against Mrs. Sinclair consisted of a couple of Haye-annotated letters. Nothin' more. If he shoved those documents into her handbag, the cat would be out of that handbag with a reverberatin' yowl; and some women (he didn't know this one) are inclined to talk too much to the police. But there was all the low-down on Peter Ferguson, her husband, gained by Haye through kind remarks of Mrs. Sinclair."

Here H.M. blinked over his spectacles at the calm-faced Bonita, who was smiling at him.

"Y'see, ma'am, you didn't really believe Peter Ferguson was dead. Now, did you? Otherwise you'da collected that insurance-policy that was such a trap for you. Haye didn't believe he was dead. But he couldn't be asked to the party, because nobody knew where he was. So Charles Drake decided to take the quick-lime and phosphorus (relics of Ferguson's old burglar's kit, preserved by you and obtained by Haye) and shove them into your handbag to underline the connection between you and Ferguson."

Bonita Sinclair lifted her shoulders.

"It is not so late in the evening," she smiled, "that I am ready to talk confidences. But may I ask a question? Suppose Drake himself were invited to the gathering? What if Haye invited him?"

H.M. stared at her. "Oh, my wench!" he said. "*And spoil the joke?* Spoil Haye's beautiful scheme? How could he let Drake know he suspected without either tippin' off the Judith Adams game or at least lettin' Drake know Haye's ideas about him? Oh, no. I ake knew he was safe there.

"Well, when Drake received the word, 'Tonight's the night,' he was ready. He arranged to call on Haye, *circa* six o'clock. You've guessed why? Haye would be dressin' for dinner and swillin' a cocktail before he went out. Drake therefore had admirable excuse, or could make excuse, to renew the ice in the refrigerator.

"His 'burglary' of the office he must have managed between six-thirty and, say, ten-thirty, after the staff had gone home. Whether he stole Haye's securities then, or whether he'd pinched 'em a long time ago (as I conjecture) we don't know now. He broke the lock of the deed-box, fooled about with the window, and was off again.

"He was certainly in Great Russell Street before ten-thirty. He was goin' to sneak into the flat and wait for the guests' arrival. Simple, even in a flat—when you have a wardrobe as big as an alcove in the bedroom. I think he'd got a duplicate key to Haye's flat, but he didn't need it. The door was open, because Timothy the caretaker was inside guzzlin' whisky in the kitchen.

"Charles Drake got into the bedroom and waited. He didn't prowl about much, except (after Timothy had reeled out) to disconnect the telephone in case somebody should get to it before the atropine worked, and give a premature alarm. Then he hid in the wardrobe.

"You know what happened. His worst moment was when Peter Ferguson suddenly appeared in the bedroom, and began takin' an energetic dekko through the door to the living-room. Drake didn't know Ferguson or what in blazes he was doin'. But Ferguson, whoever he was, might 'a' been a harmless clerk from downstairs—as he looked—and Drake wasn't worried. Ferguson had seen the people in the other room: he hadn't seen Drake, or so our solicitor thought. And Ferguson slipped out just before the whole company keeled over with atropine poisoning.

"Humph. Well. Drake's fault was that he worked too fast. He put the articles in various persons' pockets. He made a mighty effort, and nerved himself, and struck Haye through the back with the umbrella-swordstick. Then he wanted to get out of there, fast. He wasn't used to that sort of thing, you understand.

"But he didn't altogether lose his nerve. His artful purpose was to suggest that one of the 'drugged' guests had crept out of there, gone to Gray's Inn, burgled his office, and returned. He damned near did plant that immutably and finally in our minds. That was why he left all the doors open behind him—the door of Haye's flat, the back door of the building. That was why he left the swordstick propped up conspicuously up on the stairs.

"The offices of the Anglo-Egyptian company were dark. He didn't know Ferguson was followin' him. But you see Drake's (again) artful scheme in goin' to Gray's Inn. He didn't mind bein' seen in that neighborhood, provided nobody saw him too close. Somebody *was* going to Gray's Inn, in case any stray idler noticed it and the police checked up on it afterwards. But—"

H.M. broke off and looked at Schumann.

"I say, son. You were tellin' the chief inspector that Ferguson knew Charles Drake personally? You said so this afternoon, didn't you?"

Schumann nodded. "Yes. I have heard Ferguson talk about it as much as ten years ago. He said that Drake's rolling walk, like a sailor's, was distinctive. I suppose that was how Ferguson spotted him when he went out of the building."

"Out of the building," said H.M. with sour amusement. "Sure. Ordinarily, of course, Charles Drake would'a gone straight out the front door instead of the back. Less trouble. Naturally. But—he looked out through the glass front doors, and he saw—" H.M. turned to Marcia. "You, waitin' there under the lamp dead in front of him.

"By the way, my wench, you obstructed justice in another way. You didn't know there were four watches in your old man's pocket until after you and Dr. Sanders discovered the 'bodies' upstairs. While he was down telephonin' to the police and for an ambulance, you found the watches in Denny's pockets. You knew what they meant. So, when the doctor came upstairs, straightaway you told a wild story about him borrowin' 'em before he left home that night. The art of misdirection, y'see, to prevent us thinkin' of pick—well, never mind.

"We were talkin' about Drake, and the story's nearly told. Drake had a brief look round at his own office, just to prove there was somebody there; and also, like a thorough-paced artist, really to fool with the catch on the window and show it was an outside job. At a quarter-past twelve he went home to Bloomsbury Square, only ten minutes' walk away. Naturally (as you've guessed) it was really the pursuer Ferguson that the night-watchman saw climbin' out of the office window at just twelve-thirty. By that time, a'course, Drake was home in time to answer the telephone-call from the night-watchman, screamin' about a burglary.

"He must'a wondered what in blazes was up, with the night-watchman sayin' the burglar left at twelve-thirty and providin' a rare alibi for himself. On his way to investigate the burglary—he told Sergeant Pollard he got dressed and went to his office soon afterwards—he nipped up into Great Russell Street. His intention was to phone from a public callbox and tell the police there was somethin' wrong in Haye's flat.

"But he knew the murder would be out before long. He saw Marcia Blystone and Dr. Sanders first arguin' under the lamp, and then going into the building.

"The rest of it Masters'll be able to fill in with routine detail. Ferguson had gone back to Great Russell Street, as his manuscript says. He was there at the discovery of the murder. He wasn't quite sure of it all; the things in people's pockets bothered him horribly; but he knew Drake was a murderer. And the next day he got in touch with Drake with beautiful schemes o' blackmail in his onion. Obviously he wouldn't share such a rich vein of gold with his wife. When she had been taken to Scotland Yard, he invited Drake to

Cheyne Walk for a chat. Drake was ready for that too. You know how.

"But the saddest part of it all was that the firm of private detectives, the Everwide, the firm Drake employed himself, had traced the poison to him before either Haye or Ferguson was murdered. When they knew what had happened they didn't know what the devil to do. But, since it was a matter of murder and they value their reputation, they first told Drake they had information—and then went to the police. When Masters and I heard they had tipped Drake off, we knew it was time to hit Drake hard with the facts and a reconstruction o' the murder (he was with Pollard and Wright, forcibly, in the other room). We had got from Mr. Schumann here the rest of the evidence. He not only knew of Haye's Judith Adams game, but—"

"I was the last to lose consciousness at this table," said Schumann very quietly. "I thought I saw him come into the room before I was gone. It might have been an atropine hallucination; though I know now it was not. But, God help me, how could I speak without giving myself away for—for other things?"

He reached out and struck the table. Then he drew a shaking breath, and they were all quiet.

Outside it had begun to rain, softly at first, and then with a deepening rustle, until it sounded like the rain of two nights ago. Sanders remembered another thing, too. Two nights ago he had wrestled with a problem at the Harris Institute: the last thing which had perplexed him before he walked into this case. It was the Smith case, and the problem was how arsenic had been introduced into ice-cream. Now he knew.

In the midst of their silence Lady Blystone got to her feet. Since certain frank words of H.M. a long time ago, she had not spoken.

"Do I understand," she said quietly, "that this case will come to trial?"

"That's right," said H.M., and looked at her without expression.

"This horrible—this mud—all these things about my husband, will be mentioned in court?"

Blystone was wry-faced, but he smiled. "Never mind, Judy," he soothed her. "I can take care of myself. I don't mind. I've learned how to laugh at it."

"But I mind," she said. She was in a quiet and strong rigidity of rage. "I have not learned how to laugh, if you can find consolation in that. I don't think I care to learn. Why do you believe I have endured all this? Coming here tonight, even? Endured you? Endured other things? Because I will not have disgrace in any family with which I am concerned. I cannot stand it. It would kill me."

"But look here—Judy! Our cruise—"

"That plan was made," said the other, "when I believed the matter would be decently hushed up. Now I cannot say that I look forward to it. Good night, Dennis. Good night— gentlemen. No, Marcia, remain where you are. I shall in- struct my solicitors to file divorce proceedings tomorrow. It will hardly be necessary for me—" she did not look at Bonita Sinclair—"to mention the name of the co-respondent here. Then at least I can disassociate myself with the matter as soon as possible, if technically only."

She walked out of the room, not hurrying. Blystone jumped to his feet and strode after her.

"Yes, go after her," said Bonita Sinclair. "Go after her, and lose the rest of your soul and peace of mind. Be nagged half to death and never be easy even with your own daughter. Or stay with what you're pleased to call a mercenary harlot like me, and take the chance you know you have of being happy. I never lived until I met you. You never lived until you met me. Do as you like, and be damned to you. But, whatever you do, first try to say a word of thanks to a friend who may chew tobacco and shock your illiterate acquaint- ances with bad grammar, but was the only one who would reach out and try to help you when you really came to harm."

H.M. was making sputtering noises of general rage and wildness, the one time in his life when Masters had ever seen him completely at a loss. But Sanders was then looking at Marcia. She disengaged her hand quietly from his. She cleared her throat. She reached over with an almost furtive air and touched the other woman's arm.

"Mrs. Sinclair," said Marcia. "I'm sorry. I beg your par- don."